This is Richard Breakell's first novel, a dream realized after many years of pushing and prodding by his family. It is with great sorrow, this will also be Richard's last novel with his unexpected passing during the publication process.

Father, Grandfather, Brother, and great friend to so many, he was loved, and respected in numerous circles in many countries. Of spiritual and religious belief, he was a daily inspiration to his family, friends and colleagues.

He lived a well-rounded life, which included careers in broadcasting, international real estate, telecommunications, and his last years spent as an entrepreneur dabbling in numerous business ventures, including pursuing his goal of publishing this novel.

He is deeply respected for his mentoring, and sponsorship of dozens in Alcoholics Anonymous, of which he was involved for almost 40 years. His wisdom, friendship, love, and positive outlook impacts their lives to this day.

Richard has now joined his middle Son on the next great adventure, and is survived by two of his three Sons, seven Grandchildren, two Sisters, and the hundreds of souls he touched. As his eldest son, my brother and I hope you enjoy my Father's first novel, a subject of which he had deep concern and impacts all of us daily.

R.I.P. Dad/Dick…you are loved by many.

To my Mother: I should have said 'thank you' more often.

Richard Breakell

Murder by Prescription

AUSTIN MACAULEY PUBLISHERS™
LONDON • CAMBRIDGE • NEW YORK • SHARJAH

Copyright © Richard Breakell (2020)

All rights reserved. No part of this publication may be reproduced, distributed, or transmitted in any form or by any means, including photocopying, recording, or other electronic or mechanical methods, without the prior written permission of the publisher, except in the case of brief quotations embodied in critical reviews and certain other non-commercial uses permitted by copyright law. For permission requests, write to the publisher.

Any person who commits any unauthorized act in relation to this publication may be liable to criminal prosecution and civil claims for damages.

This is a work of fiction. Names, characters, businesses, places, events, locales, and incidents are either the products of the author's imagination or used in a fictitious manner. Any resemblance to actual persons, living or dead, or actual events is purely coincidental.

Ordering Information:
Quantity sales: Special discounts are available on quantity purchases by corporations, associations, and others. For details, contact the publisher at the address below.

Publisher's Cataloging-in-Publication data
Breakell, Richard
Murder by Prescription

ISBN 9781643782096 (Paperback)
ISBN 9781643782102 (Hardback)
ISBN 9781645366898 (ePub e-book)

Library of Congress Control Number: 2020908362

www.austinmacauley.com/us

First Published (2020)
Austin Macauley Publishers LLC
40 Wall Street, 28th Floor
New York, NY 10005
USA

mail-usa@austinmacauley.com
+1 (646) 5125767

For years, my eldest son told me to write,

                        So, I finally did!

For years, my middle son tried to alert me about Big Pharma,

                        So, I finally am!

For years, I have waited to thank my youngest son,

                        So, I finally can!

You are my three best friends.

                        ***

All I needed was the spark to get started. That spark happened one day over lunch, when my friend, Chet, a published writer, said some magic words that lifted me "off the starting blocks".

Thank you, Chet!

                        ***

When the plotline seemed at an end, I would wander down the street to my longtime friend, Lin, and she would "prop me up" with her wisdom and support.

After a few chapters, I asked her to give me an honest assessment – am I a writer?

The answer was yes and that "lifted me off the runway".

                        ***

Reading about writers, I never understood the reverence paid to editors…until now. I assumed that because I could write, then it followed that I could edit.

After my fourth edit, I finally accepted the kind offer from my good friend, Pam, a retired editor, and thirty-nine hours later, we have this finished product. I am forever grateful.

And finally, to my anonymous friends, whose comments kept me staying the course and doing the next right thing.

Table of Contents

Prologue	11
Chapter 1	12
Chapter 2	22
Chapter 3	32
Chapter 4	43
Chapter 5	49
Chapter 6	56
Chapter 7	67
Chapter 8	76
Chapter 9	83
Chapter 10	92
Chapter 11	99
Chapter 12	105
Chapter 13	117
Chapter 14	124
Chapter 15	133
Chapter 16	139

Chapter 17	**153**
Chapter 18	**177**
Chapter 19	**185**
Chapter 20	**192**

Prologue

Marty sat staring at the wall. Three weeks and three days ago, he had been sitting in a cubicle musing that his squirrel cage existence looked permanent. A chance encounter and he was launched into 17 days of fulfilled dreams, conspiracy, intrigue, failure, death, and success. He felt like he had not had time for a deep breath.

Chapter 1

The job market was bleak for Marty Cooper when he had graduated college with his master's in both biochemistry and computer engineering. After many interviews, he finally accepted a junior position with a mid-size pharmaceutical company, basically factchecking other people's work.

His penchant for research still held top priority. In his off times, during the three-year daily drudge, he pursued his research and could only hope that one day, he would be discovered.

One evening, Marty was explaining his dream over drinks with Tim Franzden, an old college buddy. Tim was impressed and introduced Marty's work to the executive assistant of Derek Maurrel, the president of Chiles, Arken, and Associates, a major player in the Pharmaceutical Industry. Two months passed and Marty's normally optimistic nature was taking a beating. He seemed destined to toil in obscurity forever. He had all but forgotten about the incident when he got a call requesting an interview.

The heavy traffic on the Dallas Toll Way the morning of the interview, combined with blustery and rainy weather, advertised an omen of misfortune. Convinced he was going to be late, Marty thought, *Great... how to blow a lifetime opportunity*.

Cutting off a woman heading to a parking space, he arrived on time. The elevator doors opened on the 15th floor and he was presented with the opulence of a major corporate player. The receptionist desk seemed bigger than his current office with serious and determined people buzzing around, which did nothing for his confidence.

"May I help you," asked a stunningly beautiful receptionist.

"Uh... Yes... thank you. I am here to see Derek Maurrel... I have an appoint..."

"Of course, Mr. Cooper, Mr. Maurrel is expecting you. My name is Crystal. Please follow me." He couldn't help admiring the view as she led him down a short hallway, entered a code at the doorway, and was admitted to an array of glass and mahogany.

Feeling like the new arrival at the zoo, Marty followed Crystal down the middle aisle past offices on both sides, being met with curious secretarial stares. Stopping near the end, Crystal announced his arrival to the attractive thirtyish gatekeeper, Kelly, and thanking Marty, turned and left.

"Hello, Mr. Cooper," smiled Kelly, "Nice to meet you. Your fiend, Tim, has spoken highly of you. May I get you something to drink." She got up and led him to a sofa beside the office door.

"N… No, thank you," stuttered Marty

"Mr. Maurrel will be with you in a moment." His nervousness was all too apparent and Kelly said, with a comforting smile, "Mr. Maurrel is excited to meet you."

Marty took a deep breath. "Thank you," he said.

The door behind Kelly opened and a six-foot, dark haired, handsome man approached Marty. "Marty," he said, extending his hand, "Derek Maurrel… nice to finally meet you. You have created quite a stir around here. Come in."

Marty was struck dumb. "Uh… Nice to meet you, Mr. Maurrel."

"No…No… The name is Derek, please," he said as he ushered them into an office the size of Grand Central Station. Derek pointed at the sofa arrangement in one corner.

"Sit down, Marty. Kelly," he yelled, "bring us two coffees. How's the family, Marty."

Marty was dizzy. He had prepared for the usual, formal give-and-take introductions. Not this 'hail fellow – well met' routine.

Reading his thoughts, Derek said, "Please, excuse me, Marty. I shouldn't be so forward. Let me explain that you have been thoroughly 'vetted', so I know quite a bit about you. The truth is I was excited to meet you and when I get excited, I tend to go overboard. Please, forgive me."

"No problem, sir," said Marty

"SIR?" boomed Derek, "I thought we had settled this. It's Derek. Now, then… tell me about yourself."

"Well," began Marty, "I *am* married, and have been for 3 years. We have a little two-year-old girl named Cara."

"Wonderful," exuded Derek, "starting out with the all-American family. Before long, you'll have two, three children and be a bona-fide citizen."

They both laughed as Kelly arrived with the beverages.

"Thank you, Kelly. Please close the door and we don't want to be disturbed"

"Yes, sir."

"So now, Marty, enough chitchat. You're probably wondering just what this is all about. First of all, I want to apologize for the delay in getting back to you. Frankly, I didn't get to see your research until about a week ago. Somehow, it just kept slipping through the cracks. My fault. But I want you to know that I was very impressed with what you have accomplished. Let me get 'right to the meat'. As I said, we have vetted you and are completely satisfied with all the attributes you will bring to the industry. Yes, I did say, 'will bring'. We want to help you activate the research plan you have worked on so hard."

If Marty was overwhelmed before, he now was completely unable to react. He sat with his mouth open, staring at Derek.

"Marty," said Derek, "are you all right. Say something."

"I... um... Of course... uh...thank you... I think."

Derek roared with laughter. "I know I am unorthodox, Marty, but it saves time and bullshit. Just so you don't think I am completely off my rocker, let me tell you that I am a believer that nothing happens by mistake and the timing of your research could not have been better. We have been watching the growing 'push back' from the, how shall we say, 'natural medicine community.' Frankly, I wish we could ignore them completely, but that would not be prudent. We need to get out ahead of them and create and launch a comprehensive program debunking their supposed experts and letting the world understand that the drug industry is their best friend with the best solutions. Your thorough research into the new media and 'Big Data'[i] has fleshed out our sketchy knowledge and made us aware of new tools to help in the launch of our products."

"Thank you, Derek."

"No... Thank *you*. Not only have you shown us a whole new avenue, but you have given yourself a new life."

"A *new life*?"

"Yes," Derek barked, "and we are going to work that life out, right here and now"

Derek shifted to face Marty square on, "We are prepared to facilitate the launching of your own company. You will have your own people, your own office and total autonomy. Why are we doing this? Because we believe there is a need for a company that the entire Pharmaceutical Industry can turn to when it needs quick, comprehensive, and expert responses to any 'push back' from the 'natural medicine' naysayers. Your company will be creating the 'front line' defense to put these 'do-gooders' *down*. Does that sound like a winning program.?"

Barely able to open his mouth to respond, Marty squeaked out, "I think it's wonderful, but…"

Derek slapped the coffee table, "The word, I want to hear, is *fantastic*."

Marty's head was spinning. This whole thing was moving way too fast. Before he could put any thoughts together, Derek continued.

"Now let's talk financing!" he rose from the sofa and moved to his desk, grabbing a sheath of papers, "read these over tonight and then we will talk again tomorrow. I think you will find this a sufficient beginning and I stress *beginning*. Marty, I think this demonstrates that we have total confidence in your talents, your vision, and your enthusiasm and are excited to begin a long and mutually productive relationship."

Marty stood up as Derek handed him the papers and they shook hands. "Thank you, Derek,"

"Nonsense. My thanks to you. Please, set a time with Kelly and I will see you tomorrow." As if on cue, the door opened and Kelly ushered Marty out.

The elevator reached the ground floor long before he did. He was on a cloud. He had quickly peeked at the first page of the papers and all he could see was the number… $200,000.

***

Immediately after the meeting with Marty, Derek punched the CEO, Tom Chiles' intercom.

"Well," snapped Tom.

"Perfect," replied Derek.

"Great. Come on up and fill me in," replied Tom, smiling as he leaned back in his chair. *Things are moving right along,* he thought.

CEO, Tom Chiles came from humble beginnings and was truly a self-made man; having graduated summa cum laude with a master's in microbiology from a major ivy league school, he then moved on to a doctorate and subsequently acquired an MBA. These combined achievements garnered much interest from major international pharmaceutical companies. Upon selecting InterPharma, he quickly moved up the ladder and pioneered breakthroughs in healthcare research.

Reaching his ceiling after only five years, his ambition, together with his financial participation in many patents and the acquisition of financial partners, allowed him the wherewithal to form his own company – Chiles, Arken, and Associates.

With his education, experience, funding, and unbridled ambition, he quickly propelled his company into the highly profitable and competitive world of big pharmaceuticals (*Big Pharma*).[ii]

"Come in. I want to hear all about it," Tom said enthusiastically. Accepting the offered glass of Scotch, Derek smirked at Tom.

"Yes… A well-earned celebratory drink. He bought into it all. I almost feel sorry for him. He left the room with stars in his eyes."

"Good work, Derek. What's the path from here?"

"We will hear from him tomorrow, no doubt, accepting the offer. We'll set him up with that suite of offices on fourteen, and commence the plan," Derek said smugly.

Tom frowned, "We need to make sure he is covered under a non-disclosure/ non-compete agreement."

"Of course, he will be tied down completely. Tom, I assure you, this kid is perfect, or I wouldn't have given him the offer. His research has been flawless and I don't want him talking it over with anyone else. He's an ideal mixture of talent and naiveté. He will be so knocked out with the offer that suspicion will not even enter his head. By the way, I am going to have their home wired, just to be safe."

"What about the wife… what's her name… Myra?"

"She is the perfect 'Stepford Wife.' No problem."

Tom leered, "Would I like her… just kidding."

"Are you…?" they both chuckled.

Tom stared out the window for a moment. "First, you were right. I have from sources he is a very likable guy and that's what we wanted. I am a little concerned that he might be too green for what we need."

"I am convinced that I can toughen him up and still keep that naïve nature," Derek contended, "let me work with him for a few months and you won't recognize him. Besides, even if we must jettison him, we will have enough on him to get our money's worth. I am working with 'legal' to be sure that we are totally transparent and separate from his company… Cooper Consulting."

Tom paused, "Do you see any 'downstream' problems?"

Derek shook his head, "No. But if anything should develop, we can always come up with an exit strategy… like a moral claim or something."

Tom chuckled, "*That* kid… You've got to be kidding."

***

On his drive home, Marty felt like the car was floating. He kept looking at the folder on the seat. He wanted to pull over and digest the contents, but decided to do it together with Myra. He picked up his cellphone. Myra answered breathlessly, "Well"

"My he called her by his nickname for her…are you home yet?"

"Pulling into the driveway."

"Good… get the best bottle of wine open and… better still, I think we have some champagne. Put it in the fridge and I'll be home in about twenty minutes."

"*Marty*… this isn't fair. What happened?"

"Nope … You have to be patient."

"I hate you"

"Noooo … you love me more than ever. See you in a few," he clicked off before she could whine any more.

He opened the garage door to be greeted by Myra holding 2 spiffs of champagne. He grabbed her and twirled her in the air, spilling champagne all over the floor. She shrieked in laughter and howled… "Tell me… tell me… tell me."

He held up the file, "We are going to learn together. I only know that I have been offered something way beyond what I could have hoped for."

Breathlessly, Myra said, "Let's go sit in the living room."

"I'd rather tear your clothes off and ravish you."

"Later, macho man."

Settling on the sofa together, Marty gingerly opened the file as if it would shatter. They both scanned the first page. The opening paragraph explained that Marty would be forming his own company – Cooper Consulting Company and confidential 'startup financing' and credit lines, if needed, had been arranged. Just as Marty had seen, his suggested annual salary was $200,000.

They looked at each other in disbelief. This was double his current income. Nervously, Marty turned the page. Following was an itemized list of additional points.

Marty held his breath, *Please, God, let there be no 'deal breakers.'*

'50% ownership.

Total autonomy in annual increases.

Five-member Board of Directors.

Marty, plus one of his choice, as a Board Member.'

The rest was just 'boiler plate' that he would go over later. They both sat alternating between looking at the page and looking at each other. Neither one could speak. Finally, they both let out their breath.

"Marty," whispered Myra, "how did you do this?"

"My, I swear, I didn't do anything. I walked in and before I could even start to talk, he handed me these papers and, basically, that was it. I am to get together with him tomorrow and move 'the venture' forward."

"Do you believe this! It's almost too good to be true. What's the catch?"

"Honestly, My, I don't know if there is one. I will know tomorrow when I go back."

***

Marty's eyes snapped open from the alarm. Damn it! It was such a great dream. He reached over to touch My, but the pillow was empty. Then he smelled the coffee. He quickly threw on a shirt and wandered downstairs.

There she was, looking as radiant as ever, and just out of bed. He walked over and wrapped his arms around her and nuzzled her neck. "Please, tell me that I am not still in my dream and last night was real," he murmured.

"No… it was not real. It was *unreal*. You have to warn me when you are going to be an animal."

"I beg your pardon. Who was the animal…? A second bottle of champagne? How risqué!"

Myra blushed, "…and you… On the bathroom counter? You must learn to control your libido."

"Me…? And dancing nude is *your* idea of control," Myra waved her hands in surrender. "Enough… enough! You told Derek last night when he called, that you would be at the office at 10. Now stop molesting me and get ready. I laid out your suit and tie. I'll make some breakfast. Hurry… hurry!"

Could anything be better, thought Marty. He could visualize their future rolling out like a magic carpet

***

He pulled into the underground parking. The attendant looked at him and then the picture on his desk and the gate rose. "Good Morning, Mr. Cooper," he said. Marty was dumbfounded. They already had him in the system? "Your parking space is number 242, just straight ahead, on your right."

Marty couldn't shake the nagging feeling that this was all too good to be true. So, it was with apprehension that he followed the receptionist to Kelly's desk, who looked up with a happy smile.

"Hello, Mr. Cooper. Nice to see you again. Your meeting is in Mr. Chiles' office," she said as she pushed the intercom. "Mr. Cooper is here… Thank you… Just follow me" she said, rising from the desk. "Mr. Chiles and Mr. Maurrel are waiting for you."

They started up a wide, semicircular stairway which opened to a lavishly furnished waiting area with flanking hallways down both sides. In the center, behind the reception desk, were mahogany double doors manned by Pam Styles,

"Pam Styles," said Kelly, "meet Mr. Marty Cooper."

Marty nodded.

"Thank you, Kelly," said Pam, dismissing Kelly with a wave.

"Hello, Mr. Cooper. Nice to meet you."

Marty had never seen such magnificent furnishings, both furniture and human. Pam, rising from behind her desk, opened one of the opulent doors to see Derek striding toward them. "Marty… glad you could make it on such short notice."

"No problem, sir… ah… Derek."

Derek guffawed, "Now you've got it!"

As they entered the office, Marty was once again overwhelmed. The office was larger than his house. In one corner, with floor to ceiling glass walls, overlooking the Dallas skyline, was a living room, complete with a fireplace and an obviously well-stocked bar.

A second corner featured a round table with plush chairs for eight. Feeling as though he were in a quiz show, Marty glanced to corner number three which featured some obviously expensive original art pieces overlooking a cozy den-like nook, with two plush leather chairs facing each other over a small and rare teak coffee table.

In front of the center glass wall, commanding all of this, was a strangely small, but stylish, glass-topped desk almost completely bare except for the Intercom and phone. Emerging from behind the desk was a tall, tanned, and obviously fit Tom Chiles. His stylish, long grey hair and expensive suit made Marty feel that he was meeting the President.

With his hand outstretched, Tom said, "Marty… Tom Chiles. Nice to finally meet you. Derek has told me so much about you, I feel as though we have already met."

"Mr. Chiles. A pleasure."

"Marty," said Derek, "Tom has been brought totally up to date on your research and, of course, is privy to your vetting. I don't think I am overstating that Tom is more than impressed with your academic history and your subsequent patience in 'earning your chops,' as they say in the music business."

"Absolutely," chimed Tom, "when Derek brought you to my attention, I couldn't help but wonder, why no one else had seen this diamond in the rough."

"Thank you, sir," mumbled Marty.

"But enough chitchat," chided Tom, "let's get down to cases," he said as he walked over to the living room setting in the corner. "Have you digested the opportunity."

"I have and I must say that in light of my limited experience, I was surprised at your generosity."

Tom laughed, "Derek and I both understand. We knew there were more experienced candidates but, in all candor, your potential was your selling point. Specifically, your insightfulness gave us a glimpse into the nature of 'Big Data'[iii] and how to keep ahead of these individuals and groups that fight us with such ferocity. We need that kind of talent, tempered with pragmatism, in order for Derek and I to continue to satisfy entities like the FDA, NIH, AMA, CDC and congress."

"Plain and simple, Marty," Derek added, "we need you in the 'front lines,' feeding us and using your research to soften, if not remove, the resistance."

Marty swallowed, "Gentleman, first let me say this. I accept, with gratitude, the opportunity and I can promise you that you will not be disappointed. I understand the risk you are taking and your confidence is not misplaced."

Tom rose, "Fabulous. You and Derek can work out the details."

"Marty," said Derek as they walked to the door, "I am going to have Kelly take you down to the 14th floor so you can start planning your next physical steps. I need to speak with Tom for a moment and then I'll be down."

"OK," replied Marty.

Pam rose as the door opened. "Just go down the stairs, Mr. Cooper, and Kelly will show you to the 14th floor."

Back in Tom's office, Tom paced, "Now what about Dr. Kenmore. Has he been prepped?" asked Tom.

"Yes. As you already know, he is a full-fledged, bought and paid supporter. His pragmatic view is that a few deaths on the road to world health is more than acceptable. He's the perfect 'egg head' degreed academic. He not only believes that our products will save thousands of lives, but I think he may have his eyes on a Nobel," snickered Derek.

Tom pointed at Derek, "As we discussed, to maintain his neutrality, we don't want him attached to us in any way, nor the money supporting his rise to stardom."

"We will introduce him to Marty ASAP so that Marty can speak with more authority and reference the Dr. in his releases"

Tom nodded his head, "Good. Are we continuing the campaign to push him as the world expert"?

"Yes, and that will be enhanced as soon as Marty fleshes out his program," replied Derek

"The thing I am most excited about is the reception the Dr. is receiving within his peer groups. I noticed in Marty's report that he is being quoted on a much more frequent basis. Good work on that."

"Thanks, Tom. After we finish with Marty, let's' talk about the long-view plans. I have some thoughts."

"I'm meeting our lobbyist tonight, so let's wait for another time."

"Nothing serious, I hope?"

Tom frowned, "I don't think so. Just some loose ends with the FDA that need to be addressed. One of the new Congressmen is asking too many questions."

Chapter 2

Kelly and Marty stepped out on the 14th floor. He had expected to have to do a 'build out' from a former office. Instead, it was like someone had said, 'OK… everyone out' and they took their personal effects and left.

It was a completely functional, ready-for-business, facility. Marty crossed to the inside door and pushed it open to behold at least 4000 sq. ft. area comprised of one major office of maybe 500 sq. ft., five more offices of approximately 300 sq. ft. each, secretarial desks, a lunch room, two bathrooms, and a room he couldn't see.

"Shocking, huh," said Kelly.

"That doesn't cover it. What is all this?"

Kelly laughed, "It's your *domain*!"

"Ok, wrong question. *What was it?*"

"It was a company that went under and Tom knew that someday he would expand, so he worked out a great deal and it's been sitting here for six months."

"…and you are saying this is *my* domain."

"Yes… Officially, this is Cooper Research and Development."

"But, Kelly, I will not, in a million years, use this space."

"Oh, yes, you will, if what I have been seeing and hearing happens," Kelly said quietly.

Marty turned and looked at her, "What do you mean?"

"Marty… I'm sorry… Mr. Cooper…"

"No… No, please call me Marty."

"Marty, I hope I am not being too presumptuous, but this is going to become a huge operation. You are not going to be consulting only with Chiles, Arken, and Associates, but thanks to Mr. Chiles and Mr. Maurel's contacts with other major Pharmaceutical companies, they will be 'pounding on your door.' You will impact the entire Pharmaceutical Industry. I should have told you… I read your research. It's brilliant."

Marty didn't know whether to be angry or flattered and muttered, "You realize that it was supposed to be confidential."

"I'm sorry again. Mr. Maurrel left it on my desk by mistake. Please, don't say anything to him." She looked like she was going to cry.

"Your secret is safe with me," sympathized Marty, "...and I thank you for your comments."

Just then, Derek came rushing into the offices. "Well," he said, spreading his arms wide, "what do you think? Can you function here?"

"Function! ...are you kidding. I could move in here with my family," gushed Marty.

Kelly said, "I'll leave you gentlemen"

Derek started toward the big office, "OK, Kelly. See you upstairs."

Marty said, "Thank you, Kelly."

She turned, and as she passed Marty, she leaned into him and whispered, "Thank *you*... be careful."

***

Kelly was still blushing as she sat down at her desk. She was so embarrassed. What the hell was *that* about. She hardly knew the man and here she was, trying to warn him. *Typical Kelly,* she thought, *always trying to be the caretaker.* Her mother's words rang in her ears, *Kelly, you can't fix everybody.*

Maybe that was why she was still single at twenty-seven years old. She had certainly had opportunities. She knew she was attractive and had no problem initiating interest from men. But it always seemed that when it came down to commitment, *he* just wasn't quite right.

It wasn't that she was interested in Mr. Cooper, although it had crossed her mind, but he seemed so vulnerable, which was not a good quality to take into a relationship with Derek Maurrel or Tom Chiles. She had been sitting at Derek's door for three years and one thing she knew for sure. You did *not* exit his office without some 'skin' missing. The worst part was that usually the victim didn't know until it was too late.

She had prepared all the documents and she knew anything that Mr. Cooper did from hereon was independent of and completely deniable by Chiles, Arken, and Associates. In other words, he would be manipulated by the company in all his activities and yet, totally liable for any results. It was the perfect set up.

Maurrel and Chiles *always* had a plan and she had heard and seen enough to know that Mr. Cooper was part of a 'plan' and could be and, probably would be, tossed to the 'wolves' when the time was right.

Kelly knew that she worked in an amoral environment and rationalized the decisions that were being enacted *for the greater good*... at the expense of her conscience.

Like everyone else that was associated with Chiles, Arken, and Associates the remuneration exceeded the going market, which maintained loyalty, not to mention that it enabled a standard of living beyond her means. She knew it was economic slavery, but she needed the money.

These decisions affected millions of lives and that knowledge, with its accompanying guilt, had to be quelled! The more than comfortable lifestyle usually did the job... Most of the time!

But this time, something was different. It was *personal*! She didn't know why, but there it was! She was passively participating in allowing another new drug, with very questionable pedigree, to enter the marketplace. Notwithstanding that she was now abetting the destruction of a good man and his family.

She was not a martyr or a dreamer, but something unfamiliar was stirring in her. Maybe it was time to challenge her amoral existence. Maybe it was time to take a stand!

***

The rest of Marty's day was taken up with contracts and other administrative necessities. In reviewing the documents, he confirmed that he was a major shareholder of his own research company. Marty looked up from the documents with a questioning look,

"Derek, what is the purpose of my own company? Why am I not just a department of the company?"

"Very simple, Marty. When we quote 'research' in our press releases from our 'sources,' yours is an independent viewpoint. No bias! Your company officially will have no connection with ours except as a consulting service. The startup financing for your company will be private and anonymous and your revenue stream will come from consulting contracts with other pharmaceutical companies and industry organizations. Should the jackals from the media start attacking, we don't want you to be vulnerable. Your research needs to be unquestionably neutral."

"Excellent," acknowledged Marty.

When Kelly finished drafting the necessary consulting documents for Marty, Derek asked Kelly to leave the office and, after the door closed, he turned to Marty.

"Marty, the reason we wanted the agreements 'roughed out' here is so that we are in agreement on where we are going, but I'm sure you understand that these have to go to an attorney for finalization."

"Of course," said Marty.

Derek stared intently at Marty, "Just to maintain our separation, I think it would be wise if you be the only one involved in the preparation of the final documents. I hope you understand."

Marty nodded, "I understand."

Derek continued, "Because of their knowledge of our industry, I would recommend the law firm of Johnson, Lavin, and Bales. They handle a lot of clients in the pharmaceutical industry. Understand?"

"Absolutely."

"…and lawyers being lawyers, I think you should advise them you would like the documents to be basically untouched, other than what little technical changes they may wish to do. We, of course, would not be privy to the incorporation, unless you choose to allow it, and we need to make sure that the consulting documents are dated after the formation of the company."

"Yes… yes," agreed Marty.

"All right then," nodded Derek, "now when will you be able to take occupancy and begin your new career?"

"Well, I don't want to burn any bridges, but I suspect that once I give notice, they will want me out immediately."

"Yes. That would be the prudent thing. All right, just keep me posted. From now on, any contact with us will be from Cooper Consulting. You have the contacts for the investors' law firm and you can make financial arrangement with them for immediate funding."

"Yes… Derek, I don't know what to say except 'thank you' for this opportunity."

"Not necessary," said Derek, "but you're welcome. Remember this is a two-way street. We are receiving just as much as we are giving."

Derek walked into Tom's office with a smile on his face, "If it wasn't for the importance of this venture, it would be comedic."

Tom looked up from his desk, "Everything done?"

"Yep. He's on his way to his attorney tomorrow to get the incorporation done and then start dealing with the investors. Are they ready for him?"

"Well, *we* are, and the others are on standby to give him the money," advised Tom, "you're sure he doesn't know the source of the funds?"

"Positive, Tom. He is so high that it didn't even occur to him to ask who they were. Barry, the lawyer, knows, but it's all papered over and I cautioned Marty and Barry that I don't want the attorney to 'screw around' with the deal."

Tom pursed his lips, "How long do you think before we will see some real results."

Derek looked out the window for a few seconds. "Oh… I would think somewhere within the next few weeks."

"Good. We should be well into the launch of Sistophan by then. Anything new from the labs?"

"Nothing that we can't handle," bragged Derek.

"That reminds me," said Tom, turning from where he had been looking at the skyline, "remember when I said I had to meet our lobbyist the other day?"

Derek nodded.

"Well, it seems that a certain congressman, chairing the committee controlling the FDA, has been asking some tough questions about our last success… namely Tamsitor, and has also brought up Sistophan."

"Oh, oh," exclaimed Derek.

"Yeah," said Tom, "I mentioned to the lobby group that we are working with a new consultant and perhaps the congressman and the consultant could meet when they both happen to cross paths on the industry Mediterranean cruise in a couple of weeks."

"Oh… you mean the all-expense paid 'research cruise?'"[iv] chuckled Derek.

"That's the one," Tom smiled, "do you think Marty is up to it this soon."

Derek stared off into space, "Before I commit, let me have a session with him and I will let you know in the next day or two."

"Great, and let's have Dr. Kenmore on the cruise as well," Tom turned to look out at the skyline again as Derek left the office, reflecting that with the launch of Sistophan, Chiles, Arken, and Associates would be recognized as one of the senior 'members' of *Big Pharma*.

He remembered early on, when they were forming their lobbying group, the Safe Drug Council (*SDC*), the innumerable meetings with competitors wrangling about their share of the spoils, completely missing the total picture. Many had become victims of their short-sighted greed while the majority had shelved their avarice for the long haul.

One of the biggest hurdles had been the development of the internet. The speed of transference of information had, for a time, looked like it would wield a deathblow to their vision, but thanks to people like Tom, they persevered.

Tom was continuously surprised at the fundamental greed in human nature. The human ego just needed to be massaged and pampered and inevitably, the thin moral veneer eroded. He smiled as he remembered that these developments with Marty had been fundamentally the same when he discovered Derek.

Derek's naïve morality, from his father, had been unfortunately welded with an unquenchable need for acceptance from his mother, which manifested in the schizophrenic character development of a 'nice guy' with a terminal case of *more*.

When Tom met Derek, he instantly recognized that Derek's magnetic personality, combined with his drive for material success, would be extremely useful in Tom's plans. The only additional requirement was a more refined pragmatic approach to drug development. With a 'carrot and stick' management technique and the ever-increasing material satisfactions, together with the constant reinforcement of 'the means justifies the end,' Derek had developed into the perfect senior pharmaceutical executive.

Many of Tom's competitors had attempted to *buy* Derek, but his sense of loyalty, together with stock options, had assured his allegiance. Tom wondered if Derek realized that his development of Marty was a carbon copy of Derek's own history with Tom.

Tom took some pride that Derek had discovered Marty at this early stage and that Derek understood that Marty was dispensable.

Tom often pondered if Derek realized that he, also, was dispensable. No matter… things were moving forward as planned and that was priority.

***

Kelly looked up from her computer to see Marty standing by her desk. "Oh… you startled me. I didn't see you… Can I help you?"

"No… No… I just wanted to tell you, 'Thank you for all your extra efforts.'"

"My pleasure, Mr. Cooper… And if there is anything I can do for you, just call."

The urgent look on Kelly's face as she spoke was rather baffling to Marty. What was she saying with that look and the previous 'Be Careful' comment?

As she watched Marty walk away, she hoped that she hadn't shown her worry. She was musing on that thought when Derek called from his office, "Kelly, could you come here, please." *Please,* she thought, that wasn't his usual request, *Wonder what's up?*

"Kelly, I just wanted you to know that I really appreciate the efforts you have put in today. I'm sure you have realized how big a development this is for our company. I think it's time to review your situation here. I am authorizing a pay raise of $500 per month, effective today."

"Mr. Maurrel… I don't…"

"It's done. You're welcome. That's all."

Kelly was stunned as she turned to walk out.

"By the way, Kelly, I am sure that we don't need to talk about Mr. Cooper and our recent meetings. And could you please purge all the files from today's work as well as previous appointment notations."

"Of course, Mr. Maurrel," she replied knowingly.

***

Marty's text arrived as Myra was exiting Neiman Marcus: 'Better than expected – home shortly.' She almost dropped her bags.

Mary Margaret looked at her, "Are you OK?"

"Yes," she choked, "just some good news from Marty."

"Well… Give it up, girl."

Myra held out her cell as Mary Margaret read the message. "Wow. It sounds like things are moving fast."

"Yes… I hope not too fast. It all seems like a dream."

Mary Margaret held up her hand, "Wait… Are you looking this gift horse in the mouth?"

"No… No. It's just… I don't know. Marty is suddenly jettisoned up to a whole new level that normally takes years. How does that happen?"

"Maybe you're underrating Marty's talents?"

Myra nodded, "Yes, I'm sure that's what it is. I better get home. Thanks for the day and lunch. Say hi to Ric."

"Will do. Love ya!"

***

Something was nagging at Myra that she couldn't place. As she drove home, she tried to identify her feelings. All that kept popping into her mind was, 'it's too fast.' But who was she to question the decisions of a multibillion-dollar company?

Marty arrived home before Myra and surprised her with 'takeout.'

"Oh, thank you. I just didn't feel like cooking tonight. Is Cara upstairs?"

"Yes, I just sent the babysitter home. C'mere… give me a hug." Myra flew into his arms and couldn't help breaking into tears. Marty panicked, "What is it… what's wrong?"

"Nothing… I am just so overwhelmed with… whatever you have to say."

Marty started laughing, "How can that be… You don't even know what's happened."

"…but your text said…"

"I know and it's all great."

Cara came screaming into the kitchen, "Daddy… Daddy," and jumped into his arms. Marty rained kisses all over his daughter and then reached for Myra. "Daddy wants to give Mommy a bunch of these."

Myra screeched, scooped up Cara and went running into the living room. "We need to get away from this monster," screamed Myra. Cara giggled and screamed.

Marty ran after them, roaring like a bear. They all tumbled onto the sofa. Marty growled into Myra's ear, "The monster will take care of you later… right now, this little girl needs a good tickling."

Cara yelled, "Mommy, help me." But it was too late as the monster started tickling her and she laughed till she was out of breath.

"OK," said Myra, "let's eat."

Dinner was finished, Cara was in bed and Marty and Myra snuggled, sitting on the backyard patio. Myra broke the silence, "Marty, I am *so* proud for you. I watched you putting your research together and I must admit, I didn't grasp the vision you had… and now it has catapulted us into our own company, doubled our income, and allowed us to be in control of our own future."

Marty smiled contentedly, "To be honest, I didn't know if anyone else would grasp my vision. I knew a long time ago that with the dramatic advances in medical research and development, there were going to be people who would mistrust and question *Big Pharma*. It just seemed to me that someone had to be out ahead of the curve and utilize the new tools of Big Data with social media and aggregate all that information with my algorithms to counter adverse publicity. I had no idea that those ideas would dovetail with the vision that Tom and Derek were developing. By making us an independent researcher, and their connections in the industry, they have added a dimension beyond my vision, allowing us to be the leading authority for the pharmaceutical industry. It's mindboggling."

Myra raised her head and gave Marty a kiss, "It seems like everything we ever hoped for."

"I just pray that I can live up to expectations."

"I don't think that will be a problem. Now… I have some expectations," Myra murmured, "come to bed."

Marty grabbed her, "Those expectations don't necessarily have to be reached in the bedroom."

***

Kelly sat on her balcony watching the moon rise, sipping on her margarita. She was in a jumble of emotions, mainly fear.

The bravado of her decision to act had been dissipating rapidly. She looked around her condo and thought, *I could be putting all this in jeopardy… and for what? Some misguided sense of 'justice.'* What could one person do in the face of the evil in which she was a participant. 'Tilting at Windmills' was the old saying.

No matter how much they manipulated and 'sugar coated' the lab results,[v] there was no question that there were serious issues that had not and were not being addressed in the launch of not only Sistophan, but of previous generations of drugs. She also knew that this was not isolated to Chiles, Arken, and Associates, but was practiced by the entire pharmaceutical industry.

The public trusted that the FDA, AMA, and the CDC were protecting their safety and, in many areas, they were. However, with *Big Pharma* being the largest single lobbying entity in Washington[vi] and contributing the majority of the FDA budget,[vii] was it any wonder that some questionable decisions were being enacted.

But, of course, like almost everything else done in Washington, facts like these never saw the light of day through any of the Mainstream Media (*MSM*).[viii] Kelly knew deeply that she was 'selling out' her conscience. She thought of the old line about prostitutes… 'we've established what you are, we're just dickering over the price.'

Watching Derek maneuvering Marty down the same path was making her ill. She knew, from experience, the power of rationalizations through the benefits. She was surrounded by coworkers who had completely swallowed the 'Kool-Aid.' How she was even able to think these thoughts was a miracle.

She had just finished watching a documentary regarding the training of doctors.[ix] It had been difficult for her to even begin to accept that *Big Pharma* had been influencing medical training since the early 1900's.[x] Talk about a long-term game plan!

No wonder the public, informed only by the complicit media, blithely accepted whatever their doctor said. Through the decades, the public had made the doctor their God. Whatever he/she said was gospel. As the knowledge load exponentially exploded, together with the development of pharmaceuticals, the teaching institutions and their graduate doctors had no option but to trust the drug companies. Surgery and pills had become 'healthcare.' They looked to the FDA as inviolate.

Through the educational institutions, with the help of *Big Pharma*, the doctors were reduced to the equivalent of butchers and pharmaceutical 'pez dispensers.' Adding to this was a continuous degradation of historically proven alternative healing techniques.

Kelly acknowledged that she was no Joan of Arc, but that didn't alleviate the guilt. *There must be something I could do,* she mused… *why not anonymously?*

She had access to the files. If she could redact any reference to Chiles, Arken, and Associates then there would be no way to trace back to her.

"…Hmmmm."

Chapter 3

The last few days had been chaos for Marty. As predicted, his old firm did not want him around once he had submitted his resignation.

The formation of the company and the consulting agreement had gone flawlessly. Marty's new lawyer, Andrew Carson, from Johnson, Lavin, and Bales, was extremely helpful in educating Marty on things that could arise as he moved forward.

The subsequent meetings with the investors' law firm had been interesting. He was informed that they preferred to remain anonymous because of their status and all arrangements would be done 'in trust.' That arrangement was a little disquieting, but the urgency of moving forward overrode any prudent deliberation.

So… here he sat at his new desk, in his new office, at his new company… prepared to do… what? He laughed to himself. *Well, a staff would be helpful! Before I go to an agency, I wonder if Kelly may know someone with industry experience that she could recommend?*

"Hey, Kelly… It's Marty Cooper."

"Hello, Mr. Cooper. How are things going?"

"Very fast, thank you."

Kelly laughed, "I'll bet. What can I do for you?"

Marty sighed. "I realize this is 'off the wall,' but before I go to an agency for an executive assistant, it occurred to me that you may know someone in the industry that would be a fit for my needs. It would help to not have to educate someone."

There was silence!

"I hope I haven't put you in a bad position."

"No… No," replied Kelly, "I'm sorry, my mind immediately started searching. If you could give me a couple of hours, I am sure I could come up with something."

"That would be wonderful, Kelly. I will wait to hear from you… and thank you."

"Mr. Cooper…? um… I would suggest this just be between you and me. Not that there's anything wrong, but perhaps it could be misconstrued."

"Of course, Kelly… and thanks for your forethought."

Kelly hung up the phone both elated and frightened. If her previous thinking were going to develop, this could be a boon, but there could be complications. She would have to be careful.

Circulating in the industry all these years, she, of course, had come to know several women who were very knowledgeable and resourceful. Some had opined that they were open to a new situation. One, in particular, came to mind. Her name was Nancy and she had worked her way up from just another 'backroom body' to the personal assistant to the CEO and Founder of a medium-sized pharmaceutical company. Word had it that he verbally abused her while she did all the work and he took the glory. She and Kelly had struck up a bit of a personal relationship and Kelly felt like she would be perfect.

She looked through her old notes and found her name and number: Nancy Stone. She dialed the cell number and immediately a woman answered "This is Nancy Stone"

"Hello, Nancy. This is Kelly Freeman. I don't know if you remember me…"

"Of Course, how are you, Kelly?"

"Great. It's been a long time."

"Yes… let's see… about two years?" queried Nancy.

"Something like that. Am I interrupting anything?"

"No. I'm just cleaning out my desk."

"*What?*" blurted Kelly.

"Yes… I am leaving Levin and Jones."

"Wow. May I ask, why?"

"Thank you. You are being kind, but I know you know what I have been living with and I've had enough… so I gave my notice this morning and he said, 'You're 'outa here, *now.*'"

"I don't know whether to say I'm sorry or congratulations."

Nancy laughed, "It's the latter."

"Well, you are not going to believe why I am calling. This is too freaky! I have a contact who has just opened an office, is very well funded and is about to make big waves in the industry. He has just acquired offices and needs a, …what shall I say… an 'everything person' to help start and grow the company."

It was Nancy's turn to screech, "You're *kidding!*"

"Nope... and he needs someone now. Why don't we meet after office hours and I will 'fill you in.'"

"That would be fantastic. What time and where?"

"How about the Fox and Hounds at 5 o'clock?"

"That works," agreed Nancy, "see you then... and thanks for thinking of me, Kelly. You're a doll!"

"Let's hope it works out. See you shortly."

Kelly stared at her cellphone as it disconnected and sighed. "Please, let this be the right thing to do," she whispered to herself.

***

Kelly had never been a 'bar person.' She always felt that she was being assessed as a prospect for the dating slaughter. It seemed that nothing had changed. All male eyes swiveled her way, whether they were with a date or not. She was confident enough to not care where she landed on 'the scale.' Those insecurities had faded when she passed 25.

Finding a two-top table against the wall, she sat down just as Nancy came through the door. Kelly remembered being impressed with how she carried herself with such confidence and class.

"Kelly... so nice to see you. You look as successful as ever."

Kelly smiled, "Thank you. I would say the same to you, but considering your events today, I am not sure it applies."

They both laughed and sat down just as the waiter arrived. "What can I get you, ladies"

Nancy looked up, "I'll have a Margarita, please."

"Make that two," responded Kelly

Nancy removed her jacket and settled in her seat as she spoke, "Kelly, wherever this conversation goes, I just want you to know that you saved my ass today. I was trying to be the brave 'wonder woman' after Mr. Asshole finished with me, but I must admit your phone call saved me from plunging either into murder or suicide."

Kelly smiled ruefully, "I don't blame you, although from what little I know about him, I don't think the murder option would have been so bad."

"You're sweet," said Nancy, "but through it all, I knew that I was not a victim. I volunteered for where I was. I always could have opted out but I just could never find the right moment until today. I am still in shock. Frankly, I'm scared shitless. I have a little backup, but my standard of living is going to be altered dramatically."

"Well, let's see if our meeting can bring some hope to your life," said Kelly as she saw the swirling emotions behind the tears. "Let me start at the beginning, but first we need to agree that this meeting is confidential."

"Of course, my lips are sealed."

Kelly continued, "You know as well as I do that in this industry there are always secrets or gossip or conspiracy theories galore. I have learned to keep my head down, my eyes closed, and my mouth shut. So far that has kept me in good stead. I don't quite know why, but for some reason, I instinctively trust you, so I…"

"Thank you," responded Nancy.

"You're welcome. But that 'thank you' may be at a risk you may not be willing to take."

Nancy's eyebrows shot up, "What do you mean?"

"To tell you about this opportunity, I have to give you some background on my situation and see if you are somewhat of the same mentality. I am exposing myself for what I believe to be honorable reasons and if they don't 'jibe' with your philosophies then we can just move on with no consequences."

"Wow… this sounds very mysterious."

Kelly nodded, "In a sense, it is… but let me get this out because my confidence is seeping. I need to ask you a question before I continue. Have you ever had any doubts about the morality of this industry?"

"Oh, my God… *yes*! …but I knew better than to *ever* voice them."

Kelly smiled, "Well, then you understand. I, too, have doubts and that's why I am nervous about this conversation. The scenario I am going to explain is only just developing. Over the years, I have been fortunate to engender a fairly high level of confidence with my bosses. They trust me as far as they can trust anyone. As a result, I have been able to pick up a lot of information that I am not happy that I know. I think that is as far as I want to go. I don't want to be overly dramatic, but it can be dangerous to think too much in this industry. Better we 'drink the Kool-Aid' and shut up."

Nancy's head had not stopped nodding, "I know I am on a different level than you, but what little I have seen and heard has certainly caused me to wonder."

"Well, just remember… head down, eyes closed, deaf ears."

"Yeah!"

"…Anyway," Kelly continued, "if I haven't turned you off, let me continue."

"…No …No …go ahead."

"Recently, my boss… do you remember where I work?"

"Yes. Chiles, Arken, and Associates."

"Yes. My boss is Derek Maurrel, the president. Anyway, he found a man in the industry who is on the rise and decided to bring him, in a sense, on board."

"What do you mean 'in a sense?'"

"I'll get to that in a moment. He wants to 'groom' him in his image and likeness."

"Ahaa…" laughed Nancy, "the inevitable Male ego emerges."

"You're surprised?" scoffed Kelly… "anyway, I am ashamed to say, but I have let my personal feelings about this man interfere with my good judgment."

"Oh… oh," chided Nancy.

"No… No… not in that way. It's just that he is brilliant, has a wonderful family, but… is very naïve about our industry. I believe he is in way over his head. He is being manipulated and he doesn't know it."

"Who isn't in our business," Nancy tittered.

"Tell me about it," agreed Kelly. "So, what they have decided is that they want his brilliant research and marketing ideas to become the 'go to' standard in the industry. They are setting him up with his own company, completely independent of Chiles, Arken, and Associates, but they will control him with consulting contracts. They are funding him from unknown sources and purging any history of their association with him."

Nancy sat staring at Kelly as though she had grown horns, "My God, Kelly, that's positively Machiavellian."

"At the very least," said Kelly. "So, I hope you can understand why I am feeling like I would like to do something for this guy. I am telling you all this because I would like him to have someone on the inside to help when he needs it."

Just then the waiter arrived. "Another…?" he queried, looking at them both.

"Sure… why not!" answered Kelly.

Nancy stared into her glass. Her enthusiasm had certainly been tempered, but Kelly did not know that she, too, had been going through a crisis of conscience on a smaller scale. But size didn't matter… right was right and wrong was wrong.

She had been asked to turn a blind eye to some things that her company had been a part of and it had been eating at her. The thought of, in some small way, retaliating, had never occurred to her... until now. It was very titillating, but scary.

Nancy paused, gathering her thoughts. "I am intrigued and yes, I have some thoughts about the industry. You have been very candid with me so I will be with you. If it weren't for the money and the 'perks,' I would be gone... oh... wait... I am gone," she said, breaking into laughter, "...but I am ready to 'drink some more Kool-Aid'...and the truth is, money 'sooths the savage beast.' Am I prepared to hoist the flag and charge into battle? Hardly! ...but..."

"Precisely where I am," responded Kelly, "I, frankly, don't consider myself a hero... but entertaining these thoughts has given me a strange sense of fulfillment and excitement. If I am not prepared to be a 'flag carrier' then maybe just being a foot soldier is enough."

Kelly took a sip of her drink while they both pondered their respective positions.

"If I were to consider working with this guy, assuming he would offer me the job, how do you see this happening?" asked Nancy.

"I don't have a clue," frowned Kelly, "...Well, that's not exactly true. I did contemplate something, but it hasn't exactly reached the stage of a plan. My thought before I called you was that if you were to work with Marty... oops... one too many drinks... with him, and we were of generally the same mind, the pooling of our information could be valuable for anything that develops down the line. As they say... information is power. I do know that whatever we decide to do or not do, we need to not be seen together. Any further contact would have to be covert, although our respective positions would give us some 'cover' for contact."

Kelly clarified further, "Derek's not so subtle message, with the order for me to expunge all previous communication, was very clear."

"Which was?"

"Don't fuck with the big boys. This is above your pay grade!"

"Yikes!" exclaimed Nancy.

"I don't want to unduly alarm you Nancy, but these people play for keeps. Anything or anyone that comes in their way gets dealt with severely. If we were perceived to be working against *Big Pharma* in any way, our ass is grass and they have the lawnmower."

Nancy shivered, "I'm not sure I have the chutzpah to do something like this."

"Me either, Nancy, but I just feel I have to do something, and collecting a little information surely wouldn't be noticed, especially when we would be at the center of the flow."

"But why are we doing it?" asked Nancy

"Well… for one thing, we may be able to help this guy somewhere down the road. The rest I'm not sure yet, but I know something for sure. We will have a lot of information and 'information is power.'"

***

The next morning, Kelly dialed Marty.

"Marty Cooper."

"Mr. Cooper, it's Kelly Freeman. Do you have a minute?"

"Of course, what can I do for you?"

"I think I may have someone that you could be interested in."

"Splendid."

"I have known her for several years. She just recently left a mid-sized pharmaceutical company and would be available immediately."

"Sounds very interesting, Kelly. When could I meet her?"

"I would have to check. I, of course, did not disclose anything in our conversation, but with the few generalities I laid out, she expressed interest. I'll see if I can set an appointment whenever you are available."

Marty couldn't hide his excitement, "Great… the sooner the better."

"I may be able to get her in this afternoon. Does that work for you?"

Marty looked at his calendar, "Absolutely. How about 3 o'clock?"

"Let's assume that's confirmed, unless you hear back from me. By the way, her name is Nancy Stone. Should she come to your new offices?"

Marty chuckled, "Yes, if she doesn't mind the mess"

"Well, considering she may be the one to help clean it up, it seems appropriate," laughed Kelly.

"Touché… and Kelly, thank you for this. If it works out, I owe you one."

"Not at all. It's my pleasure and I hope it works out. I think you will find her more than what you are looking for."

"I hope so. Talk to you soon."

After hanging up, she dialed Nancy.

"Hello… Nancy Stone."

"What? …after baring my soul, my name is not in your contact list?"

Nancy snickered, "Thanks… I just spewed coffee all over my iPad. What's up?"

"You're on at 3 with Marty Cooper."

"Wow! That was fast."

"Do you know him?" asked Kelly.

Nancy paused, "I don't think so."

"No matter. Just take your resume, your good looks, and knock him dead." Kelly described where the office was and where to park. "Good luck, Nancy. I think this could work."

"Thank you again, Kelly. You don't know what this is doing for my sanity."

"No problem. Keep me posted."

"Will do."

***

Nancy had no problem finding the building and the underground parking. Walking to the elevators, she started feeling 'the butterflies.' What did he need? Did she have the qualifications and experience? What did he want? Could she handle it? Would she like him? Would he like her? "…Stop it…" she yelled to herself. *It is either going to be or not to be. Accept it now and the rest is easy.*

The elevator stopped at 14 and she stepped into utter chaos. Boxes, furniture dollies, moving blankets, and big, sweaty men. She surmised that to the left was her destination. Slipping around the furniture and through the door, she spied a casually dressed man waving directions to one of the movers. Assuming him to be Marty Cooper, she walked over.

"Mr. Cooper," she said hopefully.

"Nancy?" responded Marty.

"Yes… Nancy Stone."

"Nice to meet you, Nancy… Marty Cooper."

Marty couldn't resist an up and down assessment of Nancy. She looked so elegant in her black Versace, just enough makeup to accent her beautiful high cheek bones and the most penetrating green eyes he had ever seen that were assessing him as well.

Having both finished their mutual perusal, Marty said, "Let's go into what will one day be my office." They skirted the activity and found Marty's office with two chairs.

"Excuse the elegance," chuckled Marty.

Nancy laughed, "Very chic."

As they sat down opposite each other, Marty couldn't help looking at her legs.

Well, he's definitely a man, thought Nancy.

"So, Nancy Stone, tell me a little about yourself."

Nancy took a deep breath, "Well, I am 29 years old, single and… out of work."

Marty broke into laughter, "That's a great beginning… How did that happen?"

"Until yesterday, I had worked for Arthur and Associates, a small pharmaceutical…"

"I know that Company," interrupted Marty, "the CEO is… umm… Rod Arthur… right?"

Nancy froze! *Are they friends? Am I already cooked?* "Yes, that's right," she answered. There was silence.

Finally, Marty spoke, "Is there a problem?"

She could see only one way through this. "We had a… what shall I say… difference of opinion and I chose to leave." It hung in the air like a bad odor.

Marty was impressed that she chose to address this immediately. He also was kind of pleased. He had met Rod Arthur a couple of times at various events and had not been impressed. He was an arrogant ass and had belittled Marty when he found out that Marty was a mere employee.

"I think I understand. I have been in his presence a few times," he smiled.

The air whooshed out of her. "Oh… anyway I have known Kelly Freeman for a few years and she suggested that maybe my background could be of help in your new enterprise."

"What were you doing with Mr. Arthur?"

"I was his executive assistant for four years. Basically, I coordinated everything within the company."

"Did you have any experience with social media, media relations, PR, advertising… those areas?"

"Very much so. Those were predominately where Mr. Arthur had me focusing. Being a small company, I had to develop and strengthen relationships. It was often difficult because sometimes the personalities didn't mesh."

Ah… thought Marty… a diplomat. She was saying the company could have grown were it not for Rod Arthur's boorish personality. Marty liked that she wasn't 'badmouthing' Arthur.

Nancy continued, "I worked with all the various media genres, preparing launch information, countering negative attacks, researching, clarifying opinions, contacting experts, etcetera."

Marty's eyebrows raised, "You really were in 'the trenches,' weren't you?"

"Yes, and, in the process, I developed relationships with most of the industry's top people."

"Do you think those relationships will survive your leaving?" asked Marty.

"Actually, I think they will be strengthened, and I will leave it at that."

"Nancy, I am impressed. What about the mechanics of setting up and running a company of this nature?" Marty posed.

"Well, first, it is not strange to me. When I started with Mr. Arthur, there was no infrastructure at all. He was basically a loner and didn't appreciate the need for support. As a result, I had to set up not only the systems but the physical necessities as well. I guess, the short answer is… this would be easier. There are no entrenched biases in place."

Marty stood up and started pacing. "As you can see, I am starting from scratch. Whoever I hire as my assistant will be leaned on heavily. I will be trusting them totally in all areas of the company. Would this concern you?"

"Not at all. It's not foreign to me," replied Nancy confidently.

Pacing again, Marty stopped and turned to Nancy, "Let's get something out of the way. What would be your expectation of remuneration?"

Nancy paused. She had not expected the first interview to reach this level.

"This is all so sudden. I haven't really given that any consideration. I don't feel as though I am in a position to negotiate," she smiled, "I am at your mercy."

Marty laughed, "Yes, it is rather sudden. Initially, I am very impressed. I am sure you can appreciate I need to do a background check, but assuming it pans out, I would be willing to offer you $75,000 a year plus expenses with stock options and bonuses to be negotiated as we move forward."

"That's more than generous."

"Great. Text me your full name, address and social number. I will order the background today and should be back in touch with you within a couple of days."

Nancy stood and accepted his handshake. "Thank you, Mr. Cooper. You will not regret this decision."

"I believe you," said Marty while leading her through the maze of furniture to the elevator. "Oh… when could you start?"

"Should I start moving furniture now?" She said, laughing.

"Could you *please*?" answered Marty.

***

"Wheeee," screamed Nancy into her cell, "Kelly, I love you. It went awesomely. What a guy! You were right. I can see why you are helping him. He's so… approachable. He's going to do a background check today. Assuming that's OK, I have the job. Girl, I owe you *so big* I'll never be able to repay you."

Kelly couldn't stop smiling, "You don't owe me… just don't embarrass me."

"Not a chance."

"When do you start?"

"Now."

Chapter 4

No sooner had Nancy left, Marty's cell chirped. "Hello, Derek."

"Marty. It looks like I am needing your services sooner than expected."

"Good. What can I do?"

"We have a congressman who is going on an industry Mediterranean cruise in four days and we need some massaging. Are you and your wife able to arrange to be on the cruise for eight days. It's a cruise full of industry people so you will be able to make a lot of contacts as well as settle the congressman down. It appears he has received some bad research results on Sistophan."

"Whoo…" Marty grimaced and paused.

"Is there a problem?" asked Derek.

Marty detected some irritation, "No… No… I was just running through the stuff I need to move around. Of course, we will go. I just need to call Myra and alert her."

"Splendid, Marty," Derek responded in a much cheerier tone, "when the consulting agreement is completed, we'll get together and I will fill you in on the details. You'll be leaving on Sunday the 12th in the morning."

Marty hit Myra's speed dial.

"Hey, handsome… What's up?"

"A lot. Are you sitting down?"

"I can't stand up in the car, dummy… Wait, is this good or bad?" probed Myra.

"Good, with some problems."

"Hmmm… Give me the good first and I will figure out the problems."

"In four days, we are going for an eight-day cruise in the Mediterranean."

"Stop kidding around. What is the news?" she demanded.

"Seriously. We are."

There was dead silence.

"Hello."

"Marty, if this is some kind of joke, I'll…"

"My! It's true. All-expenses paid."

"…but…what about a baby sitter… your office…"

"Don't worry, we'll work those things out. I just heard. We leave on the morning of the 12th. I have to run. I'll give you more details when I get home, but I wanted to give you a heads-up right away."

***

"Pam," Tom Chiles bellowed. Pam Styles strode into the office in her usual elegant, yet aloof manner.

"Mr. Chiles?"

"I thought we had reached an understanding that I was not to be bothered with any calls from Norm Arthur."

"Sir. He insisted that he speak with you and became rather belligerent. That's why I put the call through."

"Who do you work for… me, or COSM?" (*Council on Safe Medicine*) Pam didn't flinch, didn't move… just stared at him with her smoldering black eyes. *Damn her* he thought, *if she wasn't the most sought-after executive assistant in the industry, he'd fire her ass.*

She was the perfect gatekeeper. Stunningly beautiful, totally unflappable, highly educated, and dreadfully imposing. She could bring any visitor to their knees in ten seconds flat.

Tom acquiesced, "OK… OK. I *do* understand, but, Pam, this guy is giving us fits and until Derek can get Marty up to full steam, we need to cool Norm down."

Pam eyed him warily, "What are you suggesting?"

"I don't know… I do know that he is quite taken with you. Could you, maybe, offer to have a drink or something with him?"

"Mr. Chiles. We have been through this before. I…"

"Wait… wait. I don't mean anything untoward. Just a casual conversation to reiterate our stance on Sistophan. It would be extremely helpful." Again, Pam just stared.

"…Tell you what," started Tom, "I know that you have been putting in a lot of extra energies these last few weeks. How about we book you on that industry cruise to the Mediterranean in four days. You could use the break." Pam turned to go. "All-expenses paid," burst out Tom.

She paused. "Let me see if I can fit it in my schedule," she said… and closed the door.

Pam had always maintained an aloofness, particularly about her private life. Although she had grown up in a privileged environment, she had been badly damaged psychologically and physically and, therefore, trusted no one. Her beauty, and what appeared as superiority, kept her apart from close personal relationships, when, in fact, she was lonely.

Her one attempt at a relationship ended with his infidelity, which only strengthened her mistrust of men. She withdrew even more. In the process, she learned that her looks and obvious excellent upbringing, together with her quiet demeanor, opened doors much more effectively than conversation.

She had spurned propositions many times in many ways, but this time, perhaps out of fatigue or curiosity, she decided to consider Mr. Chiles' suggestion.

***

Myra was at the garage door before Marty could get out of the car. "When, where, how, who, and why?" she yelped.

"Can't I even get in the house?" begged Marty, laughing.

"Well… I guess so, but no more stalling."

As he walked in the door, a human missile flew into his arms. "Daddy… Daddy… let's play monster." Myra grabbed her, "Mommy and Daddy have to talk, Cara. Daddy will play in a minute." Heading to the bar, Myra said, "Let me get us a drink."

"Yes… thanks."

Myra carried their drinks to the sofa, "OK Mr.… Talk!"

Marty laughed, "There really isn't that much to tell. Derek called and said there was a problem with a congressman and I needed to try and clear it up. He is going to be on an eight-day pharmaceutical cruise in the Mediterranean starting on the 12th and I am supposed to try and sway his thinking. He wants us both there because it is a chance for us to mix with some of the 'who's who' of the pharmaceutical industry. It really is an incredible opportunity."

Myra's head was bobbing, "Oh, Marty, it really is. I am *so* excited, but I'll be a nervous wreck."

"Why?"

"Well… all these giants of the industry and us."

"Hey," snorted Marty, "what are we… 'chopped liver?'"

"No… you know what I mean. A couple of weeks ago, you were just a paper pusher at a little tiny company."

"Thanks," whined Marty.

"You know what I mean," scolded Myra again.

"I know what you mean," Marty said as he stroked Myra's hair, "something we both need to realize is that we are in the 'big leagues' now. These guys are going to be using my services."

"Our services?"

"Of course, …Sorry."

Myra leaned over and pecked Marty on the cheek. "I love you. Now let's have dinner. Oh, we will probably have to use my mother to baby sit."

"Oh, Great," groaned Marty.

"I'm sorry, Marty, but I can't get anyone else on such short notice."

"I understand."

There was silence, then Marty spoke, "Oh, Derek's assistant, Kelly, had me meet one of her contacts to be my executive assistant. She came over to the office this afternoon. She's perfect. Worked for the CEO of Arthur and Associates and just quit yesterday. She has everything I need and more. So, subject to her background check, I have hired her."

Myra gave him a funny look.

"What?" asked Marty.

"That's rather impulsive, isn't it?"

"Perhaps, but I need someone *now*, being as I am leaving in four days and she has done a 'start up' before, so there is no learning period."

"Well, I hope you're right. You said she has everything you need and more. Just don't let 'more' get out of hand."

"*Myra*!"

"…just kidding."

Marty slapped her on the butt, "Well, no more of that!"

"Yes, sir!" she laughed.

***

Nancy ran and caught the call on the second ring. "Hello, …Nancy Stone."

"Nancy, this is Marty Cooper. I hope I'm not imposing."

"No… not at all."

"Well, Nancy, I just wanted to let you know that your background check came out just fine."

Nancy started jumping around. "Oh, I'm so glad. I was afraid the attempted murder charge would show up," she chuckled.

Marty started laughing, "Well, actually it did, but because the shot missed, they didn't think it mattered." Nancy roared with laughter.

"So… with that out of the way, this is my formal offer to come 'on board' as my executive assistant."

Nancy hoped her voice wouldn't fail her, "Thank you, Mr. Cooper. I accept with gratitude"

"There in one piece of news that I need to tell you."

Nancy's heart skipped a beat, "Yes?"

"I unexpectedly have to go on an eight-day business trip in four days. Need I say that this puts a lot of pressure on us both?"

"No pressure for me, Mr. Cooper. I can hold the fort."

"Excellent," responded Marty. "Can you come in tomorrow morning and we'll clear up the paper work and plot our next moves."

"What time would you like me there?"

"Let's get an early start… Say, 8? On the way in I will pick us up some breakfast and we can eat while we start the day."

"Sounds great," enthused Nancy.

"Oh… and Nancy… just wear jeans or something casual. We'll be working in a mess."

"No problem, Mr. Cooper. See you at 8 and thank you again."

Nancy punched Kelly's number.

"Hi, Nancy."

"I got it!"

"Congratulations!"

"Thanks to you. I start tomorrow morning at 8… guess what? He is going away in four days on an eight-day cruise."

"Well, nothing like starting with 'a bang.'"

Kelly set the phone down and smiled. *Well,* she thought as a famous detective novelist once said, *the game is afoot.*

***

As arranged, Nancy arrived at 8 and Marty was already at his desk with bags of takeout. The next hour was taken up with eating and planning.

"Nancy, just so you know where we are heading, although in competition, the pharmaceutical companies all face a common enemy: Namely, the entities that are never satisfied with the research results and are always attempting to stop or delay the launch of new products. Our job is to constantly feed the media with data and scientific opinions that not only refute but may, on occasion, malign the natural medicine experts. Are you OK with that?"

"Of course. I am assuming our experts and the FDA are far more accredited than theirs," speculated Nancy.

"Exactly! Experts, the FDA, and the AMA are the three key points that we will be pounding. In that regard, I will be spending some time on the cruise with Dr. Arthur Kenmore and a congressman from Colorado. The agenda is to strengthen the congressman's commitment to previous products as well as the Sistophan launch."

Marty continued, "As you become familiar with our research on the various social media and how it is utilized, I will be looking to you more and more to activate that research. The central issue for us is that we can never be caught 'flat footed' by our adversary's charges. I have an old sales axiom that I was taught: 'Remove the objection before it arises.'"

"Our research and sources need to feed us notice of objections that will appear in the mainstream media and then we can be 'out in front'. As they say, we only get one opportunity for a first impression. Our first impression is that our research results, together with the FDA approvals, are the protectors, and any negative reference by our adversaries to those approvals, from our perspective, is careless, irresponsible, and just plain propaganda."

Nancy was nodding her head in agreement, "I understand."

"Nancy, these adversaries can be very convincing and I need to know that despite what you hear or see, you are committed to staying the course. Always remember that, no matter what, we support an industry whose major motivation is to solve medical problems. As in any honorable venture, there may be tragic setbacks, but we must accept that the end justifies the means in drug research."

"You can count on me, Mr. Cooper."

"Great... Now let's work on what's going to go where in this mayhem."

Chapter 5

Dr. Arthur Kenmore was a handsome man. He strode into Tom's office with the imperious air of academic superiority. His tall, thin physique, topped by his long, speckled grey hair spoke of knowledge that you challenged at your own risk.

Tom Chiles had first met Dr. Kenmore at a cocktail party some years earlier and quickly realized that the Dr.'s ego, combined with Tom's manipulative proficiency, could breed a strong ambassador for *Big Pharma* generally and Chiles, Arken, and Associates specifically.

Dr. Kenmore's alignment with the pharmaceutical industry had been a principled decision predicated on the noble ideal of saving lives.

Whenever possible, *Big Pharma* publicly extolled Kenmore's academic achievements while introducing him to the splendor of libertine living. That allure inevitably indoctrinated the Dr. to the pragmatic acceptance of 'the end justifies the means.'

His learning, refinement, knowledge of the science, accomplishments, and esteem gave heavy corroboration to the FDA approval process, at the same time trumping alternative arguments.

Entering the room, the Doctor was not accorded his accustomed greeting and a perturbed look crossed his face. "Tom," his deep voice boomed.

Quietly, Tom spoke without looking up, "One moment, please." …and continued to read some papers. Inwardly, he smiled. It was a cheap gesture, but with an ego of this size, it was effective. The Doctor sniffed the air as if in the presence of human offal, but to no effect.

Tom finally looked up, "How are you, Arthur," furthering the slight with the first name. The startled look on Dr. Kenmore was proof of the effect. Before the Doctor could rebuff Tom, he rose from his desk.

"Have you confirmed your veranda suite with the cruise line?"

Doctor Kenmore hesitated. Tom jumped in, "No problem. I'll have Pam handle it." He waved at the seating area, "Sit down."

They moved toward the seating area. "Arthur, I just wanted to have a little chat about your upcoming interview with the World-Wide Network (*WWN*)… and, by the way, congratulations! I understand you have just been appointed as their new medical expert."

Arthur's chest puffed up, "Thank you… Thank you. It's a great honor and…"

"Well earned, I'm sure," interrupted Derek. Both understood that Tom was a good friend of the chairman of WWN. Dr. Kenmore's name had been 'dropped' at a social event, which precipitated the announcement. "Your credentials are earning you quite the notoriety in medical circles and the appointment to the President's commission didn't hurt at all either," suggested Tom.

This prompting as to where his loyalties should lay was not lost on Dr. Kenmore. In a feeble attempt at salvaging some dignity, he muttered, "Well… If it weren't for Chiles, Arken, and Associates, who knows where I would be." The sarcasm was not lost on Tom.

"Exactly," retorted Tom, "and we are grateful for your views on our products. Now… on to other matters."

"We have struck a consulting agreement with a new and exciting company… Cooper and Associates. The CEO is a gentleman by the name of Marty Cooper. He will be on the cruise with you, as will Congressman Chet Barnes from Colorado, who heads the committee regulating the FDA. It seems that the congressman has developed some difficult views regarding one of our previous creations as well as our new product – Sistophan, and we are hopeful that when he is educated on your views, he will be more positive in his perspective. Marty, with his media expertise, will assist you in developing a wider familiarity with the lab and FDA results. I'm sure, with your knowledge and articulation, Congressman Barnes will see the light."

The Dr. puffed up, "I am familiar with the congressman's views and I look forward to clarifying his heretofore resolute stance."

Oh God, thought Tom, *please deliver me from this pompous bloviating ass.* Instead, he perfunctorily offered, "Wonderful."

On cue, the door opened and Pam spoke excitedly "Mr. Chiles, I am so sorry to interrupt, but Mr. Carter from Goldmans needs to speak to you. It's an emergency."

"Please, excuse me for a minute," Tom said as he stepped to his desk and took the call.

"What is it, Arnie," listening intently, he smiled, "that sounds like very good news. Why don't we go ahead and make an offer? That should cause some buying. When will you announce? ...Tomorrow afternoon just before the bell... sounds excellent. Good work, Arnie."

Tom set his phone down. "Now, where were we...? Oh, yes. So, can we count on your help with Congressman Barnes?"

"Most assuredly!"

"Arthur..." Tom winked, "I know I can trust your integrity, but I need your assurance that you did not hear that phone conversation just now."

Arthur shrugged his shoulders, "I know not to what conversation you refer."

"Good. Are we done here?" asked Tom as he rose. "If I don't talk to you before, have a great trip"

"Thank you, Tom."

As the door closed, Tom winked at Pam, "Good timing."

His psyche badly damaged, Arthur, once again, swore that this was the last time he would subject himself to these boorish barbarians. This debasement had to end.

Acquiescing to the discussion with the congressman was a golden opportunity to score one more major triumph in his quest to be honored with 'a chair' at an Ivy League school.

Unfortunately, this was all under the patronage of Tom Chiles, whom he despised, which justified the use of the *accidental* information he had just overheard. *Accidental? who am I kidding,* he thought.

His offshore trust would be receiving a 'buy' instruction.

Although Tom Chiles had some clout with 'the association,' his diplomatic skills needed to be sharp. An extremely secure meeting had been called unexpectedly to deal with the rising public criticism of the FDA, the NIH *(National Institute of Health),* as well as the CDC *(Center for Disease Control).* Tom had accepted the challenge to handle any issues and now his fellow members of *Big Pharma* wanted answers.

"Tom," said Albert Ashbury, CEO of the second largest pharmaceutical in the world, "you promised us six months ago that these issues would soon be behind us. What the hell is going on?"

"You're right, Albert... I did, and they will be. As you know, the political arena has been altered and we have had to introduce some new solutions."

Frank Morrison, CEO of Brinkly Salsman, the fourth largest drug company, slammed his fist on the table, "Give us that in English, Tom"

"It means that the election brought us a new congressman that we have not, as yet, been able to corral. Next week, there will be some news that will change the picture considerably," said Tom.

They both looked curiously at each other and, finally, Frank spoke up, "Can you fill us in?"

"No," said Tom, "...and that's the only answer you would want."

***

Marty pushed away from his desk and started pacing, wondering if he was going to survive to see his vision reach fruition. The pressure from Derek had been crushing.

With the upcoming cruise, Marty had been prepping with every contact and internet source available in anticipation of the meeting with the congressman. He realized that Dr. Arthur Kenmore would be doing the heavy lifting, but Marty needed to have the very latest information at Kenmore's fingertips.

He continuously thanked God for Nancy who had basically built the office single-handedly. A receptionist had been hired and interviews were underway for additional staff. Bank accounts had been opened and office equipment and supplies were being stocked. The telephone and electronics were functional and almost complete.

Nancy leaned into Marty's office. "Mr. Cooper?" ...startling Marty from his brooding, "the IT people are here and we need to meet."

Marty hung his head... "OK. Are they in the boardroom?"

"Yes."

"Good. I'll be right there."

The IT company had been recommended by Tom Chiles and, unbeknownst to Marty, had extra instructions.

As Marty and Nancy finished the briefing on all the equipment and its operation, Nancy noticed some suspicious anomalies. She was certain there were listening and tracking capabilities on everything. She knew this because what had not shown up on her background check was that, in her teen years, she had developed a strong interest in computers and became an amateur 'hacker.'

She knew what she was looking at and her first impulse was to raise the issue. Then it occurred to her that this was powerful knowledge. She would have to talk to Kelly.

Kelly answered on the first ring.

"Kelly! I need to see you. Where are you?"

"I'm in the building coffee shop."

"Are you alone?"

"Yes… but…"

"I'll be right there," and she hung up.

Nancy rushed in, spied Kelly, and strode purposely to her table and sat down. "I just confirmed some original suspicions I had," said Nancy excitedly, "the IT people have finished. Every piece of equipment has been tampered with and it is very sophisticated. Whatever transpires in our offices will be available to whoever had this ordered."

With a startled look around, Kelly responded under her breath, "I don't think we should be seen together here."

"Oh, damn. I never thought about that."

"Well, don't worry about it this time. Now start at the beginning."

"I don't think I told you I have a little knowledge with computers and software in my history."

"No… I didn't know."

"Well, I have. Yesterday, when we were working with the IT people, who, by the way, were recommended by Derek, I noticed something disturbing. After they left, I checked and found that every telephone, computer, laptop, and tablet has been altered to be remotely monitored. In other words, everything that happens in that office is public knowledge to someone."

Kelly gasped, "You're kidding. This is like the conspiracy theories that we laugh about."

"I wish I was kidding… and furthermore, I think we may be wired for voice monitoring as well."

Kelly sat stunned, "But *why*!"

"You tell me!" blurted Nancy, "we obviously need to be careful and I want to do some thinking. You live in Plano. Right?"

"Close! I live up in Frisco."

"Today is Thursday. Let's meet on Saturday at 3. Do you know that little coffee shop in the Shops at Legacy? I forget the name…"

"Java Jive Joint!"

"Yes," said Nancy.

"Works for me. See you then."

For the life of her, Kelly could not fathom the surveillance that Nancy had discovered. It obviously was in anticipation of some sort of fallacious activity. But what? By who?

On occasion, she had read what she thought was mere conspiratorial twaddle about mysterious events and even deaths associated with the pharmaceutical industry. But even if there was any element of reality, what could that have to do with Marty's office. He was merely gathering information for the support of the drug industry's products. It was information available to anyone if they used Cooper Consulting.

The only hypothesis she could visualize was that it was for internal surveillance. If that was true, then Marty was the main target and, by default, Nancy.

This obviously was a precautionary defensive action. The IT group had to have instructions from Derek. She remembered on occasion she had heard him recommending the IT company to other companies and individuals.

Then 'the light went on.' She had been asked to purge any records of previous association between Chiles, Arken, and Associates and Marty.

Cooper and Associates was a service for the entire industry, not just Chiles. Any confidential information communicated to Cooper in competitors' consultations would covertly be available to Chiles. She reflected further. The spectacular growth of Chiles, Arken, and Associates now began to come into focus. What other furtive operations had been enacted over the years.

The scope of the malfeasance was astonishing! She began to revisit her intentions. If her speculations had any validity at all, she was in a 'game' for which she was ill-equipped.

***

In three days, on Sunday, Myra and Marty were to fly to Venice. Myra was madly preparing which included some new outfits. Northridge Mall was not far from Marty's office, so she thought she would 'pop' in the office and see how things were coming along.

Stepping off the elevator, she was shocked at the progress in the last few days. The reception area was ready for whatever decorations were arriving. She saw Marty and a woman conversing in the board room with some workers.

Marty spied her through the glass and waved her over. As she approached the door, the woman turned. Myra almost gasped. She was stunning. Jealousy flooded her body.

Marty came to the door. "Myra... what a nice surprise." He hugged her and then turned and said, "Nancy Stone, meet my wife, Myra... Myra, meet Nancy Stone."

"Mrs. Cooper," beamed Nancy, "I finally get to meet you. I have heard about you nonstop. Such a pleasure."

There was slightly awkward pause, then Myra spoke, "Thank you." She replied brusquely, "I could say the same thing about you. From what I understand, you have single-handedly brought this office to life. My congratulations." She said haughtily.

The silence was deafening

"What brings you here?" enthused Marty.

"I was just doing some shopping for our trip," she said as she glanced again at Nancy.

Feeling some discomfort, Nancy demurred, "Let me get back to the IT guys. Great to meet you, Mrs. Cooper."

"Let me show you around," offered Marty.

Myra couldn't help herself. "She's very attractive, Marty," she said scornfully.

"…and extremely competent," Marty bristled, "…and what kind of tone is that?"

Myra flushed "…I'm sorry, Marty, she just caught me by surprise."

"It's not like you to be rude," chided Marty, "that was embarrassing."

Her blush deepened. "Oh, God… I am so sorry. Do you think she noticed?"

"I don't see how she couldn't. Myra, she has been a godsend to me… us. I could not be anywhere near where I am without her. Is this going to be a problem?"

"No… No… Should I apologize or something?"

"No. Let's let it lay and maybe later you can find an opportunity to make it up to her."

"…So," Marty continued, "…what do you think? Fabulous, isn't it?"

"I can't believe it, Marty. It's like it was just sitting here, waiting for us."

"Exactly. Now I've got to go and finish with the IT guys. Do you want to wander around for a while?"

Myra shook her head, "No. I should go and besides, I'm embarrassed."

"Don't worry. If it comes up, I will smooth it over and then you girls can start of on a different foot."

Myra leaned into him and gave him a long hug and kiss. "Thanks Marty. I love you."

"I know," Marty smiled, "I'm very lovable."

She smacked him with her purse. "See you back at home."

Chapter 6

When Tom had heard about the congressman's new hardened position, together with the added pressure from his peers, there was only one answer, which made him uncomfortable. However, comfort was not in the equation.

He had placed a call to his contact yesterday and awaited the return call on his 'burner phone.' He smiled ruefully, remembering his contact had warned him never to trust the telephone system.

The 'burner' cell buzzed. "Yes," answered Tom.

A quiet, deep voice said, "Are you available now?"

"Yes," responded Tom.

"Pipi's at Park and Preston in thirty minutes. Ditch the phone." …click!

Cloak-and-dagger had never been Tom's forte but… 'when in Rome… etc.'

He pushed open Pipi's door and the hostess smiled cheerfully, "May I help you?"

"I am meeting someone," responded Tom as he scanned the restaurant. By the window, sitting alone with a low-slung hat and a newspaper was the man he only knew as Monk.

"That's him. Thank you," he said and walked toward the table.

The man did not look up as Tom sat down, but said, "Did you ditch the phone?"

"Yes."

"Here's three new ones. One per call," he said as he slid a paper bag across the table. Still not looking up, he growled, "Tell me quickly about the job."

"A gentleman, by the name of Chet Barnes, will be on a cruise with you starting on Sunday. The details are on this paper," Tom said, sliding the folded sheet across the table.

Monk stared at the paper, "You mean Congressman Chet Barnes, don't you?"

"Yes," replied Tom.

Monk pushed the paper back to Tom, "This is not a normal deal."

Tom raised an eyebrow, "Is it the money?"

Monk paused. "Partly," he said, gazing out the window. "...Are there multiple stops on the cruise?" he asked. Tom was stumped. "I suppose so... yes," stammered Tom

"Good!" ...another long pause. "Now, to the money!" he said, taking back the paper.

"I understand your difficulties and the need for haste. I also understand the substantial positive financial repercussions after the fact."

He raised his head slowly, "The price is one million dollars. Half upfront, wired in the usual manner when I call you, and half on completion." A shiver went through Tom as he stared into the cold, dead eyes. The look said 'we are *not* negotiating.'

Tom nodded, "What do you need from me?"

"Nothing. I will contact you when I have made arrangements." Monk rose and walked away.

Tom stared at the receding figure, realizing that he knew very little about Monk, A friend of a friend had recommended him some years ago, and he had proven to be efficient and dependable, albeit expensive. There had never been the slightest hint of trouble.

Even if Tom had tried to do a background check on Monk, he would have hit a wall. Although he had no formal training in the worlds of espionage, assassination, covert operations, or any other aligned enterprises, Tom would have been surprised to know that Monk's expertise had been acquired right there in the Dallas metroplex.

He had grown up in the Lake Highlands area in a middle-class home, but, definitely, not typical. His full name was Franklin Carol Monkman. He was an only child and was extremely gifted. There was nothing that Monk, as he became known, could not learn. His inquisitiveness was legend and great things for him were forecast.

Alas, all things were not as they seemed. From the moment he was born, he was introduced to violence, both in and out of the home. His father, a former military man of unknown origins, was secretly employed, on a piecemeal basis, by the underworld and had no qualms in exposing his son to the workings of that dark underbelly of society. As expected, Monk became a seething, ticking timebomb, with an incredible intellect.

On one occasion in his early twenties, he had run afoul of the law and been indicted on a felony charge of manslaughter in the death of a young woman. A good lawyer and some well-placed intimidation had led to an acquittal. However, during the process, Monk had learned two things:

He vowed never to be careless and be caught again, and that the world of eliminating people was a very lucrative business.

After a mysterious fire at his home, in which both his parents burned to death, the rumor surfaced that his father had reneged on a huge debt to some shady people and the organization had paid someone $50,000 for the 'hit' and Monk was rumored to have done the job.

After the incident, Monk stayed just long enough to show, as best he could, his sorrow at the loss of his parents and then proceeded to drop off the face of the earth for more than twenty years during which time he perfected his acting and killing talents. The reason for the disappearance was well known. The contractor for the hit considered Monk's father's debt to be a family matter inherited by the son.

***

Tom finished his coffee as his musings were interrupted by the waiter with the check. He paid the bill and headed to his car. Suddenly, it occurred to him that having made this decision, the cruise agenda was irrelevant, but for appearances, it would be wise to continue the charade.

Pam was leaving Tom's office as Tom exited his private elevator carrying the small paper bag of phones. It surprised her that he didn't look his usual, confident self. In her history with Chiles, Arken, and Associates, she had never seen anything but certitude in his manner.

"Pam, get me Derek," he barked and slammed the door to his office.

"Mr. Maurrel's office," answered Kelly.

"Mr. Chiles for Mr. Maurrel," said Pam. Kelly connected to Derek.

"Derek… get up here," Tom barked.

"Be right there."

As forceful a personality as Derek was, there were times in Tom's presence that he was intimidated. Usually it was when asked to follow through on something that transcended his personal boundaries. As always, he could vindicate those decisions with the balm of rationalization: *We are saving people's lives.* He approached Tom's office, wondering if this was another one of those times. He rapped on the door and entered. Tom was sitting in the corner 'library' and waved him over to the other chair.

"How's our boy doing?"

"Marty? He's doing great. His office is close to fully operational, the systems we talked about are being installed as we speak and he has an executive assistant that is very effective and, I might say, drop-dead gorgeous. If he wasn't going on the cruise, I am sure he would be staffed up in a week or two."

"That's what I want to talk to you about."

"What? Staffing up?"

"No… the cruise." Tom resettled in his chair, "how confident are you as to how Marty would be under pressure?"

It was Derek's turn to shift, "Uh… What kind of pressure?"

"What if he were to come under some legal scrutiny of a criminal nature?"

Derek paused, "I guess that would depend on whether he had done something and was trying to hide it. I don't think he would 'hold up' if he was asked to lie."

"But if he hadn't done anything and didn't know anything?"

"I think he would be very indignant in voicing his innocence."

"Good," muttered Tom.

Confused, Derek ventured, "What's this about?"

Tom hesitated… "There may be an incident during the cruise. Suffice to say that it is positive for us. He will not be involved, but there's no doubt that there will be an in-depth investigation and I just wanted to get a feel for his stability under duress?"

Derek smiled, "Well, if he doesn't know anything, then he doesn't know anything. Right?"

"So be it," Tom grinned. "Now on to something else. I have decided Pam should be on the cruise. Her workload has been rather strenuous lately and she needs a break. I just wanted you to be aware. Perhaps as Marty is circulating, he could introduce her around."

"I'll apprise him," agreed a now paranoid Derek. *Very odd,* he thought, '*Is Tom using Pam to monitor his people?*

***

The past five days had been an absolute nightmare for Marty. The industry cruise could not have come at a worse time. Between training Nancy, completing research for Dr. Kenmore and Congressman Barnes, and helping Myra get ready, he felt like he was being torn apart. In addition, he now had learned that Pam was joining the cruise.

Although this did not directly affect Marty, he could not help but wonder if she was there to report his actions to Tom Chiles.

The news that Norm Arthur of COSM was also on the cruise had pleased Marty because it would give him a chance for some 'one-on-one.' He had toyed with the idea of having all the parties involved get together and cover the issues in one session, but had thought better of it. Divide and conquer was a better game plan. He would have to do some serious scheduling.

They were two days away from their flight to Venice and Myra was in full panic mode. Marty, understandably, was of no help. She had been 'ticking off' the prep list but still was uncertain of the required attire, so she had 'contingent packed' for everything.

His load in getting ready for the business end of the trip had eroded a lot of the excitement for her, but she did not begrudge him that, hoping it was not a precursor of the entire trip.

Thanks to Nancy, Cooper Consulting was developing nicely. Interviews for three researchers were completed. After cursory discussions with applicants, Marty and Nancy deliberated. They agreed on two of the applicants and Marty foisted the hiring on to Nancy, with instructions for them to report on the day Marty returned. He and Nancy had agreed that she had more experience 'in the market' and, therefore, should negotiate the pay scale.

He did explain to Nancy that he believed in slightly overpaying people for two reasons. One: it commanded loyalty, and two: it dissuaded poaching. Nancy smiled secretly, totally understanding Marty's philosophy. *He maybe 'green,'* she thought, *but he isn't stupid.*

Nancy could not have been more pleased with her decision to join Cooper Consulting. She had sensed some attitude from Mrs. Cooper, but that was a customary reaction from women and particularly, wives.

Mr. Cooper had given her the freedom she had so desired in her old position and she could demonstrate her abilities with unfettered execution.

She studied Mr. Cooper's research relentlessly and realized the opportunities that Derek had seen. The amalgamation of all the new social media sectors was a daunting undertaking that she could see could evolve into a propaganda giant.

As her horizons widened, she now understood what Kelly had actualized… That anyone utilizing this new technology accorded themselves an incredible edge in media management and thus, public perception.

The diabolical plan was brilliant. As the industry companies contract Cooper, Derek and Tom, with their covert espionage, would be privy to all participating companies' information.

Pam routinely was in and out of Tom's office retrieving instructions. She noticed today he seemed distracted. As usual, she was conscious of his furtive glances, but this time, there was a subtle difference. Picking up a sheath of papers, she started to leave when he looked up from his desk.

"Only two days to the cruise. Are you ready?" he ventured.

"In what way?" she responded.

What is it with her! Once again, he felt off-balance, "I meant... packed, and... whatever."

"Yes. I'm ready. Will there be anything else?"

"Have you thought anymore about my request regarding Norm Arthur? You may not be aware, but the *Council on Safe Medicine (COSM)*, ergo Norm Arthur, is one of our largest adversaries, so I hope you can find an appropriate time to speak with him."

She met his eyes, "I would assume the close confines of the ship would present some opportunities to meet him."

"...yes...well... I hope you will also meet and speak to Congressman Barnes."

"That would be nice," she offered.

"OK," he muttered. In a feeble effort to retain some authority, he interrupted Pam as she turned to exit the office. "Pam. Are you contented here?"

She turned, "I beg your pardon?"

"Are you contented with your job?"

"Have I done something wrong?" she said.

"No... No... I just want to be sure we are on the same team."

"Of course, sir" she replied coolly as she exited. *What the hell was that all about,* she thought. In all the time she had been with Chiles, Arken, and Associates, she had not seen this level of apprehension. Something was up! She would have to keep her wits about her on the cruise.

***

Derek had spent Friday night tossing and turning and now driving to the office, he weighed Tom's comment about an incident on the cruise. Whatever he was meaning, his lack of knowledge would afford him some protection if there were consequences, but he wondered if he might be caught in a web of circumstances not of his making.

His tenure with Tom, if nothing else, had revealed there was nothing that would deter Tom's compulsion to attain his goals. Derek had previously seen Tom's duplicitous methods executed with success and he was sure whatever was unfolding now would achieve the same end.

Derek had certainly participated in some questionable events in the past which, as usual, were justified for 'the sake of the children' or 'the means justifies the end,' but those old platitudes, for him, were showing their age.

He knew from experience it was useless to review the past, with its myriad of regrettable decisions. That would only lead to the usual banal recitations of 'the ultimate good we are doing.'

These 'sleepless night qualms' were invariably followed by recriminations. *But it's a little late for those*, he thought.

When his conscience had been breached, the power of the rewards metastasized the greed, and fear engulfed his psyche. Fear of loss, fear of shame, fear of discovery, fear of the law were now his constant companions. His only exit was to stay, feign compliance, complete the walk, and empty the pot at the end of the rainbow. Perhaps later there would be time to salvage himself.

No sooner was Derek sitting at his desk than Kelly buzzed. "Yes, Kelly."

"Mr. Chiles would like to see you."

"Thank you." Again, this reaction of foreboding! He walked up the staircase.

"Mr. Chiles is waiting for you," said Pam.

Derek opened the door and was met with a big smile, "Derek… come in." If nothing else, Tom was a master at 'the off-balance opening.'

"How are things going," he queried.

Derek nodded and warily responded, "Great… what's up?"

Tom covertly observed Derek. One of his principal assets was gauging human nature and his antenna was aquiver. They walked over to the den area in the office. Tom continued, "The other day, you suggested that we have a conversation directed toward our long-term goals."

"I did… I did," responded Derek.

"Was it something specific or were you just thinking generally?"

Despite the years they had been together, and no matter how Derek steeled himself, Tom was always able to disarm whatever defense Derek erected. A discussion would begin on equal footing and immediately devolve to Teacher / Student.

It was time to 'grow a pair.'

Derrek began, "First, let me again express my appreciation for what you have done for me over these years. I couldn't be more grateful to you for mentoring me on this journey capped with the presidency. Having said that, it has been some time since we addressed the issue of additional stock options. The launch of Cooper and Associates, together with my shepherding through the FDA, the recent successes of Tamsitor, Saxitoxin, and now Sistophan, leads me to suggest the time has arrived."

Tom turned and stared into the fireplace. He didn't dare look at Derek for fear he would reach out and grab his throat. *The ungrateful bastard! A nobody, plucked out of the herd. A whelp, barely able to shave, brought from obscurity to be president of a Fortune 500 company earning in excess of fifteen million a year plus existing stock options...* and he wanted more!

He had a moment of compassion. At least Derek had the balls to ask. How he wanted to respond was, 'don't let the door hit you in the ass.'

Instead, he gathered his senses. This was not the 'hill to die on' with Derek. That day would come, but with all that was developing, he needed him at peak performance. This required diplomacy, tact, and just plain old 'bull shit.' Tom stood up. "Follow me," he said

They both walked to Tom's desk. Tom opened a door behind the desk and entered a code on the safe, pulled open the door, and pulled out a stack of files. Setting them on his desk, he culled through them and then handed Derek a bound file.

"Read this."

Derek took the file and sat in one of the chairs at the desk. Opening the file, he saw the letterhead from a major accounting firm. The file was titled 'Future Projections for Chiles, Arken, and Associates,' containing, what looked like five pages, and marked 'Top Secret.' He started scanning the projections and his eyes widened. Tom stood by the window watching Derek's reaction.

"My God," whispered Derek, "Tom, this is unbelievable..."

"...but how does it relate to your question," interrupted Tom, "...well, here's how! First, let me address your comments. Yes, you did guide our recent products successfully through the FDA and you are moving forward with Marty's project. But, Derek, to be perfectly blunt... you did what you were paid to do."

Derek leaned forward to speak.

"Hold on, Derek. Don't get all 'knotted up.' That is not a reflection on you or what you have achieved. It's just the simple truth. But... what you *have* done is pave the way for what you just read. You can see that our plan for the aggregation of the media is solid gold."

"For either you or I to consider any major shift in our current situation would be foolish. You, above all, know the flack we currently are receiving for our remuneration. Any increase, at this time, would not be a good PR move. Further, you can see the stock projections in that brief. What are your current options going to look like when those projections reach fruition?"

Derek leaned back. What Tom was saying was true. They were receiving considerable outrage over their compensation and a negative PR bump could affect both the current and future share price. Begrudgingly, he nodded his head, "With this new information, I have to concede that you make perfect sense."

Tom turned back to the window to hide the smirk. *This was so easy. Now for the carrot.*

Spinning back, he said, "Now look… this in no way closes the window. We will all be able to improve our position when things have settled down."

He smiled, "It's Friday. Let's have a drink." He buzzed for Pam

"Yes, sir," answered Pam.

"Pam. We'd like to wish you 'bon voyage.' Will you join us for a drink?"

She frowned, "Thank you. No. I have Kelly here. As you know, she is filling in for me next week and I need to bring her up to speed."

Derek's head snapped up. In his anxiety, he had forgotten about sharing with Kelly. "Bring Kelly in here so we can all get up to speed" ordered Derek.

"… uh …we were in the middle…" fumbled Pam.

"Nonsense," said Tom.

Pam opened the door and waved at Kelly. As Kelly hesitantly walked in, Derek said, "Pam, I apologize. We should have had this session sooner." Kelly looked at Derek and smiled awkwardly.

Tom walked over with his hand outstretched, "Kelly, it's nice to see you again. I understand we will be seeing a lot of you in the next week."

"Yes, sir," nodded Kelly.

"Great… looking forward to it. Pam, do you see any issues we need to cover right now?"

Pam paused, "I have shown Kelly the basics for her to function. If you request something that she can't manage she can always reach me on the ship. The only other thing I would ask both of you, is your patience if, on occasion, Kelly is at the other desk if you happen to call unexpectedly."

"I'm sure Derek and I can work that out," laughed Tom, "you know, Kelly, we had talked about getting a temp in here, but Pam assured me that with your experience with our company and the industry, that it would be a waste of time. By the way, I understand you were instrumental in bringing Nancy Stone aboard with Marty Cooper."

A shiver went through her as his piercing blue eyes bored into hers. *Does he know something? How is that possible? Did Nancy say something?*

"…uh …yes. Nancy and I have known each other for a few years and I happened to talk to her the day she resigned as executive assistant to Rod Arthur of Arthur and Associates. From what I had learned from Mr. Maurrel, I knew that Mr. Cooper was needing an executive assistant."

"Very insightful of you, Kelly."

Kelly couldn't divine whether he was being sarcastic or complementary, but she did know she would not underestimate Mr. Chiles.

It was going to be an interesting week.

***

Saturday dawned with Marty and Myra already up and scrambling. It was going to be a day full of preparation for their flight in the morning. Periodically, Marty would pull out his cell and text a message to Nancy as new ideas would hit him. He smiled to himself. She was going to be tired of these by the end of the day.

"Marty… Please. I need you to tell me what you want packed," rebuked Myra.

"OK… OK…" retorted Marty.

They continued through the morning, trying to anticipate the requirements on the cruise. Finally, after a quick lunch, they were done around 3 o'clock and could take some time with their daughter, Cara, and get to the airport to pick up Myra's mother, Dorothy.

Dorothy had long ago worn out her welcome in the Cooper household. It had taken Myra years to purge herself of the feelings of inadequacy born from her mothers' constant criticism. She still found it difficult to maintain boundaries in her life and so tried to keep Cara's exposure to Dorothy at a minimum.

Because of the short notice, Myra was forced to resort to her mother, which prompted Dorothy to bemoan that she hadn't been asked sooner. Despite Myra's explanation, Dorothy was convinced that she had been a last resort.

They arrived at Terminal C with ten minutes to spare and they both tried to relax as Cara bounced around in the backseat.

Marty started walking as he saw Dorothy come through the exit. Dorothy waved and then pointed at the luggage so as to remind him of his duty. He turned and raised his eyebrows at Myra and then waved back.

Walking past the two cars in front, she leaned to look in the passenger window, "Too bad, you couldn't have been car number one."

"Hello to you too, mother," said Myra.

Cara started squealing, "Grandma… Grandma!"

"Hi, peanut," Dorothy said, reaching through the window and giving her a big hug.

As Marty loaded the luggage, Dorothy called, "Careful with those." Marty winked at Myra, who was scowling in the mirror.

"How are you, Dorothy?" asked Marty.…Big mistake!

"Well, I'm fine now… no thanks to the airline. Myra, isn't there another airline you could have chosen for me. I swear, they might as well put us in pens like animals."

They headed away from the airport, navigating 635 East, with Myra almost amputating her tongue. The flood of memories was nauseating. Years of therapy was a thin defense when faced with the brutal, constant onslaught of Dorothy's negativism.

***

Having confirmed the payment, Monk had caught the overnight flight and then the train to Venice and arrived rested on Saturday morning.

He checked into an out of the way Hostel close to the Cruise ship port and settled in to rehearse his plan again. Simplicity had always been his forte and this job was no exception.

His five additional identities were secreted in the double lining of his valise. The other assets were disguised as medical needs.

The only problematic issue was the timing for the finish, but he knew that would be resolved as the event unfolded.

Chapter 7

Kelly and Pam agreed to meet at the office for a final check. Saturday morning traffic was light and Kelly arrived a little early. She set her purse down on her desk and turned to sit down when she heard the crash of glass from above.

Puzzled, she slowly started up the winding stairs. Turning the corner, she could see straight into Tom's office and there was Pam, down on her hands and knees, with blood dripping from her head.

As Kelly was running toward the office, she heard the door at the end of the hall 'whish' closed.

She reached Pam as she was rising from the floor. "Pam... What happened? ...are you alright... Should I call an ambulance?"

"No... I'm just a little woozy. He just missed me. Did you see him?"

Kelly shook her head, "No, I just heard the door at the end of the hall close. What happened?"

Pam grabbed a tissue and started dabbing the cut on her head. "I wish I knew. I came up here early to get set up for you and I noticed both the office door and the door to the safe were open. I heard a noise behind me and tuned just as this guy swung the glass globe at me. Fortunately, I ducked just in time and it only grazed me."

"Pam, he could have killed you. Did you see who it was?" Kelly asked breathlessly.

"No."

Kelly pulled out her cell, "We better call the police."

Pam waved her hand, "No... Let me think for a minute."

They both deliberated. Finally, Pam spoke, "He must have been here when I arrived, but how did he get past security?" They both paused.

"Unless he knew the codes," theorized Kelly.

"Which means we don't want the police involved," Pam pronounced.

Kelly began to pick up the glass pieces while Pam finally staunched the bleeding. "I'm going to call Mr. Chiles," declared Pam, "he will know what we should do." Kelly shivered involuntarily. She hadn't planned on any interaction with him this soon.

"Mr. Chiles... this is Pam. Sorry to bother you, but I am in the office and we have been broken into."

"What do you mean 'broken into?'" asked Tom.

Pam continued, "I came in about fifteen minutes ago, your door was open and I noticed the cabinet door to the safe was open. When I started to walk over to it, someone came up behind me and hit me on the head with the glass globe... Yes, I'm OK, just a cut, but he got away. Kelly arrived just as he left through the hall exit."

"Have you done anything or called anyone."

"No, sir... just you. Kelly is cleaning up the glass."

"Good. I am going to have Rob Schafers come over and talk to you and we'll see where we go from here. You did good in calling me first, Pam." Tom disconnected and then hit speed dial.

"Schafe... it's Tom. It looks like we are in business again. Are you free right now? Good! I have had an attempted break-in at my office. ...Just now. Pam is there right now and she will fill you in. When you know the details, call me and we'll see where we go from here."

"I'll go over right now. I am on the tollway and can be there is a couple of minutes," responded Rob.

"Thanks!"

After leaving the Force Recon Marines, Rob Schafers, like many Vietnam vets, had a hard time finding his niche. Becoming intimately acquainted with the electronics field in his military career, he quickly perceived the potential and attached to the rising star of computers. Over the years, he continued to maintain his physical condition while becoming an electronics and security expert.

Tom and Rob had gone through all their training together and developed a deep bond which was further cemented when Tom anonymously funded Rob's startup security firm – 306 Security. Only Tom and Rob knew the meaning of the name and never revealed it to anyone.

Their motto was: 'We Will Do It / Find it / Protect it – Anywhere / Anytime,' and their track record proved it.

The security officer at Chiles, Arken, and Associates greeted Rob with a big grin.

"Hey, boss, what're you doing here?"

"Just visiting," said Rob, "...Harry, have you been here all morning?"

"Sure have. I punched in at 5:57. Everything OK?" he inquired.

Rob clapped him on the back. "Everything's great. I'm going upstairs for a while."

The doors opened on 16 and Rob stopped just inside the lobby.

Kelly peeked around the corner from Tom's office.

"Hello, Mr. Schafers. We're so glad you are here."

Rob smiled, "Hi Kelly… you can come out now." They both laughed. He walked into the office and stopped to survey the situation. Some of the glass was still on the carpet. Then he saw Pam sitting in the living room area holding her head.

"Pam, are you alright?" he quizzed.

"Yes… I think so. Just a cut and a bump."

Rob walked over and knelt. "Let me have a look" He pulled her hair back and saw the inch-long cut atop the knob. "Whew…you are one lucky girl."

"…uh… I guess so."

"Do you feel up to telling me what happened?"

Pam sighed "Sure… I guess. There isn't all that much to tell. I had just come in and I was downstairs at Kelly's desk when I heard a noise at the top of the stairs. I thought, *Ohh… Kelly's up there*, so I went up the stairs and saw Mr. Chiles office door open. I thought that's weird, so I walked into the office and just as I noticed the cabinet door to the safe was open, I heard a sound behind me. I started to turn just as something hit me on the head… that's all until Kelly came in to help me."

Kelly jumped in, "I had just come in and was downstairs when I heard some glass shatter. I went up the stairs and saw Pam on her hands and knees with blood dripping from her head, and as I was going into the office, I heard the door at the end of the hall close."

"Did either of you see the person at all."

They both shook their heads. There was silence for a moment, then Pam said, "I do remember seeing a shoe as I turned."

"Can you describe the shoe?" Pam frowned in thought, "I think it was a blue-and-white, tennis type shoe."

"All right. Nothing else?" asked Rob. They both shook their heads.

"Well, you both reacted in the right way by calling Tom. I think, with the sensitivity of everything around here, it is best if we just keep this to ourselves. The authorities would just cause us a lot of unnecessary problems," Rob continued, "…by the way, what were you both doing here this morning?"

"I am going on the industry cruise, starting tomorrow," responded Pam, "and Kelly is going to fill in for me. We were here to bring her up to speed."

Kelly looked at Pam, "…but I think you should get your head examined." They all stopped and then started laughing. "…Well, you know what I mean."

"No. I'm fine," said Pam and then turned to Rob, "should I still plan on leaving in the morning?"

Rob smiled, "I don't see any reason why not, but let's check with Tom." He pulled out his cell and as he walked out into the lobby, Tom answered, "Hey, Schafe."

"Tom, someone broke into your office, but everything is fine. That's the main thing. He hit Pam with the globe on the desk, but she's OK. She would like to go home, but wonders if she should still plan on leaving tomorrow. I have talked her and Kelly through and I see no reason why not. Whoever was here, tried unsuccessfully to get into the safe. We can brainstorm later today about what we should do."

"Do you think you're getting the whole story from the girls?"

"Yes. They are both pretty shook. They didn't see who it was, but Pam did see a blue-and-white tennis shoe. She got quite a knock on the head, but she's fine. They have talked to no one."

Tom hesitated for a moment as he mentally scrolled through the information, "OK. Tell her to go ahead with the trip."

"Good. I've already got some preliminary thoughts, so do you want to get together this afternoon?"

"Yeah. I'm just about to tee off, so I should be done around 4. Why don't you come out to the club?"

"Great."

Both girls were just walking out of the office. "Go ahead and go on the trip, Pam, but be sure and stay in touch."

Kelly looked at Pam, "Pam, I'm OK, why don't you go home and rest and get ready for your flight."

Pam looked relieved, "Thanks, Kelly. I think I will. Are we done here, Mr. Schafers?"

"Just one more thing," he said with a steely voice, "this is all between us and no one needs to know."

Both girls nodded in agreement.

***

Derek couldn't stop shaking. He had never attempted anything like he had just done. Playing business hardball was one thing, but performing a criminal act was another. What in the hell had gotten into him? The other day when Tom had pulled the file for Derek to read, he had watched Tom carelessly enter his safe combination and automatically committed it to memory. Tom had left the other files on his desk for a moment and the top one had a label… 'Derek Maurrel.' It had tormented him ever since.

Working with Tom as long as he had taught Derek there was *always* a motive in everything Tom did and he needed to know what the motive was for Tom to have a file on him.

After stewing for the past couple of days, the solution had finally bubbled up. Saturday was Tom's regular golf date; Pam would be home, packing for her cruise. There would be nobody at the office. He would slip past the security guard, enter his code and be upstairs alone. The key to Tom's door was in Pam's desk. He would read the file, go to the security room and erase his keyed entry, and be home in an hour. Simple!

What the hell had Pam been doing there anyway? The fear of getting caught in Tom's safe had been so overwhelming he had just acted out of sheer panic. He had heard her coming and just had time to pick up the globe and slip behind the door. Even now, the reality of clobbering her with the crystal globe sent loathing through his system. When he had heard someone starting up the stairs, he only knew flight.

He still wondered if anyone had seen him exit the hallway and… how was Pam? Had he killed her? Another shudder racked his body. A murderer!

But the real problem lay ahead. He had not had time to erase his entry code. The only solution he could come up with was hope that when everything had settled down, he would go back, enter the normal way, pick up a file, erase the code and then leave.

***

Rob pulled up to the club, gave the keys to the valet kid and went around the back, taking the short way to the locker room. A couple of guys waved hello as he weaved his way through the tables to where Tom was playing Gin Rummy.

Rob looked at the score card, shook his head, and said, "…and the slaughter continues." He looked across the table at Barry, Tom's opponent, and said, "Aren't you ashamed of yourself, taking money from the handicapped?" Everyone roared.

Tom finished and totaled up his losses. "Can I make monthly payments," he joked, "thanks, guys… Sorry… I have to leave."

He and Rob ordered a drink and then went over to a quiet corner. "So," opened Tom, "what's the scoop?"

"Well, at first blush, it's a pretty amateur job. He was going for your safe when he was interrupted by Pam. The perp was able to get behind the door and then hit her from behind with the crystal globe that was on the coffee table. It shattered when it fell against your desk. The perp then must have heard Kelly coming up and was able to get out and down the hall to the door just as Kelly arrived at the hallway. She said she heard the hall door close. Nobody saw him except Pam, who saw a blue-and-white tennis shoe before he hit her."

"So," started Tom, "…there was no material or information loss that we know of?"

"Correct."

Tom sipped on his drink staring into space. "I don't get it," he said to Rob, "how would someone get into the building and into my office without security seeing them?"

"My question exactly. When we finish here, I am heading over there to do some checking. My first guess is someone in the company."

"Yes… my thought exactly. But it's stupid. Everyone knows we have videos, keypads, onsite people… what were they after? You don't just bust into somewhere without knowing what you are after and no one knows what is in my safe, except me." …Tom paused and then a wry smile crossed his face.

"What?" asked Rob.

"Damn!… It had to be Derek. The other day, we were talking and I got a file out of my safe and he was standing by the desk. I must admit, I was careless when I opened the safe and he very well could have seen the combination."

"But why would he be going into the safe. Just to rummage around? It's not worth that risk."

"…hmmm …good point," mumbled Tom. They both fell silent, pondering the next move. Finally, Tom spoke, "I was just running through my mind the contents and I realized there is a file in there with the title 'Derek Maurrel.' He may have seen that file."

"That makes sense, Tom. I think you have commented before that Derek always was a little paranoid. He could have decided he needed to see that file and his paranoia overcame his good judgment."

"If that's the case, then there would be an entry in the entry log," opined Rob, "would he know enough to erase the entry?"

Tom thought for a moment… "I think he might."

They both looked at each other. Rob picked up his cellphone. "Harry, its Rob Shafers. Are you on duty right now…? Has Derek Maurrel come in this afternoon? When?"

He looked at Tom. "He came in about ten minutes ago, and is still there." They both jumped up and started for the door when Tom stopped dead.

"Rob… Are we assuming there can be no other suspect?"

Rob turned back, "I would say that's a 90-10."

Sitting back down, Tom said, "OK, that's good enough odds for me. Now let's think this through. One question first. If the entry code were removed, would you be able to tell?"

"With some work… yes."

"OK… OK. This may be a situation we can take advantage of."

"How?"

"I don't know… yet, but we have an advantage. We can let him think he got away with it. We lose nothing," Tom continued, "can you go by tonight and check if the entry has been erased?"

"Sure… as long as you buy me another drink."

***

Pam laid down when she arrived home and woke up with a startle. It was 6:30pm and her flight was at 11:09 in the morning. She had done some basics but needed to complete her packing. She rose and the world started spinning. She had almost forgotten. She sat back down till the dizziness subsided. She had not even had time to consider the earlier events. She would sort that out later. Right now, she needed to finish.

Through it all, she was excited. She had never been to Europe and a luxury cruise; all-expenses paid was certainly the way to start. Then she thought of the unstated price. She was expected to do some 'schmoozing.' There was an unfamiliar element of anxiety, being a corporate event and not just a chance encounter, but she was confident she could fend off unwelcome advances.

***

Derek had successfully performed the entry code erasure and 'hung around,' waiting for fallout. It was to no avail and he finally left around 5:30 with a deep sense of foreboding. He was plagued with questions. *Who cleaned up? How was Pam? Were the police called? If so, then at who's direction?*

Later, sitting in his bachelor pad watching the sunset, the enormity of what he had done seeped in and fear, the internal cannibal, devoured his confidence.

Pam must not have gone to the hospital, or he, as president, would have been called. Either Pam, or whoever came up the stairs, must have called Tom. If so… why hadn't Tom called him. Unquestionably, something was amiss.

He lurched and spilled his drink when the cellphone buzzed. He looked at the number while trying to dab up the spilled liquor… It was Tom!

Having been in tough emotional and physical spots in the past, nothing approached the terror that fragmented Derek's entire system. He gawked at the obscene cellphone as it insistently buzzed. His eyes could only stare at the blinking name… Tom… Tom…Tom.

At last, the dragon was silent and the 'beep' for a message sounded. The phone weighed 20 pounds as he picked it up.

'Derek, I don't know if you heard, but we had an incident at the office this afternoon. Call me back.'

Derek gazed out the window. He didn't detect anger or agitation, which gave him some solace. Maybe he had a chance to escape this nightmare. Taking deep breaths, he dialed Tom.

"Derek… How are you?" The relief almost took Derek to his knees. His body was 'all prickly' as he tried to form words.

"Hey, Tom. I was on the other line. What's this 'incident?'"

"Someone tried to break into my safe at the office. Pam was in the room and she got hit from behind. She's OK. Kelly was there as well. We decided not to call the authorities because we don't need the trouble."

The relief continued to flood his body, "When was this and why didn't Kelly call me?"

"I asked her not to. Pam called me first and once I determined she was fine, I decided to seal this up and have Rob handle it."

"Rob Schafers?" squawked Derek.

"The same," said Tom.

Derek frowned, realizing that this wasn't over. "Well… I wish someone would have called me."

"I made the decision. I didn't want to bother you on a Saturday."

"OK. I'll see you on Monday."

Tom smiled as he closed the call. *It's good to have insurance,* he thought.

The precariousness of Derek's situation was further rattled by the upcoming Monday meeting. The angst only intensified Derek's feelings of vulnerability, and if there was one thing you did not want to be around Tom Chiles, it was vulnerable. He was like a shark and could smell fear 'in the water.'

All Saturday night, he had not been able to calm his foreboding. *Did Tom know I had seen the file? If so, then the jig was up. But why wouldn't he have brought it up?*

The only option on Monday was to plead total ignorance. He hoped that Rob Schafers would not be there. Derek was never comfortable around him, particularly when he and Tom were together.

Chapter 8

Sunday morning dawned... the typical Dallas winter day. Forecast for grey and more grey, but at least there was no 'norther' blowing in from Canada.

Marty and Myra had finished their obligatory visit with Dorothy through a flurry of negative comments about the flight time, the airline, the time change, ad infinitum, and were having some alone time with Cara. She was happy to be with 'Nanny' and content with the promises of gifts when they returned.

The limo arrived at 9:30am which, being Sunday morning, quickly whisked them to DFW airport in record time. They checked their luggage through and took the escalator to the departure level and entered the surprisingly short security line.

This portion of travel was always stressful for Marty. He viewed the security personnel and the entire system as ludicrous. Strip searching a seventy-five-year-old woman based on a head count was beyond his reasoning powers.

However, they checked in at the American Airlines Presidents Club lounge with no incidents and settled into a quiet corner.

"Marty, will we see anyone else you know?" asked Myra.

"Probably Mr. Chiles' assistant, Pam," answered Marty, "I heard she was coming. I don't think you have met her. She's kind of aloof, so don't get 'bent' if she seems cold."

Myra looked puzzled, "Why would she be on this trip."

"I don't exactly know, but you can bet she has been assigned some mission by Mr. Chiles."

Pam arrived at the parking area just before 9:30 and reached the terminal at 9:50. She had been pleasantly surprised when her ticket showed a first-class flight, which meant she could relax in the American lounge for a while.

After clearing security, she approached the lounge wondering if she would see Mr. Cooper and his wife. Her interaction with Mr. Cooper had been next to none and she wasn't adroit at idle chitchat.

The reality was that she desperately wished she could be more conversationally adept, but she allowed her insecurities to force her into silence, which manifested as snobbish and cold.

From the corner of her eye, entering the lounge, she instantly spied Marty and his Wife but continued to the check in counter. Feigning fumbling with her purse she walked to the other side of the room and settled in a comfortable lounge chair, pulled out her cell, and dialed her mother.

"Hi, Mom. I'm at the airport in Dallas, waiting to fly to Venice. …yes, Venice, Italy… It's a business trip on a cruise for eight days."

Her mother was always keenly interested in everything that Pam did. Pam could never quite figure out if she had any real interest in her life, or she was just envious.

Pam had left home ten years earlier, in a less than joyous atmosphere. She had called a cab and as the door slammed, her father was still yelling his perpetual dirge… *whore… slut… no good… never will be… good riddance…* while her mother stood behind him, wringing her hands. Pam had long ago inured herself to their dysfunctional world.

She had worked hard to reach a level of comfort with herself. Nevertheless, she longed for a close relationship. Pam finished her superficial conversation with a perfunctory 'I love you' and hung up. She wondered if she really meant it or even if she knew what love was at all.

She glanced up from her phone as Mrs. Cooper approached.

"Miss Styles?" asked Myra.

Pam stood, "Yes."

"I'm Myra Cooper," offered Myra, "we noticed you come in and wondered, being as we are on the same flight, if you would like to join us."

Pam paused, hoping she was not being rude but trying to sort out a response. "How very kind Mrs. Cooper. I have a few things I need to clean up," she said, holding up her phone, "but I would be glad to join you in a few minutes."

"Wonderful," Myra said cheerily, "just come over when you can." She pointed to the corner where Marty sat.

"Thank you. I will be over in a few minutes."

As Myra walked away, Pam started to breathe again. She was swirling in conflicting emotions. The last thing she wanted was to begin what could end up being a 'clingy' relationship in the first hour of an eight-day trip. Yet, it was a genuine gesture that she did not want to slight the offer, and it might be nice to have a female companion.

While she pondered her next move, she faked a phone call in case they were observing her, then slipped the cell into her bag and collected her things.

For travel comfort, Pam had chosen white capri pants and a loose-fitting silk blouse and as she proceeded across the lounge, a chorus of male heads swiveled in unison. She smiled inwardly... *Men... so predictable.*

Marty and Myra rose as she approached. "Pam... I am so happy you are joining us," Offered Marty.

"Well, thank you for asking me. I must admit I was feeling a little alone, especially in the face of the long flight ahead."

Myra waved her hand to a seat. "Please, sit down," she offered just as an attendant walked up. "May I get you anything to drink?"

"I could use a coffee," said Pam.

"Make that three," suggested Marty with a questioning look at Myra, who nodded approval.

"So, Pam... Are you on the trip for fun or work?" asked Marty.

Pam paused, then smiled, "Purely pleasure. I have never been to Europe and Mr. Chiles suggested I come... So, here I am."

"How nice," said Myra with a surprised tone. Pam turned her head to Myra with her disconcerting stare.

Myra paled.

Pam had been told many times that she sometimes unconsciously exhibited a look that bordered on defiance and she knew this was one of those times. She quickly offered, "Yes, I thought it was extremely generous of him." She continued, "What about you... have you previously traveled abroad?"

"No," answered Marty, "it's the first time for both My and I and we are very excited. However, I will be involved in business discussions throughout the trip."

Pam turned back to Myra, "Good! That will give us some time to enjoy the cruise."

Myra, still a little shaken by Pam's mannerisms, smiled, "Yes, that will be nice."

The attendant arrived with the coffee and some Danish treats and updated their boarding time to forty minutes.

"Do you know Dr. Kenmore," inquired Marty.

"Not really," replied Pam, "I have met him on a couple of occasions at the office, but that was only introductions."

"I am looking forward to sharing our views with him."

Good luck in penetrating that ego, reflected Pam. "Yes… I imagine that will be exciting," she said.

The next thirty-five minutes were taken with idle chitchat and finally, their flight was called.

After stowing their carry-ons, Marty and Myra settled into their plush first-class section, as did Pam, one row back and across the aisle. Flight time was ten hours and twenty-five minutes, which would put them in at 4:30am Madrid time for a two-hour stopover.

Thank God for Wi-Fi, thought Marty. After takeoff, he immediately opened his tablet and started updating his research. Myra buried herself in her book. Across the aisle, Pam stared out the window, watching the diminishing landscape and wondering what the next week would bring.

Something told her this was not going to be just a nice, quiet vacation.

***

Kelly woke early Monday morning after a fretful night. The attack on Pam, together with her upcoming double duty had played on Kelly's mind all night. She really had no idea why someone would decide to commit a robbery in the middle of the afternoon. Whoever it was, knew where the safe was. How? To her that said 'an inside job.'

Well, at least she was in the clear. Her key entry would show she had just entered the building. Oh, well… not her problem. She had her own obstacles to deal with.

Traffic was easy this morning and she arrived a little early at her desk. Mr. Maurrel had not arrived yet. She started toward the break room for coffee when the lobby door swung open to Rob Schafers. There was always a reason he was on the premises. The rumor mill was normally ahead of his arrival, but in this instance, everyone was baffled.

All eyes followed him as he entered the break room behind Kelly, greeting her with a smile, "Good Morning, Kelly. Did you manage to get some sleep?"

"Hello, Mr. Schafers and yes, I did. Thank you."

He glanced around to make sure they were alone. "Kelly, I wondered if you had any further thoughts regarding the Saturday incident?"

Kelly wrinkled her brow. "No… not really. I did wonder why someone would do that in the middle of the day."

"There's no telling what's in a criminal's mind. Anyway, if you think of anything, please get hold of me and please remember, this whole thing is just between us."

"Yes, sir," she said as she walked back to her desk to find Mr. Maurrel opening his office door. "Good Morning, Mr. Maurrel."

"Oh… you startled me, Kelly. How are you?" Then his eyes widened as he saw Rob climbing the stairs to Tom's offices. He recovered and turned back to Kelly, "Can you come in, Kelly?"

Kelly entered first and Derek closed the door. He didn't waste any time, "Were you here on Saturday when the break-in occurred?"

"Yes, sir," she responded, "I had just arrived to meet Pam for an update. I heard a noise upstairs and, thinking it was her, I went up just as I heard the hall door close."

Derek steeled himself for the next answer, "Did you see anyone?"

"No… I just heard the door close at the end of the hall."

Relief prickled through his body. One worry allayed. "Thank you, Kelly."

"Mr. Maurrel, I hope I haven't broken my word to Mr. Chiles. He asked me to not talk about the incident with anyone, but I assume that did not include you."

Derek controlled the shock he felt. "No, Kelly, you did the right thing."

"I also wanted to remind you that I am working with both you and Mr. Chiles this week."

"Yes… thank you. I'm sure there will be no problems."

Kelly walked out to the front desk. "Crystal, please refer any calls to Mr. Chiles through my desk while Pam is gone."

"Yes. There have been no calls this morning."

"Thank you," she said and headed for Mr. Chiles' office.

Tom walked into his office from his private elevator with his cell at his ear, went straight to the door, and pointing at Kelly, said, "Kelly, please come in."

"Yes, sir," answered Kelly.

"Has Derek arrived yet?"

"Yes, sir."

"Please have him come up."

She picked up the intercom just as she saw Mr. Maurrel coming up the stairs.

"Kelly, do you know if Tom has arrived yet?" he asked.

"Yes. I was just going to call you. He would like to see both of us."

They both started toward the office as Tom arrived at the door. "Morning, Derek," barked Tom, "come on in."

They both followed Tom into the office and saw Rob Schafers seated in the living room area. *How did he get here?* thought Kelly, *he must have used the private elevator.*

"I'd say let's get a coffee, but we won't be in here long enough," said Tom, "the four of us, plus Pam, who is on the plane to Venice, are the only ones that know about the break-in on Saturday and I just wanted to caution us that we want it kept that way."

Derek worked hard to keep his face neutral and not register the panic that was consuming him. *Was Tom going to drop 'the other shoe?'*

Everyone remained perfectly still as Tom, one by one, looked everyone in the eye. They all nodded in agreement.

"I know you probably have questions, as do Rob and I, but now is not the time to waste while we are going to be coordinating information from Marty as well as continuing the ramp up of the Sistophan launch. Rob will continue to look into the incident, but the rest of us just need to 'move on' and do our jobs."

Again, everyone nodded in agreement. "That's it!" said Tom as he rose. Derek and Kelly started to leave. "Kelly, why don't you mainly work from Pam's desk this week so I can have closer communication. Is that alright with you, Derek"?

"Certainly," responded Derek, "I can always contact her quickly."

Kelly hesitated… "Let me run down to my desk and get some things and I'll be up shortly."

"Good… Good," replied Tom.

Kelly started to collect some of her necessary things while Derek went into his office. He was befuddled by the results of the meeting. Why were Tom and Rob not asking about the office door and the door to the safe being open?

How long was he going to be left twisting in the wind?

"Mr. Maurrel, is there anything I can do before I go upstairs," enquired Kelly.

Derek shook his head, "No… I'll get hold of you if I need you."

She hurried up the stairs just in time to see Tom's office door close. Obviously, she was not needed at this moment.

***

The cell in Tom's drawer buzzed

"It's Monk… Confirming that we are go!"

"Confirmed." Tom threw the phone in the trash and nodded at Rob, who had a troubled look.

"You know I am not comfortable with this, Tom," mumbled Rob. Tom scowled, "Rob, don't assume that you know what you're talking about."

"Tom… How long have we been together? Don't fuck with me. You hire me to 'have your back' and I am telling you that you are entering an arena that you may not be equipped for."

"Ok… Ok… don't get 'in a wad.' We have been through tougher times than this might be. I can't just sit back and jeopardize what we have worked for. The 'flack' is getting heavier by the day and it's affecting the stock price. Recently, we've lost ten million dollars in capital value and we can't continue, especially with our launch in a few weeks."

Rob granted, "I understand, but this is 'federal' you're messing with."

"Don't worry, we're working with the best."

Chapter 9

It had been a long, tiring trip. It was just after noon, Venice time. Marty, Myra, and Pam exited immigration in Venice and saw their 'welcome' sign.

Walking with their porter to the limo, they noticed down the walkway a cluster of what appeared to be a press conference. Marty assumed that the congressman had arrived. Then the crowd parted and he saw it was Dr. Arthur Kenmore addressing the adoring media with his usual, imperious manner.

Marty excused himself and walked down to the crowd, waiting until it thinned, then walked over to Dr. Kenmore with his hand extended.

"Dr. Kenmore… Marty Cooper… Cooper Consulting."

Dr. Kenmore looked down at the extended hand, then up to Marty. "Oh, yes… Tom mentioned that we should get together."

"I just wanted to say 'Hello' while I had the chance."

"Yes… Well, we will see each other later," he said and turned and hailed a taxi. Marty was left with his hand in the air, his mouth open, and a few expletives hovering on his lips. Kenmore's ego was widely known, but to experience it was quite another thing.

It occurred to Marty that perhaps the doctor needed some 'tuning up,' or there wasn't going to be much cooperation on this cruise. He double checked the time in Dallas, then pulled out his cell, happy that Tom had given him the private number.

Tom answered on the second ring, "Hello, Marty… How's the trip going?"

"Fine, sir. We just arrived in Venice and are about to board. I happened to see Dr. Kenmore just now and went over to meet him. He was, to say the least, very rude and barely acknowledged my introduction. I am alerting you to this only in the interests of having successful results from our meetings. Perhaps he has misunderstood the intent of our being together in our persuasions of Congressman Barnes."

"Interesting," mused Tom, "...to be frank, between you and I, he is a royal pain in the ass, but we need him to support our launch. Let me have a talk with him and I am sure there will be no problem. Thanks for alerting me, Marty. Have a successful week."

"Thank you, Mr. Chiles."

Tom immediately dialed Dr. Kenmore's international number.

"Dr. Kenmore speaking. Who is this?"

"Arthur, it's Tom Chiles and we need to talk."

Dr. Kenmore was taken aback. "Tom... to what do I owe this privilege?"

"This is no privilege call, Arthur. I wonder, just why you think you are on this cruise?"

"I beg your pardon," sputtered Dr. Kenmore.

"Begging my pardon won't do you a damn bit of good. Arthur, you are there for one reason and one reason only, and that is to coordinate with our consultant, Marty Cooper, and sway the congressman in our direction."

"Tom, what is this all...?"

"So... What I suggest, Arthur, is that you rewind your arrival and reintroduce yourself to Marty Cooper. He is going to be your partner in this enterprise and it would help if you could deign to at least recognize that he exists. By the way, he did not call me to whine. He called to check as to whether he had received the correct briefing."

"Tom, I am not accustomed to being talked to..."

"You *still* don't get it! You *will* cooperate, Arthur. We would not want our stock price to devalue because you chose to not understand and I don't want to have to investigate that large block of stock that was bought in the Caymans. Do I make myself clear?"

There was silence and finally, Dr. Kenmore responded, "I will fulfill my commitment."

"Thank you, Arthur. Enjoy your cruise."

***

Marty and Myra, having received their welcome package, walked up the bridge to the ship and were met by Captain Lucania Papadakis. "Mr. and Mrs. Cooper... Welcome," he said in a pleasant Greek accent. "We are happy to have you aboard and look forward to giving you a memorable time."

"Thank you, Captain, we are excited to be here," responded Marty.

Meanwhile, Pam received a call just before entering the walkway. "Hello... Pam Styles."

"Pam... It's Kelly. I just wanted to check how you are feeling."

"Oh... Thanks, Kelly. I'm fine. Just a little tender, but nothing serious. How're things there?"

"No problems so far. We had a brief meeting this morning to solidify the blackout on our... uh... event."

Pam smiled, "Yes... quite an 'event.' Any answers yet?"

"No, and I don't know if we will ever know anything."

"I've had some thoughts, but nothing concrete. I have to go, Kelly, we're just boarding."

"OK. Have a great week. I hope I don't have to call you."

"Me too. Bye."

Pam turned to start boarding and bumped into a man just starting up the ramp. He glanced at her with irritation and continued. *That's strange,* she thought, *he acted like he knew me.*

She continued up the gangway and, after being welcomed, was directed to her deck and room. Tossing her purse on the bed, she walked over to the balcony, opened the door, and stepped out to a stunning view of the Mediterranean. She was thrilled. She had never seen anything like this and she stood for a few minutes soaking it in.

In the adjoining cabin, Myra was unpacking while Marty fired up his laptop and logged into the ship's secure server. He had just started to sort through his e-mails when the cabin phone chimed. Marty waved at Myra with an 'I'm not here' gesture.

"Hello."

"Mrs. Cooper?"

"Yes."

"I hope I am not interrupting. This is Dr. Arthur Kenmore. Could I please speak to your husband?"

"Oh... Dr. Kenmore..." Marty shook his head. "...I'm sorry, he stepped out. Should I have him call you back when he returns?"

"Yes, please. My cabin number is 914 and I am looking forward to meeting you as well."

"I will have him call you."

"Thank you, Mrs. Cooper."

She cradled the phone with a smile.

"Well, somebody has been spanked," she said to Marty. They both chuckled.

"Tom works fast," concluded Marty.

"I'm going to change and go get a drink and take a stroll," asserted Myra.

"I can handle that," returned Marty, "but first, I am going to help you change." He grabbed her and threw her on the bed.

"Animal," she shrieked.

***

One deck below, Monk sat stewing on his balcony. He had made a mistake and that was very rare. When he had accidentally bumped into Pam, he had looked her full in the face. Previously, on another assignment for Chiles, he had done surveillance on some of the staff, which included her.

One of his MOs was that he *never* showed his face to anyone connected with the case. This worried him. He would have to be very careful if he was in her vicinity again.

Meanwhile, it was time to scout out the congressman's digs. He donned his first disguise of a beard and long grey hair, a light brown shirt, and brown pants. With his sun glasses, floppy hat, and his book, he passed perfectly as a professor.

The arrival of a U.S. Congressman was always an event, and this was no exception. Although the public was not apprised of his presence, the crew had been notified.

Monk looked around, immediately spotting where the congressman was assigned. Security at the stairway and the elevator was a little more than he had anticipated. The 'delivery' would need to be done on the run. He had foreseen that scenario, but he needed to scope out the dining room.

Seemingly lost, he wandered into the dining room expecting to be met, but there was no one. Monk walked over to the concierge podium. The map of the tables was marked with magic marker and he saw the congressman's table fourteen, with names marked at each seat. The table adjoining was number fifteen.

Finding his table nine on the layout, he quickly switched table numbers nine and fifteen. Checking again that no one was around, he walked over and picked up the nametags from Table nine and switched them with table fifteen, placing himself directly behind the congressman.

Meanwhile, on deck, Marty and Myra relaxed at the bar, watching the passing parade. They had sailed about ten minutes ago, and the mood was lighthearted.

Marty picked up his cell and hit the return number for Dr. Arthur Kenmore.

"This is Dr. Kenmore."

"Dr. Kenmore… Marty Cooper returning your call."

"Yes… Yes, Marty, and please, call me Arthur. I wanted to apologize for my actions when we met at the airport. I had just received some rather disturbing news and I was not myself."

Yeah… Yeah, thought Marty. "No problem, Arthur. I assume we will be at the same table for dinner tonight. I will look forward to seeing you then."

"Wonderful. I'll see you then," replied the Dr. in an overly sappy tone.

Marty clicked off as a man approached him from behind. Myra started to warn him when the man put his finger to his lips, shaking his head.

"Are you sure you are on the right ship," quipped the man.

Marty turned and broke into a smile. "Norm… How nice to see you." Marty turned to Myra, "Myra… I'd like you to meet Norm Arthur."

Myra offered her hand, "Nice to meet you, Norm."

"Norm is the Chairman of the 'Council on Safe Medicine (COSM).'"

"So nice to meet you as well, Myra. Are you enjoying yourself so far?"

"Very much, and I plan on a lot more while you boys continue to save the world," she said, which brought a chorus of laughter.

Marty edged closer to Myra, "…care to join us, Norm?"

"No. I just came to get a drink for Lin, my wife, to bring a back to the cabin. I assume we will see you at dinner?"

"Of course, we'll look forward to it." Everyone said their goodbyes and Norm strolled away.

"He seems pleasant," Myra said.

"He is a great guy. I just wish we weren't on opposite sides."

Myra looked puzzled, "Does it get nasty?"

"No. He's too much of a gentleman to let that happen. …but he can be very persuasive with his point of view. We have managed to avoid any hard feelings and I think he respects me as much as I respect him. This trip will be very interesting. Particularly with the two egos of Dr. Kenmore and Congressman Barnes. Hopefully, Norm and I will be the two buffers."

Marty's cell chirped.

"Marty Cooper."

"Mr. Cooper, it's Nancy. I am so sorry to bother you. Am I interrupting anything?"

"No. Go ahead, Nancy. What time is it there?"

"It's 9am. I hope this is nothing, but I thought I should notify you immediately. We have been attacked by someone on our server. Our security caught it, but I don't know if they got in or not."

Marty frowned, "First of all, I am glad you called. I haven't had time to introduce you to Dave Reasoner, our IT guy. You will find his number in my phone list file on my laptop. I gave you the passcode."

"Right."

"Call him and after he's done an assessment, have him get back to me with you on the line."

Nancy sighed, "OK."

"Nancy... you did the right thing."

"Thank you."

Marty closed off, "Goodbye."

Nancy was furiously scrolling through Marty's phone list when her cell beeped. She looked down and saw it was Kelly.

"Hi, Kelly."

"Hi, Nancy... You busy?"

"Kind of... but go ahead."

"I was wondering if we could get together tonight. Nothing special." Kelly remembered that they were probably being recorded. "I just thought we could have a drink."

"That sounds great. The same place at 6:30."

"Great. See you then."

She continued scrolling and found Dave Reasoner's name and punched in the number.

"He... hello..." answered a sleepy voice.

"Mr. Reasoner... I am so sorry if I woke you. My name is Nancy Stone. I am the executive assistant to Marty Cooper."

There was a rustling sound and then, "...What did you say your name was?"

"Nancy Stone. I work with Marty Cooper."

"Oh... OK... Sorry. I worked until 4 this morning." Nancy stared at the phone. She had forgotten that IT people don't work normally.

"...Um ...well... Mr. Cooper is on a business trip and I have just discovered that we had an attack on our system during the night and he said to call you immediately and have you do an assessment and then call him with me on the line."

Dave sat up in bed. "OK. I am going to go to my computer and then I will direct you how to get me on the system remotely and we will see what we can find."

***

Marty's cell chirped just as they entered their cabin.

"Marty Cooper," he answered.

"Hello, Marty… Dave here."

"Dave… Don't give me any bad news."

Dave laughed, "Well… I don't have any bad news, but I don't have any good news. Definitely, someone tried to get in. On a preliminary basis, I would say they failed to get through the security. But it seems that it wasn't just an ordinary hack. I think they targeted you."

"Wow," exclaimed Marty, "why would they be after us?"

"Well… You have some pretty sophisticated algorithms and search capacities that, I imagine, competitors would love to have. I don't know if I will be able to track anything. I would bet not, but I will give it a shot and keep you posted. In the meantime, I did not connect Nancy on this call because I wanted to discuss with you how secure you feel with her."

Marty paused, remembering the speed with which he had hired her. His 'gut' told him that she was trustworthy and no problem. "Dave, I have no reason to doubt her integrity, but why don't you keep an eye on her and let me know if you see anything that would cause us problems."

"OK… will do."

"We'll get together when I am back in a week. OK?"

"Great… see you then."

***

Pam had decided to stay in her cabin on the balcony and enjoy the fresh air, dozing from time to time. Her headaches had stopped and the wound was healing nicely. She had been able to cover it with a little hair manipulation so no one noticed.

Reading through the itineraries, she learned dinner was at 7 and her table and seat was prearranged. She was intrigued about the placements and who she was seated beside. Fortunately, she had remembered to call the steward and had her dinner attire sent out to be pressed.

After checking the time, she decided to take a jog before getting ready for dinner. Throwing on a pair of sweats, she emerged from the cabin just as Marty and Myra were walking down the hall. They exchanged waves.

"I guess we'll see you at dinner?" questioned Myra.

Pam nodded, "Yes. I'm excited. I'm just going to go for a quick jog. See you later." She hoped that this chance meeting was not going to be the norm. She planned on a lot of 'alone' time.

She had studied the ship's layout a little and knew the jogging track was on the top deck. Rather than taking the elevator, she decided to walk the two flights. As she was starting up the second flight, she glanced down the hall and saw the man she had bumped into at the boarding station. They locked eyes again for a brief moment and then both continued.

Pam couldn't understand what it was about the man that unnerved her, except that he seemed to take an unusual interest in her. She shrugged it off and entered the top deck to gorgeous bright sunshine.

***

Monk sat on the balcony staring out at the ocean as he pondered the latest occurrence. He had always been a great believer that there were no coincidences and now there had been two encounters with this woman in which, both times, she had seen his face express interest.

He smiled! Perhaps, he was getting too old and sloppy for this business. Maybe with this large job, he would finally retire. But that didn't solve the problem right now. He began to consider whether it was serious enough to work out a solution. She certainly did not know who he was and the chances of seeing her again after this job were slim... Hmmm.

Meanwhile, he had to make some preparations. Back in the cabin, he began dressing for his performance, as he liked to think of them. First the makeup and then the beard and mustache, topped by bushy eyebrows and artificial colored contact lenses, followed by the complete 'under outfit' of a grey mock turtle neck and black slacks.

Next came the slightly oversized slacks, shirt, and jacket, with a clip-on bow tie, and finally, the shaggy grey wig.

Before leaving for the cruise, he had visited his favorite doctor who specialized in euthanasia. The doctor found Monk's drug selection rather humorous, considering the name. It was called Aconite, from the plant Monkshood *(also known as wolfsbane)*, which causes arrhythmic heart function, quickly leading to suffocation, leaving only one postmortem sign; that of asphyxia.

The quick deterioration of the toxin in the body boded well for this client because proximity to a modern postmortem facility was negligible.

He had only used this method one other time, so dosage was somewhat unknown. He knew that death was inevitable, but when was a question. He had to be sure his 'getaway' was rapid.

For his previous event, he had developed a flat, handheld container that, when pressed against an object, injected the solution into the tissue.

Carefully, he inserted the small vial into the mechanism and secured the cap over the injector, then placed the device in his pants pocket for quick retrieval.

***

Myra hollered from the shower, "Have you picked out what you're wearing?"

"Yeah…" mumbled Marty as he continued his research. He wanted to be totally 'up to date' on any new blog comments. He knew this was going to be his first session with Norm and the congressman and he certainly didn't want to be 'sandbagged.'

Emerging from the shower, Myra saw Marty on the computer.

"*Marty*! We have to leave in fifteen minutes."

"OK… OK… I'll make it," he said as he popped up, stripped, and jumped in the shower.

Sure enough, he almost made it as he finished buttoning his Tommy Bahama shirt. Myra came out of the bedroom and Marty stopped dead and just stared. She was absolutely dazzling in her Oleg Cassini cocktail dress.

"What?" smiled. Myra.

Marty laughed, "Oh, nothing… I just thought you would be wearing something other than an old house dress."

She whacked him on the arm.

Chapter 10

The main dining room was majestically decorated, as were the guests filing in past the concierge podium. The cocktail bars were already active when Marty and Myra arrived. They walked through a crowd shaking hands and hugging. Marty's growing reputation and the news of Cooper Consulting had gained him additional recognition. Reaching the bar, they were met by Norm Arthur and his wife, Lin.

"Marty, Myra, say hello to my wife, Lin."

Myra reached out her hand, "A pleasure, Lin."

"Nice to meet you, Myra," Lin gave them a sweeping smile, "thank you. I have heard such nice things about you both. What a pleasure."

They all turned as the bartender asked for their orders.

The arrival of the drinks was met with a whirlwind of activity preceding the entrance of Congressman Chet Barnes. He was a dashing figure. An athlete during college, he graduated with a law degree from Harvard, followed by a four-year stint in the Military. His three-year political career was uneventful until he took up the torch to fight for stronger enforcement by the FDA after the sudden cancer death of his wife. That had taken a toll, but since then, he had returned to the spotlight, earning plaudits for his efforts.

The Congressman waved as he spied Norm and walked over to the group.

"Norm... How nice to see you. Lin, how are you."

Lin smiled, "Great. How are you, Chet? Nice to see you again."

"Lin, why haven't you left him yet. You know I am waiting for you."

Everyone laughed. Chet looked to Marty, "You must be Marty Cooper."

Marty looked surprised, "Yes. Nice to meet you, Congressman... and this is my wife, Myra."

"Please, call me Chet, and a pleasure to meet you, Myra."

Just then Marty noticed all eyes turned toward the door to see Pam walking toward them, followed by Dr. Arthur Kenmore. Myra waved at Pam while Dr. Kenmore stood basking in what he thought was his glory.

As Pam hugged Myra, "Hello," she looked over Myra's shoulder, straight into Chet Barnes' eyes. Neither one broke the gaze until, finally, Myra pushed away and said, "Pam, I want you to meet Congressman Chet Barnes."

Pam reached out her hand while Chet extended his. "Pam Styles," she said.

"Chet Barnes. A pleasure to meet you."

Marty jumped in, "Pam is the executive assistant to Tom Chiles."

"Really," exclaimed Chet, "I saw the table seating and I wondered who that name was." He looked over to Pam and paused. Her unblinking black eyes held him captive.

"I have admired your work, Congressman Barnes. It's an honor to meet you."

"Please... not so formal. Call me Chet." There was silence as they stared at each other just as the tone sounded to be seated. "Shall we eat?" suggested Chet, reaching for her elbow.

Myra looked at Marty with raised eyebrows. Marty scowled and shook his head slightly.

Following Congressman Barnes, the group strolled to their designated table. Observing the seating plan, Chet picked up Dr. Kenmore's name card, beside his, and replaced it with Pam's, while the others sorted out their location. Marty and Myra again locked eyes. *What was all this about?*

Predictably, Dr. Kenmore held back so he could be the last one to the table after everyone was seated. As he walked over, Marty rose and they shook hands, then Marty addressed the group, "I think you all know Dr. Arthur Kenmore."

Everyone nodded. "Nice to see you all again," exuded the Dr." Then, eyeing the Congressman, he said, "Congressman... I am a big fan."

Chet gave him a jaundiced stare. "Nice to meet you, Dr.," he said unenthusiastically.

Oh... Oh, thought Marty, *this is already on a rocky road.*

"Well, now... does everyone know everyone?" said Dr. Kenmore in an attempt at humor, which was met with blank stares, then muffled, polite chuckles around the table.

Being round, there was no 'head' of the table, but there seemed to be a slight separation between the congressman and everyone else, indicating an elevated importance, which was quickly altered even more by Chet moving his chair closer to Pam. To Pam's right was the Dr. then Lin, Norm, Myra and Marty.

***

Watching from the bar across the room, Monk had watched the introductions with interest and was surprised to see Pam join the group. Obviously, she was in some official capacity. He still had qualms about her and had contemplated calling Chiles for directions. He would have to be extra careful. He would make some decisions tomorrow.

He had decided that if an opportunity presented itself, the first night would be preferential. He had memorized the ship's itinerary, and knew that they would be at the port of Split, Croatia within an hour, and he would have time to catch the fastest flight to anywhere in Europe and then back to the U.S.

His 'table mates' had begun to arrive, so Monk rose from the stool, grabbed his cane, and started across the room. Pam had her back to him so he was not concerned about her seeing him.

With as little fanfare as possible, he settled himself in his seat and smiled to his table companions. Everyone nodded as the introductions began.

To his relief, Pam had not noticed his arrival. They were about eight feet apart, with his back to the Congressman. He kept his voice as low as possible.

The servers, looking like an army, marched single file from the kitchen and began to deliver the first course. As Monk did his best to 'chitchat,' he was thankful when the food arrived at the table and he could focus on keeping his head down and eating with his left hand. He had learned a long time ago that little things, like being observed as left-handed, could cause a misdirection in any investigation.

Meanwhile, at the other table, having seated himself, the Dr. immediately launched into a diatribe of the difficulties to which he had been subjected in traveling to Venice.

"I honestly don't know how these airlines stay in business," he lamented, "in my world of medicine, we don't have room for this kind of inefficiency. The rude attitudes and inept training would not be tolerated and these people would be immediately, summarily dismissed."

Marty glanced around the table, seeing the downcast eyes and the obvious annoyance on the faces of his fellow guests. It was time to redirect the conversation.

"So, Mr. Congressman, are we going to be privy to some secret legislation that no one else has learned or are you going to hold back."

The table erupted in polite laughter except for the disgruntled Dr. Kenmore, looking bereft that he had lost his audience.

"Marty, I think, in view of the disparate opinions at this table, security would be seriously jeopardized," he admonished, causing another ripple of laughter.

Marty was feeling an increasingly uneasy feeling as the atmosphere seemed to thicken. There were some powerful 'guns' staring him in the face and the Dr.'s alienation was palpable. He felt as though he were on an island.

His friend, Norm Arthur, came to the rescue and looked to the Congressman.

"Chet! For the sake of a collegial atmosphere, let's all recognize that everyone at this table agree that our motives are honorable and that any variance in our opinions is born of good intentions."

"You're right, Norm, and thank you," offered Chet, "I did not mean to 'poison the water' before we dive in."

Dr. Kenmore was reddened in the face. "Excuse me," he initiated, "it is my understanding that our discussions were going to be mainly between the congressman and myself."

Myra put her hand on Marty's arm as he stiffened.

Surprising everyone, Pam leveled her gaze on Dr. Kenmore, "Dr. Kenmore, I was asked by Mr. Chiles to come on this cruise, among other things, to help facilitate discussions between Mr. Cooper, Congressman Barnes, Mr. Arthur and yourself. I think that it would be to everyone's advantage if we just enjoyed the entertainment tonight and, perhaps, had breakfast in the morning."

There was dead silence as everyone stared openmouthed at Pam. She turned to Chet, "Shall we eat."

Dr. Kenmore was totally confounded. With his status, he was unaccustomed to this kind of treatment, particularly from a mere secretary. He was still smarting from the earlier admonishment and threat from Tom Chiles and so withheld the impulse to lash out, but instead, snorted arrogantly. Rising from his chair, he pleaded a bathroom break and departed.

Chet maneuvered his chair slightly to face Pam and his left leg was fully exposed.

***

Monk had not heard all the words of the exchange, but recognized an unexpected opportunity.

He slowly slipped his hand into his pocket, slid his hand under the holding strap of the delivery device, secured it firmly in the palm of his hand, pulled it out, and uncapped the needle.

He started to rise, putting his weight on the cane. The purposely weakened cane snapped in his left hand and pitched Monk forward, with his arms outstretched. His right hand made hard contact with the congressman's right leg, triggering the injector. Immediately, the Congressman reached for Monk to help him up, ignoring the sharp, short pain that he had felt.

"Are you all right, sir?" asked Chet.

"Yes... yes," sputtered Monk, "I am so sorry; my cane gave way. I hope I didn't hurt you."

"No. I am fine," offered Chet. The rest of the table had stood up to see what had happened. Monk rose grabbing his broken cane and apologized again and started to limp away.

"Should you see a doctor?" offered Myra.

"No... no" ...mumbled Monk. "I am fine. Again, my apologies."

Chet was rubbing the side of his leg.

"Are you OK?" inquired Pam.

"Yes, I think I got a bruise or something. Nothing serious. Let's finish our soup."

Monk continued limping out of the dining room to his cabin. All in all, it had gone very well. The injector had worked as planned when his hand had made the hard contact with Chet's leg, instantly injecting the Aconite into the blood stream. If Chet decided to look at his leg, the only thing he would see, if at all, would be a very small reddish spot. Soon, he would begin to suffer arrhythmic heart function, leading to suffocation.

Monk limped out of eyesight and then sped down the stairs to his deck. He entered his room and walked to the balcony.

It was a dark sky. After checking that no one could see him, he ripped the 'tear away' outfit off, shoved it into a bag together with the dispenser, broken cane, and all personal effects, and dropped it overboard.

Carefully walking around the entire cabin, wiping every surface for fingerprints, he surveyed his work one more time, then picked up his valise containing some jeans, a checkered wool shirt, a new folding cane, and a new beard and wig. Looking carefully out the door, he proceeded to the departure area, arriving just as the ship was arriving at Split Croatia. Standing at the rail, he watched the frantic activity to secure the vessel.

He had passed the two critical points in his escape – the table and the cabin, and this was the final one.

His heart rate was still accelerated as he tried not to appear interested in the preparations at the gate. Being first would not be wise, so he concentrated on the docking activities, ignoring the gate agents as they organized the security. He saw no sign of any abnormal movement or cell activity.

***

Monk's table was abuzz about the accident, but soon quieted down to a conversational hum as everyone enjoyed their meal.

Having missed the excitement, the Dr. returned with a subdued attitude and quietly meshed with the table talk. The table was cleared and the coffee and dessert were served as a boisterous MC introduced the entertainment.

Pam noticed that Chet seemed to be rather quiet and leaned over to ask if he was OK.

"Yes… I'm fine. Maybe a touch of sea sickness." As the entertainment continued, Pam looked over at Chet with alarm. He seemed to be having some difficulty breathing.

"Chet… What's wrong?"

"… I… I… don't know," he gasped.

His security man was instantly at his elbow, "Call a doctor."

Everyone turned to look at Chet. His face was red and he was heaving. Other tables had begun to look at the activity as the Maître' D' walked over.

Chet, grabbing at his chest, fell off his chair just as a man called out from the crowd, "I'm a doctor," and ran over to kneel beside Chet whose head was being cradled by Pam.

"He needs oxygen, *we need some oxygen*," he yelled as an attendant came through the door with a medical bag. The doctor waved him over. "*Oxygen*" he shouted again as Chet started into spasms.

Pam screamed, "Chet… Chet… stay with us… Chet," as his eyed began to roll.

The doctor started to do CPR just as another attendant ran through the door with a tank of oxygen. The doctor quickly snapped the hose onto the tank and cranked the dial as the attendant pushed the mask onto Chet's face. A stethoscope appeared and was held to Chet's chest. "Arrhythmic," the attendant said to the doctor. They both looked at each other, knowing that there was nothing more they could do.

Chet gave one final gasp and then fell back with a groan. Pam let out a sob just as the Captain came into the room and headed directly to the scene.

He immediately ordered some screens to be brought up to block off the rest of the room.

Marty, Myra, Norm, Lin, and Dr. Kenmore had sat in horrified silence as the tragedy unfolded and now rose from the table to move away and make room for the ship officials.

Pam still sat on the floor beside Chet, weeping quietly as Myra came over to comfort her along with Chet's executive assistant, who had been sitting at another table and was now in total panic mode.

The other passengers were frozen in disbelief, quietly murmuring among themselves. Any thoughts of a fun evening had obviously been dissolved, as some of them slowly, quietly filed out of the room.

***

The ship had been tied down and Monk wandered toward the gate as it was being finalized to open.

He joined the line of about thirty passengers lining up to go ashore. The gate agent had started the process to register the vacating passengers and the line slowly crawled forward. Monk, under his hat brim, was watching carefully for any unusual activity.

As the woman in front of him was registered, the phone rang and Monk was shaken. The woman proceeded down the gangway as the officer in charge answered the phone.

The agent took Monk's cruise ID while the officer was listening on the phone. The agent handed him back his documents and waved him through as the officer spoke into the phone, nodding his head.

Using his new cane and every nerve in his body tensed for flight, it was all he could do to limp slowly down the gangway.

He heard the officer hang up the phone and give some directions to the agent, followed by a groan from the people in line. He didn't dare look back, but quickened his pace and reached the end of the gangway. He heard a shout behind him as he slipped into the crowd that usually awaited a cruise arrival. He had made it.

Just to be safe, he quickly entered a coffee shop rest room and stripped off the wig, glasses, and hat, pulled off his shirt and deposited them, together with the cane, into the garbage along with the now old passport. Opening his valise, he pulled out the new shirt, wig, and beard and quickly exited to catch a cab to the train station.

Chapter 11

Antonio DeAngelo had worked the dock for five years. His job was to coordinate onshore activities for passengers of the cruise ships. He liked to sit and have a cappuccino, watching his staff interact with the tourists. As a retired police officer, his training was never far from the surface.

He noticed a limping man with a cane emerging from the crowd at the gangway heading toward the coffee shop. Antonio didn't attach any significance to the oddity, but did watch him enter the coffee shop and go immediately into the bathroom.

In a short time, another man exited the bathroom, heading back out the door and Antonio, always the old cop, noted the cab number he hailed.

The odd part to Antonio was that he had not seen anyone else enter the bathroom. He mused on this for a moment, then decided to check for the other man.

He entered the bathroom and looked under the stalls, discovering the room was empty. He stood in the middle of the room with a puzzled look, then walked to the garbage can. He tramped on the foot pedal, revealing the wig, hat, shirt, and cane.

Reaching for the items, his training kicked in and he stopped... went to the door and called Arsenio, the manager, in Italian

"Arsenio, could you please get me a pair of your latex gloves."

***

The death of the congressman was immediately transmitted to Washington. At their direction, the captain informed the patrons that until further notice, all persons were restricted from leaving the ship.

Being such a public figure, Washington immediately arranged for a secret service investigator to fly to Split, Croatia, even though a heart attack was the consensus.

The other members of the table had been isolated since the incident and were seated in one of the lounges, waiting for official release. Pam had been inconsolable and sat staring vacantly, unable to fathom the event.

A couple of media people had appeared and Dr. Kenmore took advantage of the spotlight, holding court with his remembrances of his great relationship with the congressman and his regret that they had not had an opportunity to share their points of view while Norm Arthur and his wife, Lin, sat quietly in the corner, shunning any notice.

***

Marty had immediately called Tom Chiles, who was strangely detached in his hollow sympathetic offerings.

Kelly was leaving Tom's office when Tom's cell chirped. He picked it up and turned to the window. "Yes, Marty," and paused… "The congressman? What a shame. Was it a heart attack? …He's dead? Well, this drastically alters the game plan. Just do what you can and enjoy the rest of the cruise," he said as a cellphone in his desk buzzed.

"Marty, I have to go… I have another call."

Kelly was just closing the door when she heard Tom's response to Marty. She peeked back into Tom's office just as another cellphone buzzed and she saw Tom take it out of the drawer. He listened and said, "I just heard. It will be wired shortly," and he hung up, and threw the cell in the garbage. She quietly closed the door and sat down at the desk with a scowl. She was confused! She breathed deeply and opened her computer, pretending to be working. She heard his office door open but did not look up, pretending absorption in a project. He paused for a moment, then walked to her desk.

She knew he was staring at her intently. She looked up with a surprised look and said, "Yes, sir."

He stared intently for another moment and then said, "Kelly, I have just been informed that there has been a tragic occurrence on the cruise." He watched for a response.

It was all Kelly could do to maintain a calm, inquisitive look. "What?"

"The congressman has had a heart attack and died." His scrutiny intensified.

"Oh, my God," she yelped. The tension finally burst and tears boiled from her eyes.

The tears apparently satisfied Tom and he reached over and patted her shoulder. "Why don't you go to the employee lounge and relax for a while. I'll have the switchboard hold your calls."

"Thank you," she squeaked.

He walked back in his office and flopped down on one of the lounges. *Done!* he thought. Now the only remaining 'fly in the ointment' was Norm Arthur of COSM. Hopefully, Marty would handle that.

Now to the next piece of business – wiring the money, thought Tom. He grabbed his jacket and as he exited the office, he caught Kelly just leaving.

"Kelly, I am going out for about an hour. I will let the switchboard know."

"Yes, sir," answered Kelly.

In the employee lounge, she sat and stared into her coffee. *What have I just heard and seen? How could anyone else know about the congressman at the same time they had just been told…? and what phone was that? Why did he throw it away? What do I do now!*

The limo was waiting as Tom exited his private elevator. Riding along, staring out the window in deep thought, he was about to do the transaction on his cell when it suddenly hit him. *Why am I arranging the money so quickly? What if some problems develop? Why not wait until at least tomorrow?* He leaned over and told the driver to take him to the club instead. He wanted to have a drink and do some thinking.

***

Pam had finally emerged from shock and gone out to get some fresh air. Standing at the rail, her mind was in turmoil. Something was nagging at her, but she couldn't 'pull it up.' Chet had befriended her and she did not understand the deep sense of loss. When he had taken her elbow to be seated, she felt as though they had known each other forever and when the accident at the table had happened… 'That was it!' The accident! Now she remembered. It was the same man that had stared at her when she boarded.

When he fell, his arm swung around, just missing her and she saw something in his hand as it slammed against Chet's leg. It covered the palm and was secured by a strap around the hand.

With the remembrance, she was filled with dread. Revulsion flooded her body and she vomited over the railing just as Marty arrived. He grabbed her and led her to a bench.

"Pam… let me take you down to your cabin and get a doctor." Myra joined them and she helped lead Pam to her cabin and Marty called for the doctor.

Upon the doctor's arrival, Marty and Myra said their goodbyes.

"You've had a bad shock," offered the doctor as he handed her a pill, "just take this and you will have a good night's sleep."

"Thank you, doctor… I will."

Pam laid down on the bed and tried to relax, but her mind would not stop. She shook her head. This was preposterous. Surely, this was just shock? …and yet, she knew the picture in her mind of that hand was real. What had she seen?

From what she could remember in the aftermath, someone had said he was in perfect health. She was no doctor, so who was she to question the preliminary opinion of a heart attack. And yet…

***

Antonio DeAngelo felt foolish packing the trash can findings into the plastic bag, but old police habits die hard. He was just starting out the door when he heard a commotion at the pier. He walked over to the officer in charge. "What is it, Luige?"

"We have been informed that a congressman on the cruise has just died of a heart attack and officials have forbidden shore leave."

Antonio was confused, "…but I thought I just saw people leaving."

"Yes," said Luige, "but it just happened and they stopped it after a few people got off."

"Thank you, Luige, I am going to go on board."

He walked up the gangway to be greeted by the officer at the door asking for his boarding pass. "My name is Antonio DeAngelo, the coordinator for receiving passengers. I have just heard about the congressman and I need to speak to the captain. I may have some important information for him."

The officer looked him up and down and at the bag he was carrying. "Sir, as you can appreciate, the captain is extremely busy now and…"

"Just tell him Antonio DeAngelo needs to speak with him on a matter of importance."

"…uh …One moment, please." The officer walked a few yards away and spoke into his radio, "Sir, I am sorry to bother you, but there is a gentleman by the name of Antonio DeAngelo who says he needs to speak with you on a matter of great importance… Thank you, sir."

He walked back to the door with a peeved look. "You will find the captain in the dining room on the 2nd deck," he said sharply and turned away. Antonio boarded the ship and proceeded to the elevator.

The captain, Lucania Papadakis, was waiting at the elevator when Antonio emerged. "Antonio, what a pleasure to see you again. How long has it been"?

"Oh… well… at least two years." They embraced as only old friends could. They disengaged and Antonio spoke, "Luke, I know you are under extreme stress with the recent circumstances, so I will be quick and brief."

"Thank you, Tony, I appreciate that."

"I happened to be sitting in the coffee shop, observing passengers disembarking when I noticed a rather odd situation." He finished the story and held up the bag. "So, I have collected these things and am bringing them to you. I suspect you have an investigator coming and so, I thought I would leave these with you to do with them what you want."

Luke nodded, "You're right, there is an investigator arriving from Washington in a few hours, although the preliminary report is a heart attack." He looked at the bag. "I don't know what to make of this, but let me finish checking my manifest and when the thirty or so passengers that left have returned, hopefully, we can identify who this was by their absence. In the meantime, thank you for this, Tony. It is a rather strange event."

"My pleasure, Luke. Thank you for seeing me."

Tony headed back to the elevator. "Tony," hollered Luke, "can you leave your info with the officer at the door in case we need to contact you."

"Of course, …no problem."

***

Marty laid in bed completely exhausted. The jet lag, together with the events, had completely drained him.

Myra snuggled up to him. "What happens now? Wasn't one of your main undertakings to sway the congressman's resistance to the approval process of the FDA?"

Marty sighed, "Yes… and I have no idea where we go from here. I guess I will just carry on and spend the time meeting with Norm. He was my other project anyway. But right now, I need sleep. I'm sorry… I planned on our first night on board being a little different."

Myra chuckled, "Yes, I saw the champagne in the fridge. Don't worry, we've got seven more nights. Just get a good sleep." She leaned over and kissed him, but he was already gone.

Chapter 12

Kelly parked the car and entered the Fox and Hounds. She scanned the room and not seeing Nancy, found a booth in a corner and settled in.

The waiter was blocking her view of the door as she ordered and Nancy popped out from behind him and startled Kelly. "Make it two of whatever she ordered," said Nancy.

"Hi, Deb," muttered Kelly.

"Oooo… Thanks for the enthusiastic greeting."

"I'm sorry, Nancy," Kelly said as she burst into tears.

Nancy moved around to the other side and held Kelly. "What is it?" asked Nancy.

"I wish I knew," answered Kelly, "I have this feeling of impending doom, but it's based on nothing… Well, not really nothing, but it probably is silly."

"Let's start at the beginning," Nancy offered.

Kelly smiled, "I don't know where the beginning begins. I started in the pharmaceutical industry with all the ideals of a teenager. Oh, to be able to work for the 'good of mankind' in the healing of disease. Could there be a better aim in life?" She stopped to blow her nose.

"For many years, I accepted the premise that with all their medical professionals, scientists, and research capabilities as well as the protection of the CDC and the FDA, *Big Pharma* was working for the betterment of mankind. As I worked my way up, it became obvious that *Big Pharma* was working for the big bucks and was not only big and strong, but it would entertain no competition and certainly not allow anything or anyone to jeopardize their profits."

The waiter arrived with their drinks and menus.

Kelly continued, "As science progressed, both the natural health industry and *Big Pharma* continued to uncover cures drawn from nature's secrets. They were not patentable, but with *Big Pharma*'s resources, the secrets were able to be synthetically manufactured, which brought with it all the side effects that we see on television."

Nancy interrupted "What do you mean 'on television?'"

"Well, after much wrangling in Washington, the compromise with the FDA was that as long as the drug companies disclosed some of the side effects, that was enough warning for the public and the drug companies to launch their products. In other words, don't wait for the long-range research results. Subsequently, legislation was considered that would allow the drug companies to not have to fully disclose the results of their product research."

"You mean that they could 'cherry pick' what they disclosed to the public?" asked a shocked Nancy.

"Exactly," responded Kelly, "people like Norm Arthur of COSM were considered 'loons' that still believed in medieval treatments and were denigrated without mercy and paid for by *Big Pharma* with their obscene profits and protected by the largest lobbying budget in Washington. As a result, natural medicine has been pushed to the outer edges of healthcare and are almost legislated out of existence."

"Why hasn't the medical profession helped?"

Kelly sneered, "With what they receive from the drug companies, plus virtually no training in natural medicine, they are just as blind and biased as Congress."

Nancy looked strangely at Kelly, "Wait… Why are you still working in the industry if you know all this?"

"Because I have been coopted like everyone else. When I came into this business, the remuneration and perks were above average and the opportunities unlimited. I heard the rumors, but I couldn't bring myself to imagine the scope of the evil required to believe them. I was not able to imagine that corruption could go to this level."

"…and now?" asked Nancy.

Kelly pondered for a moment, "I don't know. I haven't cemented my thinking. I just had something happen to me today that has caused me even more reason to be concerned."

Nancy frowned, "What?"

"You probably haven't heard yet, but Congressman Chet Barnes died last night on the cruise, supposedly of a heart attack."

Nancy jumped up and moved to the other side of the booth, "What? …what do you mean, 'supposedly?'"

Kelly looked up from her drink, "Well, first of all, there has been no autopsy as yet. Secondly, and this is strictly my speculation. At the time Mr.

Chiles received the call this morning about the congressman, a cellphone in his desk rang. I was just going out the door and he thought I was gone. He pulled out the cell and said, 'I just heard. It will be wired shortly,' and then he threw the cellphone in the garbage."

They stared at each other. Finally, Nancy whispered, "You don't think… no… he couldn't… he wouldn't."

"Can you think of anything else that could mean?" asked Kelly.

Neither spoke for a long time, then Nancy ventured… "Do you think Mr. Cooper could be involved… and… oh, my God… what about Pam?"

"I don't know… I don't know anything except that we better keep this to ourselves. I don't think we should pursue our little plan for now."

"For sure," agreed Nancy.

Cagily, Kelly tilted her head, "Let's just lay low and see what develops."

***

It was early morning as the helicopter settled noisily onto the pedestrian area around the gangway and Dr. Clay Dearsome of the U.S. secret service jumped off to be met by Antonio DeAngelo.

"Dr. Dearsome?" inquired Tony, extending his hand.

"Yes," yelled the Dr. over the thrashing blades. They shook hands as they started walking toward the gangway, "I'm Tony DeAngelo. Luke… uh… Captain Lucania Papadakis asked me to meet you. As you can understand, he is rather busy."

Dr. Dearsome nodded, "Of course. What is the situation?"

"Well, first, I am not privy to a lot of information, but my understanding is that there are some diplomatic and legal niceties to clean up before the cruise can continue."

"Yes, and I hope I can clean those up in the next few hours," offered Dr. Dearsome.

Tony looked at him curiously, "You are with the secret service… Right?"

"Yes."

"I didn't think this had that kind of priority."

Dr. Dearsome glanced curiously at Tony, "Well, first of all, he was a congressman. Secondly, he was a ranking member, that chaired a powerful committee and thirdly, he was apparently a very healthy specimen with no sign of health problems."

Tony pondered for a moment and then, as they were boarding the ship, he tugged at Dr. Dearsome's sleeve, "May we talk for a moment?"

They both stopped. "Last night when the ship docked..." and he continued to tell the story. ".... So, I have given the items to the Captain. I wanted to tell you this myself because you will hear it from Luke and I didn't want you to think I was holding back. I have no idea if it has any significance at all, but I thought everyone should know."

"I am curious, Tony... may I call you Tony?"

"Yes... Yes."

"What made you notice all this in the first place and why did you follow it up when there was no reason?"

Tony smiled, shaking his head, "I am an old retired cop. Once a cop, always a cop. It's just 'second nature.'"

"I'm impressed," said Clay, "could I impose on you to join me for the next few hours. I could use a 'backup' with your 'eyes.'"

"Of course, let me make a couple of calls to clear some stuff."

"You realize that you will be under conditions of secrecy."

"Of course."

Clay extended his hand "Great. Let's get to work... and call me Clay."

***

All the involved dinner table patrons, as well as Dr. Clay Dearsome and Antonio DeAngelo were assembled in the executive dining room as the captain, Lucania Papadakis, arrived.

"I sincerely hope that this meeting will enable me to continue the cruise," huffed Captain Luke.

Dr. Arthur Kenmore jumped up, "Hear... Hear. I personally have had enough of this bureaucratic nonsense. We are American citizens and..."

"*Sit down and shut up!*" thundered Clay, "I have had enough of your ill-tempered outbursts."

"Who are you to..."

"I am Dr. Clay Dearsome, special investigator with the secret service and that gives you enough of *who* I am... now what I am... is in charge of *this meeting* and *you*, as an American citizen. Now... please, sit down and respond only when you are asked. Do I make myself clear?"

Dr. Kenmore unsuccessfully tried to stare down Clay, then turned and sat down with a "hrumph."

"OK. Let's get started. First of all, Captain, unless something extraordinary emerges, I really don't see any reason you won't be able to continue the cruise after this meeting."

"Thank you," burst the captain.

Clay continued, "Our first medical opinion is that this was simply a sudden heart attack. We have taken some samples and they are on their way to be analyzed. We have been informed that holding the cruise or the passengers would not serve any purpose. However, we have an issue that has arisen."

Heads snapped up. "The captain has informed me that there is one passenger missing. Last night, before the order to stop anyone leaving the ship, thirty-one passengers signed out and only thirty returned. We don't know if this has anything to do with anything, but it is an anomaly."

Pam raised her hand.

"Yes… Ah… Miss Styles," he said, looking at his notes.

"Do you have a picture of that passenger?" asked Pam.

With a raised eyebrow, Clay answered, "Yes. Why?"

Pam hesitated.

"Miss Styles?" queried Clay.

Pam looked around the room. "Have any of you told about the accident with that guy at the next table." Everyone looked quizzically at Pam.

"What accident?" prompted Clay.

"You mean the guy that stumbled into our table?" asked Marty.

"Yes." replied Pam. She started tearing up, "I saw something. I don't know if it is anything at all."

"Tell us, please," urged Clay.

She started with the telling of the strange feeling she had when she boarded and the encounter in the hallway and, finally, what she had witnessed during the fall. Silence followed her revelation, with everyone staring at her, dumbfounded.

Clay cleared his throat, "Miss Styles… Do you think you could recognize him if you saw him again?"

"I think so," she murmured. Clay reached into a file, pulling out the passport picture from the ship files.

"Please, look at this, Miss Styles."

Pam looked at the face. She jerked back… "That's him."

The room exploded with exclamations. Captain Papadakis locked eyes with Antonio and nodded, both recognizing the discovered clothes that were found were those in the picture.

"I guess I don't need to tell you that this considerably alters our assumptions," stated Clay, "I will need to contact Washington for further direction." He turned to the captain, "I don't see that this should delay your departure much longer, but I think we need to have these folks flown back to the U.S.

for some debriefing. Before we leave, I would like to talk to the passengers that were seated at the other table."

"In that regard," said the captain, "we have found what appears to be some confusion with the seating. Although the concierge podium and the names on the table were the same, the original seating plan is different. It appears that someone switched the tables."

Clay shook his head, "Well that does it. Since the medical people have signed off on a heart attack and released the body, all of you that were at the dinner table need to fly back together with the body and myself immediately. We need to be in U.S. jurisdiction before someone changes their mind." Clay turned to Marty and said, "I would prefer to fly on a private charter, rather than take the risk of alerting anyone. Is that possible with your company and we can cover the cost later."

Marty jumped up. "Please excuse me. I will make a call," he exclaimed and rapidly walked outside, punching out a call to Derek Maurrel.

"Remember, you are under strict secrecy." yelled Clay.

"Marty. What can I do for you?" answered Derek.

"Derek, we have a situation here."

"Go ahead."

"It seems there are some issues with the death of Congressman Barnes."

Derek sucked in a breath, "What kind of issues?"

"Some serious questions about events before the supposed heart attack."

"…supposed heart attack?"

Marty took a deep breath, "The Secret Service guy is saying that our entire dinner table attendees must return with the body."

"*What? Why?*"

"Well, for starters, I am sworn to secrecy, but there was an unusual event during dinner that involved the congressman, and now there is a passenger missing that was involved in that incident. We need to arrange a charter for us all."

"Crap… OK… What city are you in?"

"We're in Split, Croatia."

"All right, I'll get back to you."

***

Derek slowly left the office and headed for the stairway to Tom Chiles' office. He was not looking forward to this meeting. Tom never liked bad news, but this was more than 'bad news.'

Kelly glanced up as she saw Derek head towards her desk, "Do you need me, sir?"

"No. Is Tom in?"

"No. He said he would be in later."

Derek paused, "We need a charter plane arranged immediately for all our people on the cruise."

Kelly tried to appear nonchalant. "Yes, sir. Where would the pickup be and for how many?"

"Call Pam and get the details, then call the charter companies on file and make the arrangements." Derek started back downstairs as he was calling Tom. He got the recording. "Tom, we have some serious developments. Call me ASAP."

***

Pam's cell buzzed as Marty walked back in the room.

"Hi, Kelly."

"Pam... I'm calling you on my cell. I just got some directions from Mr. Maurrel. He told me to arrange a charter immediately from wherever you are, for all our people and maybe others. What's going on? Do you know about this?"

Pam walked away from the group. "There are some things I am not able to talk about, but yes, I do know about this. I'm just talking to the secret service officer and I will get back to you."

"OK." They both rang off. Pam walked back to the group, looking at Clay Dearsome, "That was Kelly, Derek Maurell's executive assistant. She is ready to order a charter back to Dallas for us all. I told her we would confirm shortly."

Clay nodded his head, "Great. I am waiting for a call from Washington."

Dr. Kenmore, who had been extraordinarily quiet since the 'smack down,' finally came alive. "I don't plan on leaving the cruise. We have just begun..."

Clay started walking toward Dr. Kenmore. "Dr., I really don't want to start with you again, so I am going to say this just once." He turned to everyone, "As of now, we are treating this suspicious event as a possible crime and being as it involves a member of the United States Congress, I have the authority to do whatever is necessary. For us to expand this investigation, the victim and all individuals in this room need to be within the United States jurisdiction."

"At the moment, there is no crime, so therefore we are free to leave. The local medical examiner has signed off on the heart attack and we have permission to take the body back to the U.S. Further...with my authority, I caution you all that this is considered a matter of national security and therefore, you are sworn to secrecy."

Dr. Kenmore started shaking his head, "I am not sure that you are within your legal rights to hold us in this manner."

Clay glared at him. "Captain," he called.

"Yes," responded Luke.

"Would you please inform Dr. Kenmore that you are in concurrence with my previous statement and as you are the law on this vessel, you will enforce my statements."

"Dr. Kenmore... that is correct."

Kenmore snorted arrogantly, "Well, I want you all to know this will be addressed when we return home."

Clay surveyed the group. "I will talk to Washington shortly to confirm our schedule. In the meantime, why don't you all go and pack up while we wait for our transport. Miss Styles, you can inform your boss that we need an aircraft that can handle six as soon as possible."

His cell chirped. "Excuse me, this is Washington," he said and walked away while the rest sat in stunned silence.

It had been a long fourteen hours and the tension was now wearing on them all. Even Dr. Kenmore seemed drained of his normal pomposity as he sat morosely, fingering his beard.

The atmosphere was heavy, swirling in a potpourri of emotions. Shock, fear, sadness, but mostly, confusion. Surely, the suspicions couldn't be true! ...and yet, there certainly were some strange coincidences.

Marty's phone buzzed. He rose and walked into the hallway. "Yes, Tom."

"What the hell is going on over there?" boomed Tom Chiles. "How can a heart attack turn into a possible crime."

"Sir... we don't know anything for sure except that the secret service wants us back on U.S. soil ASAP. I believe Kelly is arranging a charter as we speak. We will have word from Washington very shortly."

"Give me the capsule version of the situation," barked Tom.

Marty spent the next three minutes explaining what had happened and what was known. "...as improbable as it sounds, it is suspected there was some foul play in the congressman's death."

Tom sighed on the other end just as Clay came back in the room.

"Mr. Chiles, hang on a moment… the secret service man has some news." Marty covered the mouthpiece and called Clay, "…any news?"

"Yes," replied Clay, "we are to leave as soon as possible. Have you arranged the charter?"

Marty nodded his head and pointed to the phone, "We are doing it right now."

"Mr. Chiles… We have been ordered back to the U.S. right now. Derek is aware of the situation and Kelly is waiting for the decision so she can order a charter."

"Who the hell is paying for that?" bellowed Tom.

"Initially… Us, and then the government will reimburse us."

Tom grunted, "What a 'cluster' this has turned into." Little did Marty know how much Tom meant those words. Rob Schafer's words were ringing in his ears, '…you are entering an arena that you are not equipped for.'

Tom continued, "…all right. I'll have Kelly arrange for a G6 and she'll call you back." He clicked off. Marty walked back to the group. Looking at Clay, he said, "I should have a call shortly, confirming our charter."

"Thank you. Good work," said Clay, "the sooner we are out of here, the better. Some bureaucrat could get it in his head to hold us here."

***

Tom slammed down his cell, startling Kelly.

"Kelly, get in here," shouted Tom.

"Yes, sir," said Kelly as she bustled into the office.

"Go ahead with the charter for the group as soon as you can."

"Yes, sir."

He needed to start a plan immediately. If the Feds were so 'into' this at this early stage, there was no time to be sitting on the sidelines. He speed-dialed Rob Schafers' number on his cell.

***

The switchboard paged Kelly as she exited Tom's office. She picked up her phone. "Yes, Crystal."

She listened for a while, "Thank you… get him on the line again for me."

Through all of this, she couldn't get the thoughts of what she had seen earlier out of her head. Could this be a confirmation of what Nancy and she had thought? It couldn't be! It was just too abhorrent to even be considered, and yet, the pieces were beginning to fit.

She answered her phone, "This is Kelly Freeman."

"Miss Freeman, this is Jim Shore at World Wide Charter. I have arranged to have a G6 at the private terminal in Split, Croatia within two hours."

"Excellent, Jim. That's fast service."

He chuckled, "We do our best. I will email you the contract and you can send me the contact information and we will go ahead with the order."

"Perfect. I will have that information to you immediately. Thank you again, Jim."

"My pleasure."

Kelly texted the information, then left the desk and went to the restroom. She made sure the stalls were empty, then locked herself in and called Pam.

Pam answered on the first ring.

"Pam... it's Kelly."

"Oh... Hi, Kelly. What a day, huh," she said as she walked away from the group.

"Yeah... listen, Pam, I don't have long to talk. I am in the ladies' room and someone may come in. First of all, I have the charter arranged. It will be at the private terminal in two hours. Save me a call and tell Mr. Cooper that I had to get something from you and that's why I called you instead of him. OK?"

"Yes."

"Pam, what is going on. Tom is, to say the least, in a bad state."

Pam frowned, "Kelly, I am sworn to secrecy about anything that has gone on here."

"...hmm. Bummer. Well, listen... I may have some additional information that I think I should talk to you about before we get too far with whatever investigation is starting."

"OK. As soon as we land, we can talk."

"Good. Have a safe trip. Let me know your ETA."

"Will do. See you soon"

***

Rob Schafers answered on the first beep.

"Rob... we got problems. Can we get together right now?" asked Tom.

"Give me an hour and I'll be there."

"Not here... Let's meet at Leon's, in Addison."

"OK."

Tom walked out to the desk just as Kelly was arriving from the ladies' room. "Kelly, I have to go out in about thirty minutes and I'll be gone for the day."

"OK, Mr. Chiles." She sat down at Pam's desk just as Derek Maurrel walked up the stairs.

"Is Tom in?" he asked brusquely.

"Yes, Mr. Maurrel. Let me call him."

Striding to the door, he said, "Never mind," and opened the door as Tom was reaching into his garbage can. He looked up guiltily, "What the hell... Do you allow people to walk into your office unannounced?"

"Sorry... but this is important. I just had a media person call me and ask about Congressman Barnes."

"*What!* What did they say?"

"Just that there was a rumor that his death was not natural."

"Goddamn media jackals. Where in the hell would that come from?" Derek scrutinized Tom carefully, "could there be any truth to it?"

"Of course not," roared Tom, "...and besides, how could anyone know anything over here when our people haven't even left the ship yet."

"Who knows. It could have been a crew member, a passenger, a waiter ...anyone."

Tom fumed, "Did you shut it down?"

"I think so. It seemed more like a feeler than having any substance."

"Well, keep on it. In the meantime, our group will be in the air within two hours. That should put them in around 7am. I want everyone but Norm in my office immediately after they land."

"Now I have to leave. I should be back in an hour or so." Tom said as he walked around his desk and headed toward the elevator, leaving Derek and Kelly scowling apprehensively.

Derek started down the stairs and Kelly went back to her work as she replayed in her mind Derek's sudden arrival. He had left the office door open and Kelly had not only seen Tom pulling away from the garbage but had overheard the exchange. Tom's outburst was strange. Why would that cause such a reaction?

She recalled the cellphone had been trashed and her curiosity got the better of her. She went into the office, closed the door, and walked over to the trash. There it was! What now? If she took it, would he recall he hadn't retrieved it? ...and what would she do with it anyway? ...but if her suspicions had any reality, it could be a major piece of a puzzle.

She leaned over to pick it up and then hesitated. What about finger prints? Better safe than sorry. She walked to the cafeteria, grabbed some medical gloves and went back to the office.

Carefully lifting the cell from the trash onto the desk, she noticed a big finger print. She tore off some scotch tape and carefully lowered it onto the print, then pealed it off. She had no idea if this was even useful.

Noting the manufacturer's numbers on the back of the cell. she grabbed a note pad and wrote down those numbers and the ones inside. Returning the phone to the trash, she walked out and sat at her desk. She was sweating and her heart rate was up. *Now what*, she thought… *call Nancy*!

"Hi, Kelly."

"Nancy. Are you terribly busy, or could you come up for a minute?"

"Sure. I'll be right up."

As she waited, she pondered why she felt this urgent need to tell Nancy.

Chapter 13

The van was waiting at the gangway as the Dallas group walked off the ship. The tension was intense, expecting at any moment a call delaying their departure. Now the only concern was clearing the departure at the airport. They all said their goodbyes to Captain Lucania Papadakis and shore coordinator Antonio DeAngelo.

Dr. Kenmore was in a continual state of irritation and was trying the already frayed nerves of his traveling companions.

As per the caution from Clay Dearsome, talk among the group was studiously avoiding the subject of Congressman Chet Barnes, but speculation was rampant.

The atmosphere between Dr. Kenmore and Norm Arthur of COSM had been simmering. Norm had managed to keep his usual dispassionate and polite demeanor until, as they rode in the van, the Dr. finally breached Norm's boundaries

"You realize, Mr. Arthur, that this whole incident is because of you and your cohort's constant interference in the natural evolvement of medicine."

Total silence enveloped the van. Norm turned to stare at Dr. Kenmore and, with a patronizing smile, said, "Dr. Kenmore, I realize that in your ivory tower, academic world, your utterances are received with awe. However, in the real world, we find it quite exhilarating to expand our mind with the exploration of alternative ideas, especially when they are supported by outside scientific facts that are available for corroboration."

"Mr. Arthur, your insults…"

"I'm not finished. The only fortunate aspect of the termination of this cruise is that we won't have to suffer further with your opinionated prattling. I would be happy to have further discourse with you at some time when we can have an exchange rather than a lecture. *Now*, I'm finished."

Norm was met with suppressed smiles as the Dr., once again, harrumphed and turned to look out the window.

Marty, although quite entertained by the outburst, was concerned. The Dr. was the strongest advocate for Chiles, Arken, and Associates and it was Marty's job to weld this rift into a solution.

His personal admiration and fondness for Norm wasn't helping. As much as he was appalled at the outburst by the Dr., he needed to facilitate a 'cease fire.' It seemed like an insurmountable mission.

***

Tom tossed the keys to the valet guy, walked into Leon's and spotted Rob reading the menu in the corner booth. "You ordered a drink yet"

"Not yet… and hello to you too."

"Niceties are not on the menu at this time."

"I wouldn't have guessed," chuckled Rob.

Tom rolled his eyes, then looked around just as the waitress came. "I'll have a double vodka martini with extra olives."

"Just bring me a Heineken," said Rob.

"You might need more than that when you hear what I have to say."

Rob just looked at him with a detached stare, then spoke, "First of all, you need to know that I have been following the news about the sudden death of Congressman Barnes and the coincident timing of this meeting leads me to believe you are planning for me to hear more."

Tom sighed… "How perceptive of you." He rejoined sarcastically, "As you know, the cause of death was a heart attack. Apparently, because of his importance, it is protocol to have the secret service sign off on things of this nature. In this case, the agent discovered some anomalies and thus has ordered the entire Chiles, Arken team returned to the U.S."

"Do you know anything about the 'anomalies?'"

"No, and that's what's got me worried. Do you recall our conversation in the…?"

"Tom," blurted Rob, "Please, don't say anymore. Right now, I am totally devoid of any knowledge other than what I have seen on the news, and I prefer to keep it that way."

Tom started squirming in his chair. "…But, Rob, you have been my confidant forever."

"Yes, I have, and I have always been able to rationalize some questionable things we have done, but I recall in previous conversations that there were some things that I did not consider within my guidelines and I told you so."

Tom reddened, "Are you telling me that you are no longer willing to work with me?"

"No. I am telling you that there are some things that I did not consider to be in my purview. Let's say that, hypothetically, you had considered a plan to do harm to an elected member of our government and again, hypothetically, suppose you attempted to discuss that with me, I would have responded with a caution that it would not be a wise decision."

Tom leaned back with a startled look.

"However, as I know nothing about this situation, this discussion is all moot."

"You son of a bitch… after all we've been through, you're going to bail on me now."

With an unwavering look, Rob retorted, "Tom… yes, we have been through a lot and seen a lot together, but in reviewing our history, I have always stayed just on the edge. I am not proud of some of the things, but I know I could swear before a judge and jury that I didn't break the law. Now, please, could we save the rhetoric and continue this in a civil manner."

Leaning forward with a menacing snarl, Tom responded, "Do you really think that you can just smile and walk out of our relationship with no consequences. Your hands are as dirty as mine. Just because I suggest a solution to our problem and you go all soft doesn't give you the right to opt out."

"I couldn't 'opt out,' as you say, because I was 'never in.'"

Tom smiled evilly, "This 'holier than thou' shtick is not going to work when the 'feds' come calling. You're up to your ass in this Congressman Barnes thing just like me and I'm here to remind you. We're a team!"

Rob stared evenly into Tom's eyes and for the first time in their long association, he saw a depth of evil that startled him. It pained him to realize he had fooled himself over the years in thinking he could blindly walk the line and not be tainted.

When Tom had suggested the removal of Congressman Barnes, Rob had chosen to not believe Tom would follow through. He was certainly somewhat culpable with his weak attempt to stop him, but his conscience was clear as to any knowledge and participation in the abhorrent act.

Rob rose from the booth and threw some dollars on the table.

"Let me buy us our last drink. This 'team,' as you call it, is no longer functional. We have stood together for a long time, Tom, and we made decisions that were expedient rather than right, but I am not, nor have I ever been a part of whatever you have done, I have watched you bully others, but I am not one who responds to threats. I wish you the best, but I am 'done.'" He turned and walked away.

"You'll regret this," shouted Tom.

Not as much as you, thought Rob as he removed the recording device from under his shirt.

***

Derek Maurrel was perplexed. Between trying to come up with his own game plan and trying to figure out Tom's game, he had purposely stayed away from any unnecessary encounters. He was fairly certain that Tom had concluded he was the 'break in' artist. The question was, *What was he going to do?*

***

With the news of the congressman's death, and Kelly informing him that the entire Dallas 'team' was returning on a private flight, Derek's imagination was running wild. He knew something untoward had happened, but what could it be that would bring the entire team home.

Maybe Kelly knew more. He picked up the phone and called her to his office. Tom's office door was open and Tom heard her responding to Derek's call. When she was done, he called her in.

"Kelly, I haven't had a chance to tell you, but we are all sworn to secrecy by the secret service regarding anything to do with Congressman Barnes and that includes Mr. Maurrel."

"Yes, sir," replied Kelly with a confused look. *Shouldn't the President of the company know something as important as a secret service investigation?* she thought.

Kelly walked down the stairs to her own desk, which had accumulated a considerable pile of work over the last couple of days. She knocked on Derek's door and entered.

Derek looked up from his desk. "Kelly... Have you had any conversations with Pam," he asked, watching her intently.

"Yes, sir. We talked about arranging a charter."

"Do you have any idea why they are suddenly returning?" Derek saw Kelly flinch.

"Mr. Maurrel, I was informed by Mr. Chiles that the secret service has instructed us that we are not to talk to anyone about the event." There was silence… "Will that be all, sir?"

He waved here away, obviously in deep thought. *The son of a bitch is keeping me 'out of the loop,'* thought Derek. *The president of the company was not supposed to know of a secret service investigation? You've got to be kidding!*

Nancy arrived at Kelly's desk just as Kelly closed Derek's office door. "We have to be careful," whispered Kelly.

With raised eyebrows, Nancy queried, "What's going on?"

Kelly perused the room. Satisfied no one was within earshot, she apprised Nancy of what she knew of the circumstances regarding the congressman's death, Mr. Chiles strange cell conversation, the disposal of the cellphone and her retrieval of the cell manufacturer's numbers.

Nancy absorbed the information in silence. Finally, she responded, "What do you make of all this?"

"I don't know what to think. I can certainly surmise a 'worst case scenario,' but it's too overwhelming to contemplate."

"What are you going to do with the cell information?"

Kelly shook her head, "I don't know. Just file it in the same place we've filed the hacking information."

With a faraway look, Nancy mused, "I wonder if Mr. Cooper or Pam know any more about this whole thing. I think I would feel safe 'feeling out' Mr. Cooper."

"…um …any disclosure of our actions or suspicions would scare me," responded Kelly.

"Me too. I'll be very discrete. In the meantime, do you think you know Pam well enough to ask her anything?"

Kelly paused, "I'm not sure. She is pretty 'closed up' and it's not as if we are good 'buds.' Let me play it by ear. In the meantime, you better go. I don't want anyone to see us together."

Nancy rose and started down the backstairs and Kelly went up the stairs just as she heard Tom's private elevator in his office open.

Whew, thought Kelly.

***

The limo arrived as the G6 was refueling, so the group had a few minutes to gather themselves and freshen up. It was going to be a nonstop seven hours but, fortunately, the seats reclined into beds. Dr. Kenmore immediately isolated himself while the rest of the group lounged in the waiting area.

"You OK?" asked Marty, looking at Myra. She had been exceedingly quiet since the dinner and Marty was concerned.

She shifted around on the sofa and then, looking squarely at Marty, replied, "I am a complete disaster. I am a jumble of disappointment that we are canceling the trip, sadness at the death of Chet, horrified of the circumstances of the death, and just plain overwhelmed. Marty, you don't think there is anything to these suspicions, do you?"

Marty smiled wistfully, "I don't know, Myra. I am just trying to move on and deal with the personality problems. I just hope I get some time in the air to settle the Dr. down."

"Do you think Norm is OK?"

"I hope so. He is a very level guy, so I don't think this will be terminal."

Myra hung her head, "Marty, the more I listen to the back and forth between Dr. Kenmore, Norm, and you, I can't help but think that you are fighting a losing battle. Norm keeps coming at you with verifiable facts while Dr. Kenmore responds with rhetoric and bombast."

Marty stared at her in confusion, "Myra, do you realize what you are saying? Our very livelihood is based on everything that I say and believe."

"Then defeat Norm by defeating his factual arguments and leave the emotion to Dr. Kenmore."

"I agree," he responded, "I have to fight on two fronts. First, I need to blunt Norm and the COSM factual arguments with scientific response. Secondly, push Dr. Kenmore's pedigree to the forefront. That leaves the public with the choice of believing a monstrously absurd conspiracy or the reasoned answers from the collective pharmaceutical research of Dr. Kenmore and other medical experts, delivered with the help of the world's finest marketing and advertising community."

Myra paused… "Marty, I understand the fundamental issue of our livelihood and the blitzkrieg of advertising and marketing to make the arguments, but… are we 'right' or are we just being expedient? I can't even begin to fathom the guilt and shame if we are supporting what Norm views as the evil being systematically delivered on mankind."

"Wow… Hold on now, Myra. Don't you think you are taking this to an absurd conclusion? 'Delivered on mankind?' Isn't that a rather egotistical view? Do you really think the pharmaceutical industry is that powerful?"

Myra hesitated again… "First of all, let me establish something. I don't want these doubts to be true. I am enjoying this lifestyle as much as anyone and watching your success is thrilling, but I am beginning to see a larger ture and it scares me! Just below this glitz and glamour, there is a ru ness that is rather frightening."

"In answer to your question, yes, I do think the industry is that powerful. Look at the history. For example; this isn't just a Chiles, Arken cruise. There are reps of the most powerful *Big Pharma* companies that supply drug products to the entire world. So, let's not downplay the scope of this industry."

Marty was astounded, "Well… you obviously have been giving this a lot of thought."

"Yes, and most of it in the last couple of days listening to your discussions and a little internet research. Marty… I'm not sure you grasp what your algorithms are going to do in the industry. Chiles, Arken have not put you in this position just 'because you are a nice guy.' Whether you are part of it or not, they are going to apply your ideas worldwide and…"

"Wait a minute, Myra. Am I hearing you say that you think they would try, in some way, to steal my proprietary property?"

"Marty, I am not smart enough to know what they can or will do. I only know that the questions that have arisen with the death of Chet have disclosed a horizon that frightens me and I want us to thoroughly examine our motives and the playing field as we move forward."

The conversation had alarmed and dismayed Marty and yet, he was strangely proud of her stance for three reasons.
Firstly, he had underestimated Myra's interest and knowledge in and of his business. Secondly, the depth of her passion to 'do the right thing,' and finally, and most of all, the courage it took to address these issues that obviously threatened their very wellbeing.

But most disturbing of all was the logic that was squirreling its way into his heretofore unshakeable belief.

His mind went to the Herbert Spencer quote:

"There is a principle which is a bar against all information, which cannot fail to keep a man in everlasting ignorance that principle is contempt prior to investigation"

Was he being contemptuous, or just operating out of self- centered fear that he would lose what he had or not get what he wanted?

Chapter 14

The flight was uneventful, with everyone sleeping most of the way. Dr. Clay Dearsome, sitting in the rear, dozed off and on while trying to string the dots together. The people on the flight appeared to be totally innocent and yet, there seemed to be a thread that went beyond the common denominator of the industry cruise. Until he could gather some forensic information, everything seemed random and coincidental; nevertheless, beyond his experience and training, his 'gut' was saying something else.

The event, seen by Antonio in the terminal coffee shop, certainly deserved a long look. He hoped the results of the forensics on the trash contents would yield some positive results.

Antonio had met with a detective friend and given him a picture of Monk's passport and asked for a follow-up on all trains, buses, and flights out of Croatia. Clay had already ordered a workup on the passport, the results of which he hoped were awaiting him in Dallas. The concierge in the dining room had informed the captain that the seating had been doctored. The cabin that Monk had occupied had been sealed for a forensics team.

Clay couldn't stop the random thought of an assassination from wandering in and out of his consciousness. He had worked many cases, but the magnitude of that assumption was staggering. If it was an assassination, then a professional was involved. That being the case, he had to be hired by someone... then, who and why? A congressman certainly would have created enemies in his career. He needed to talk with the congressman's executive assistant.

But why on a cruise? A difficult kill site. A professional could have picked anywhere... why there? Maybe it had to be done on short notice? How long had this mysterious guest been booked on the cruise?

He had a lot of work to do!

***

During the flight, Marty and Norm had been able to have a bit of an exchange. Norm pretty well maintained the COSM line, which was anchored by the strong and partially proven suspicions that the industry was withholding lab results that would prove that some, if not most, of *Big Pharma's* releases were, at the least, premature and at worst, downright deadly.

Marty countered with – the FDA would not allow drugs to be sold if they had not met the FDA requirements.

Norm responded with an almost impenetrable counter: Namely – Why, then wouldn't *Big Pharma* allow the FDA to release those results for examination by independent experts?

The nature of Marty and Norm's relationship and their respect for each other allowed for a non-combative atmosphere. They both knew when an impasse had been reached and were willing to temporarily vacate the discussion.

However, the world that Marty serviced was not of the same temperament. He knew that their viewpoint was totally influenced by the 'bottom line.' They answered to only one master… Wall Street. Classic 'laissez faire capitalism' vs. measurable, long-term scientific verification.

Marty and Norm had finished their discussion as the Dallas skyline flashed past, and the G6 touched down at the Addison Airport. Over and above their respective viewpoints, nothing had been settled. They shook hands and promised to meet again soon.

As the plane taxied, Clay stood and addressed the group. "There will be a secret service agent meeting us in the terminal. I apologize for the delay, but we will need to hold you in an isolated room until we can complete individual debriefings."

A collective groan was cut short by the bellowing voice of Dr. Arthur Kenmore, "Haven't we had enough of this Nazi jackboot treatment. We're on American soil and I will not continue to be treated…"

"…Dr.," interrupted Clay, "as I said earlier, and I reiterate, this is now a secret service investigation and you will cooperate either voluntarily or we will have you restrained. Is that clear?"

"I want my lawyer," blustered the Dr.

"When we have finished our debriefing, you can call anyone you desire. Right now, I need you to shut up."

The G6 settled at the door to the terminal, the attendant unlatched the door, and the stairs lowered. Waiting at the bottom were two uniformed officers. The group was escorted to a waiting room where, after a few minutes, Clay opened the door and asked for Pam.

She stood and followed Clay down the hall and entered another lounge area.

"Miss Styles. This is Agent Richard Guy."

"Hello, Miss Styles. Please, be seated."

She walked to the proffered chair and sat.

"Could you please tell me what you told Dr. Dearsome concerning the events before and after the death of Congressman Barnes?"

Pam repeated the strange events leading up to the accident at the table. As the story reached the description of the hand, she hesitated. An image flashed through her mind.

"He was wearing a ring," she blurted excitedly! She had not thought of it previously.

"Can you describe the ring?"

Pam fixed her eyes on the wall trying to 'pull up' the image of the ring.

"It had a diagram or symbol on it… a triangle in the middle… and… ah… kind of like arrows around it."

Clay handed her a piece of paper and pen. "Could you draw it?" he asked.

"I think so," responded Pam hopefully.

"Do you think you could pick out the symbol if you saw it?" asked Clay and Agent Guy.

"Possibly," responded Pam.

Agent Guy rose, "Miss Styles, I will be at your office in the morning and we can look at some pictures."

Pam rose, "OK… can I go now?"

Clay nodded, "Yes… and thanks. We'll see you tomorrow."

Agent Guy, along with Clay, finished the individual debriefings and allowed everyone to return home with the admonition that they were not to talk with anyone.

***

Tom was not privy to the secret service investigation, but he knew they would be pursuing the case with a 'full court press.' Whatever was feeding their suspicions, some or all of it had to come from the scene, and that meant mistakes had been made by Monk, leaving Tom with only one conclusion. He was vulnerable! If, somehow, the investigation reached Monk, he could use Tom as a bargaining chip.

Tom paced the office like a lion… back and forth… back and forth… There had to be an answer.

The terminal rupture with Rob had left him without his usual 'go to partner.' Tom could always count on Rob's steady nature to support his decisions and now he was approaching his most difficult decision ever and was losing confidence rapidly.

Finding another Monk was not an option and, with his lack of experience, going up against Monk would be suicide. The only weapon he had was money. ...and then, it occurred to him... he had a 'patsy'... Derek! He knew Derek was extremely vulnerable, so it was time to take advantage. He hadn't really come up with a plan, but first he needed to put Derek firmly in place.

Tom clicked the intercom, "Kelly... find Derek and have him come up."

"Yes, sir", she dialed Derek's number.

"This is Derek Maurrel."

"Mr. Maurrel, this is Kelly. I am calling on my cell from upstairs. Mr. Chiles needs to see you right now."

Derek, with dread, walked up the stairs. He knew that this was IT! He was about to pay for his stupidity.

"Come in... Come in," effused Tom, "thanks for coming on such short notice."

What the hell is going on? thought Derek.

"Derek, I realize I haven't been the most affable or communicative person in the world. I have had a lot on my mind, and frankly, I am ashamed and I apologize."

It never ceased to amaze Derek how Tom could completely throw him off track.

"... Ah... It's OK. No apology necessary."

"Good... Good. Thank you. Now I want to address the 'elephant in the room.' I think that you know that I know you were the uninvited guest in my office the other day."

Derek grimaced, "Tom, I..."

"Let me finish, Derek. I am sure that you were anxious to see your file you saw when I pulled it out of the safe. Let me say that I understand. I probably would have considered the same course of action had I been you. The only thing I am unhappy about is the attack on Pam. I also understand that panic ensued. So... Let's just keep this to ourselves. And by the way, here is the file."

Tom handed the file to an obviously stupefied Derek.

"You probably won't like what you read, but has anyone ever liked their life laid out for the world to see. As you know, I tend to be a little paranoid and I wanted to make sure I knew everything... just in case."

Derek started flipping through the file. The more he read, the deeper the frown. "Wow! The further I go, the worse it gets. I don't even remember some of this."

"Well, don't worry about it. It's 'water under the bridge' and I am comfortable that our relationship is such that I needn't worry."

"Thank you," mumbled Derek.

"Now… onto greener pastures." *Time to offer the carrot*, thought Tom. "I have been contemplating your comments from the other day relative to the share structure and have concluded that your argument has merit and it is time to restructure. I am prepared to go to the board with the recommendation that you be issued an additional 10,000 shares, which would bring your holdings up to just under 2%."

Derek was astonished! At the current trading price of approximately $87, that would add another $870,000 to his net worth.

"With your efforts to date, plus the addition of the Cooper piece, you have more than earned it. I just wish it could be more, but I hope this meets with your approval."

Derek could only stare at Tom with a dazed expression, "Tom… I don't know what to say."

"Not necessary to thank me. You earned it. Let's meet tomorrow and we can talk further. I have a little project that I may want you to work on with me."

With his hand outstretched, Derek started toward Tom.

Tom chuckled, "Now let's not get to carried away." They shook and Tom turned back toward his desk. "See you tomorrow."

Derek nodded and walked to the door still in shock.

***

Pam had arrived home and immediately gone to bed. After three hours of restless sleep, she called Kelly.

"Are you home?" asked Kelly.

"Yes. I am sorry, I should've called sooner but I was beat and I went straight to bed."

"That's OK. I understand." Then she hesitated for a moment.

Pam heard the hesitation, "Are you OK, Kelly?"

"…um …Yeah…I guess so. It seems like there are some strange things going on and now, with what happened on the cruise, I am having a hard time making one and one equal two."

"Kelly. I don't know if you know, but the secret service has become involved in the death of Chet… er… Congressman Barnes and we have been restricted in saying anything to anyone regarding the cruise events. I am anxious to meet and talk, but I don't want you to think I am withholding anything on purpose."

"I understand, but I do think that we should talk and I can fill you in on my end. I have talked with Nancy and we both feel there is something serious going on."

"What do you mean?" asked Pam.

Kelly sighed, "I wish I knew. Let's get together as soon as we can and maybe you can make some sense of things."

"OK. How about we have dinner tonight?"

"That's great," gushed Kelly, "I would like to bring Nancy along as well."

"If you feel it is worthwhile, then I trust your judgment."

"Yes, I do. How about 7 at Dino's, the Italian place on the Tollway."

"I know it. That fits for me. See you then."

Kelly smiled, "Thanks, Pam. It will be nice to have someone else to talk to."

"Trust me… I feel the same."

***

Richard Guy and Clay drove down to the secret service office.

"It's been a while since we worked on a case together," Clay said to Richard as he parked the car.

Clay nodded, "If I recall correctly, it was in Atlanta."

"Right… the telecom case."

Shaking his head sadly, Clay couldn't help but chuckle, "I believe that was the one that cost me my final shred of faith in human nature. I had never seen such an example of greed."

"Well, I don't want to burst your bubble," countered Richard, "but after I fill you in on some stuff, you may want to reevaluate the number one 'greed contender.'"

Clay looked at him with raised eyebrows, "Really?"

"Yep…. but we can talk about that later. Let's review what we have here and see if we can come up with a picture," he said as they arrived at the office.

"Good."

In the office, Richard walked to a whiteboard that had been set up. "OK… The first thing we are going to need to support any kind of a theory is the lab report on the Congressman's tox screen. I am hoping we will have that shortly. Secondly, we should be getting the forensics from the bag found in the trash can. Thirdly, we need to discuss the testimony of Miss Styles. By the way, I would like to get her back in here as soon as we can, just to run over her story again."

Clay picked up his cellphone, punched up Pam's number. It rang for five rings before a groggy voice answered, "Hello."

"Miss Styles, this is Agent Clay Dearsome."

There were some muffled stirrings, then, "…Oh, hello, Mr. Dearsome. My apologies… I was sleeping."

"No problem. When are you planning on coming into the office?"

"… ummm. I plan on being there in the morning."

"Great. Could you please come and see me when you arrive? I will be in the small boardroom of Chiles and Arken on the 15th floor."

"Sure… I'll see you then."

"Thank you," said Clay as he slowly hung up the phone.

"Everything OK?" asked Richard.

Clay frowned, "Yes… It's probably just my cynical nature, but I get the feeling that there is more to be learned from her."

"Well, if I recall from our previous relationship, your 'gut' always seemed to give you good advice."

"Yeah… Well, I don't want to hang anyone on my 'gut.' We'll see what she has to say."

Richard continued, "…and finally. Can we find anything that could give us a thread to learn a motive?"

Nodding his head, Clay added, "The only glaring thing so far is that Congressman Barnes was the government lead in examining *Big Pharma* and the FDA on any collusion in suppressing lab test results on new drugs. Coincidentally, the cruise was sponsored by Safe Drug Council (*SDC*), which is reputed to be totally funded by *Big Pharma*. I am having someone corroborate that. If that is confirmed, we certainly could extrapolate a motive to have the congressman removed."

Richard shuddered, "If that proves to be the case, we are dealing with a far greater issue than just the congressman's death. Think about the billions of dollars that are spent on these drugs and the millions of people who depend on, not only the company, but the endorsements of the FDA. Just thinking of the downstream legal consequences makes my brain freeze."

"What about Cooper?" asked Richard.

"Well, in my short exposure, I have not seen any indication that he is anything more than the founder and CEO of a new research company on the side of *Big Pharma*."

Richard paced around, rubbing his chin, "How new?"

"They actually just opened and haven't even had an official announcement."

"How is he funded?"

Clay paused, smiling, "I don't know, but we will find out. Principle number one – follow the money."

***

Kelly and Nancy arrived at Dino's early and were both scrolling through there emails when Pam tapped Kelly on the shoulder. Rising, they hugged hellos and then all sat in silence. Finally, Kelly spoke.

"I feel like I am in a spy movie," said Kelly.

Pam smiled dryly, "Tell me about it. These last couple of days have been an absolute nightmare."

"Pam... Nancy and I have been talking and we..."

"Kelly... Please... As I said, I am operating under a gag order from the secret service!"

"That's serious shit! I am not sure I want to hear what you guys were talking about, and what's more, if I did know, I may be under a legal obligation to tell the secret service. I'm sorry, but I don't know what to do."

Kelly's head sagged to her chest, "I don't know what to do either, but I do know I am frightened."

Once again, they all sat in silence.

Finally, Pam spoke, "I spent some time on the ship with Dr. Clay Dearsome, the secret service guy, and I found him quite nice. Maybe we should all go and talk to him."

The silence was deafening.

Kelly sighed audibly, "Well... if you trust him... maybe we should."

Pulling her cell and the Dr.'s card from her purse, Pam tapped in his number.

"Hello, this is Dr. Dearsome."

"Dr.... this is Pam Styles."

"Hello, Miss Styles. What can I do for you?"

Pam hesitated, "um… I am with my colleague, Kelly Freeman, the executive assistant to Derek Maurrel, the President of Chiles, Arken. We were wondering if we could get together with you for some advice."

"Of course, Pam. When would you like to meet?"

Pam held her hand over the phone, pointed to her watch and mouthed 'what time' to Kelly who shrugged indicating anytime. She uncovered the phone, "I realize we are meeting tomorrow morning at 10. Would 8 work for you?"

"Absolutely," responded Clay, "where and when?"

Looking at Kelly, she said, "How about 'the coffee shop' across the street from the office?"

Kelly nodded, "OK."

"See you then, Miss Styles."

"Thank you."

Chapter 15

After a restless night, a rather disheveled Tom had just arrived to the office when the cellphone in the desk drawer buzzed. He knew it could only be Monk!

"Yes."

"I am not used to being 'stiffed' on a contract."

"You are not 'stiffed.' I just need to understand what happened. There are some problems."

Monk snorted, "They are not my problems. The job is done. I want my money."

Tom swallowed, "I paid for a clean job and apparently, that is not the case."

Silence…

"Hello," Tom queried.

"This is your last throwaway cell… is that correct?"

"Yes," responded a confused Tom.

"Immediately go out the front of your building and reach into the trash can on your left. You will find a paper bag with three new 'throwaways.' If I do not get a callback immediately with the news that the balance of the funds have been wired, I will assume that we are no longer doing business and I will have to institute collection procedures." …Click.

Tom was frozen in horror, staring at the cellphone. Things were turning terribly wrong. He sat pondering whether to follow directions. If he did not, he knew his life was in severe jeopardy. If he did follow directions, at least he would have one more opportunity to arrange a meeting.

He tossed the cell into the trash can and rose from his desk just as his cell buzzed.

"Yes," he responded.

"Mr. Chiles, this is Dr. Clay Dearsome with the secret service. I wondered if it would be convenient to speak with you this morning at 10am. Would that work for you?"

Tom was stunned. What could they possibly want with him? "What is this concerning?"

"We are just doing routine follow-up on the death of Congressman Barnes."

Tom paused to try to settle his nerves....

"Mr. Chiles?"

"Yes... Yes... I am just checking my schedule. I think that would be fine."

"Great. We are working out of the small boardroom on the 15th floor. Thank you."

We! He had said 'We.' *Who else*? he pondered as he entered his elevator and headed to the 'pickup.'

Pam sat in the coffee shop across from the office toying with the spoon in her coffee. Her nerves were on fire. The events of the past few days had pushed her to the edge and the anticipation of this meeting with Kelly wasn't helping.

She stared out the window and was shocked to see Mr. Chiles exiting the building and walking to the trash bin. *How odd!*
Tom reached in and pulled out a paper bag, just as he felt someone grab his arm and heard a voice in his ear, "My other hand is holding an injector against your back. If you make any kind of a sound or movement you will join the congressman." Tom froze in panic.

"We are going to walk together to the corner where there is a car waiting. Do you understand?"

".... ye... ye... yes," stuttered Tom.

Pam watched curiously as a man seemed to be attempting to guide Tom down the street. As they started to move, the man looked back to see if anyone was behind them, and Pam got a full look at his face and gasped. *Could it be? Surely, I am wrong!*

Pam jumped up from her chair to get a better look and ran straight into Kelly.

"...what the hell?" blurted Kelly.

"Follow me," she yelled at Kelly and both ran out the door.

Monk and Tom had arrived at the car. The driver held the door open and as they entered the car, Monk looked back one more time for anyone observing.

He was stunned. He froze. Across the street, he saw two women staring at the car. ...one of them, the woman from the cruise, and she had just ducked behind a car. *How the hell is she here,* he thought... *and who is the other one?*

"See that car," said Pam, pointing to the corner, "Get the license number. I can't let them see me. Can you see it?" she yelled at Kelly.

"Not yet."

"Walk down the sidewalk."

Kelly ran down a little further and when she had a clear view, she called back to Pam, "I've got it."

"Great," responded Pam, "let's get back to the coffee shop."

Monk nudged Tom into the car. "Be careful," he snarled, "one prick of this device, and you are a vegetable."

Tom couldn't even speak. He just nodded his head. They both got in the back seat and then Tom felt the most incredible pain he had ever known. Monk was holding a Taser and with a vicious smile, he jabbed Tom again, sending him into more pain convulsions.

"Do I have your attention now," snarled Monk.

Tom had blacked out for a moment. Finally, he was able to get some control and nodded his head.

Monk was smiling an evil grin, "Do you remember an old movie where the Warden of the prison caught an escaped prisoner and said to him, 'What we have here is a failure to communicate.' That, Mr. Chiles, is the situation you are in. Look at me."

Tom had rolled his head, having trouble with his blurred vision. Lifting his head, he looked once again into the cold dead eyes.

"Good. Now we're not going to have any more discussion regarding the balance owing on the transaction. Are we?"

".... n... n... no," gurgled Tom.

"Excellent. Now pick up the bag and go back to your office and complete the transaction. I will expect a call on one of those cells by tomorrow noon, or things will not go quite as smooth as today. Goodbye, Mr. Chiles. Now get out of the car."

The door was opened and he was pushed out to the sidewalk, barely able to stand. He made it over to the edge of the building for support as the car pulled away.

"Hit it hard," Monk yelled at the driver as he ducked down behind the front seat.

Kelly caught up to Pam, "What is this all about?"

"Wait till we get inside and I..." She had turned to look back just in time to see Mr. Chiles stumble out of the car and fall against the wall.

"Oh, my God!" Pam yelped.

Kelly turned to look and blurted out, "Mr. Chiles."

"Quiet," Pam said as she grabbed Kelly, "c'mon. Get inside."

"…but shouldn't we help him?"

Pam shook her head and grabbed Kelly, "I'll explain inside."

They walked in and over to the window to see Mr. Chiles, carrying a paper bag and staggering as he headed to the front entrance, looking extremely disorientated.

"Pam… what am I watching?"

Pam smiled ruefully. "Let's sit down," she said as Mr. Chiles went into the building.

"You have some explaining to do," scolded Kelly.

They sat down and Pam held her head trying to put together what she had just seen. Kelly waited patiently until Pam raised her head.

Breathlessly, Pam said, "Write the license number down before we talk."

Kelly pulled out her cell and punched in the number.

"OK… done."

Pam began, "I really don't know what to say. As I told you, I am sworn to secrecy by the secret service as to what happened on the cruise. The trouble is that what we just saw ties in with a part of the events on the cruise. So, I am not sure what to say."

Kelly sat for a moment staring out the window. Now she was sure her events tied in with Pam's, but how could they exchange information with Pam under the secrecy edict.

"I understand," said Kelly and they both sat silent.

Finally, Pam spoke, "Dr. Dearsome, the secret service guy, is due here shortly. Let's wait and see what we should do."

"That sounds great. I think that would work," murmured Kelly.

Pam pulled out her cell and, using voice activation, called Dr. Dearsome.

"Hello, Miss Styles. I am on the way."

"Oh… thank you."

Dr. Clay Dearsome walked into the the coffee shop and spotted the girls in a corner booth waving him over. He smiled, "Well, that's an exuberant greeting."

Both women only looked at him with distressed frowns. "Thank you for coming Dr. Dearsome," offered Pam, "we really need some help."

Clay smiled, "Well, first, please call me Clay. Secondly, if you haven't done anything wrong, then there is nothing to be afraid of. Right?"

They both looked at each other with weak smiles and nodded.

"Let's start at the beginning," suggested Clay, "who wants to start?"
They again glanced at each other, then Pam started, "We have to clear something up first. You have sworn me to secrecy regarding the events on the Cruise. Correct?"

"Yes," responded Clay.

"Here's the problem," continued Pam, "Kelly has some things that she wants to confide in me that probably tie in with the events on the cruise, but I won't let her talk to me because I can't respond. We both felt that you could offer a solution and help you in your investigation."

Clay nodded his head knowingly and looked out the window in contemplation. Finally, he nodded again and looked at the women, "OK. Here, I think, is a solution. Kelly, would you be willing to operate under the same secrecy that Pam is under and then we will all be on the same page."

Kelly nodded, "Of course."

"Good," Clay paused again, "Kelly, normally I wouldn't allow you to hear Pam's testimony, but in this case, it sounds as though they may mesh. Correct?"

They both spoke in chorus, "Yes."

"OK… as I said… start at the beginning. I already know Pam's story, so let's start with you," he said looking at Kelly.

Kelly took a deep breath, "The main piece of information I have is that within a few minutes of hearing about the news of the congressman's death, I was at my desk… well, actually Pam's desk when Mr. Chiles received a call on a cell that was inside his desk, He thought I had closed the door when he answered the call and I heard him say, 'I just heard. It will be wired shortly.'"

Pam gasped!

Having been an agent for many years, Clay was trained to show no reactions, but his training failed him as his eyes bugged out and he said, "Are you sure that's what he said."

"Yes, sir. I am certain."

Clay waited. Kelly stared at him.

"…anything else?" queried Clay.

"umm… well, all of the electronic equipment in Mr. Cooper's offices have been 'tapped,' but I don't know if that has anything to do with this."

"How do you know this?" asked Clay.

"His secretary, Nancy, is a bit of an electronic and computer whiz and she noticed it the day they moved."

A smile started across Clay's face.

"What?" asked a startled Kelly.

"Remind me to always get the women on my side in any investigation."

The tension was relieved and they all laughed.

Kelly wiggled eagerly, "Well, wait until you hear what Pam has to tell you about what just happened before you got here."

"OK, Pam… shoot."

Pam proceeded to outline the recent events.

Again, Clay was astonished as he looked at Kelly, "…and you got the license number?"

"Yes," said Kelly excitedly as she pulled out her cell and showed him.

"Can you describe the vehicle?"

The women looked at each other. Their bafflement was obvious. Finally, Pam spoke.

"It was a black sedan… maybe a Japanese make."

"Well… We've got the license. Give me a minute. I need to make a call."

Clay walked outside while dialing Richard Guy.

"Hey, Clay. I've been waiting for you."

"Richard, I have just had a major break develop, but before we talk, I need you to immediately put out an APB on a black four-door sedan, license number Texas GGK-8144. Don't apprehend, just follow and get the owner location. Meanwhile, come over to the coffee shop across the street and I will fill you in."

He walked back into the coffee shop and signaled the women to follow him over to a corner booth. Looking at Kelly, he said, "I have a colleague, Richard Guy, coming over immediately and we can try and make sense out of all this. Kelly, you mentioned that you had the numbers from that cellphone in the trash."

"Yes… I have them on a piece of paper right here in my purse and on my cell, just in case."

Clay smiled. "Very thorough," he said, as he took the offered paper from her.

Chapter 16

Marty and Myra, having arrived home eight days early, had been under a constant barrage of questions from Dorothy, her mother, none of which they could answer, causing a continuous stream of complaints and grumbling. It was impossible for her to understand they were under gag orders, which she interpreted as a personal attack on her character.

They finally got to sleep around midnight and now Myra was off to the gym. She leaned over to give Marty a goodbye peck, "I have to meet Jenny. Don't forget, last night we arranged for dinner tonight with Ric and Mary Margaret. Please, try and be home early."

"Uh-huh," Marty grunted, deep into a document, "what time?"

"7:30… Gotta run… Have a good day." She picked up Cara, waved goodbye to her mother who was just entering the kitchen, and rushed out the garage door.

Marty looked up and smiled to himself. *What a life,* he thought. *Here I am at thirty-five, just home from a Mediterranean cruise (albeit aborted), living in a million-dollar house in Plano, Texas, married to my college sweetheart, a beautiful daughter, two cars in the garage, member in a prestigious golf club, six figure income, and a hefty bonus on the way. Where do I go from here?* His reverie was interrupted by his mother-in-law.

"I don't know why she couldn't have left Cara here with me," she pouted. Marty stared at her for a moment and decided nothing was his best response.

***

Kelly was just back at the office when Marty, having finished his work at home, arrived.

"Your meeting with Tom is in ten minutes. He's been asking for you."

Marty smiled, turned, and started up the ostentatious staircase to the 16th floor, carrying his finished document.

Pam pointed to the door, "He's expecting you."

Marty tapped on Tom's door. As he turned the knob to enter, he heard Tom just finishing a telephone conversation, "I don't give a shit if he's got the entire Supreme Court in his pocket. I want that son of a bitch shut down. We can't afford to have this problem just as we are about to launch Sistophan and then Testocel. Get it done, Barry."

Marty was shocked at Tom's appearance. His red face and disheveled appearance were certainly not the norm. That was the least of the surprises. Tom slammed down the phone and waved Marty in. Derek was sitting in front of the desk. Marty wasn't through the door before Tom barked, "Marty, I thought you were taking care of our problems with these lunatic homeopathic assholes."

"Yes… we…"

"Never mind the bullshit! Barry just informed me that the Council on Safe Medicine (*COSM*) is filing an injunction to stop our launch and when our best legal mind says that we have a problem… then 'we have a problem.'"

"Mr. Chiles…"

"Marty, I don't need to tell you the importance of this issue. We have been screwing around with *COSM* for weeks and you told me that you would handle it. These do-gooders could cost us millions of dollars. We have been handling the media up until now, but we can't keep dodging forever. I don't care 'what' it takes! Do what you need to do. Do you hear me!" he said, waving him out.

"Yes, sir, Mr. Chiles," Marty tried to maintain some dignity leaving the office. Pam gave him a sad smile as he walked to the elevator. Marty had never had anyone talk to him this way, particularly Tom, and his anger showed as he slammed the wall of the elevator with his fist. *Thank God, I'm alone in here.* He had not even had an opportunity to show the document, which pertained directly to Tom's explosion

He didn't understand the intensity of Tom's anger. Yes, there were problems, but Tom's normally pragmatic manner in addressing issues was definitely not on display. Nancy looked up from her desk as Marty arrived.

"That was quick," she said and then she noticed his agitation.

Marty continued into his office and sat down at his desk. He turned, staring out the window, and tried to get a grip on his emotions. After a few moments, he grabbed the report intended for Tom and decided to review it again. Perhaps he could come up with a new angle to get these people to see reason. This bombshell of a possible injunction had not been discussed.

Reaching his intercom, Marty called, "Nancy… Get me Norm Arthur, please."

"Yes, sir," came the reply.

He had no idea what he was going to discuss, but he knew he had to start somewhere.

The strange thing was that, in the back of his mind, he was sympathetic to their viewpoint and their arguments. Try as he might, he could not shake the feeling that there was validity to their claims. He, of course, could not expose these thoughts to anyone, as it flew in direct opposition to everything for which his job, his company, the industry, and the FDA stood.

Never could they entertain the thought that there may be natural answers to a myriad of medical issues. Not to mention that a financial pyramid of astronomical proportions depended on the present structure.

The *Big Pharma* view, which Marty acknowledged, was that any discussion point that was acceded to, could spell financial disaster of unimagined consequences for the pharmaceutical industry.

He had to admit that this was not the first time, over the years, he had wrestled with the hypocrisy of accepting his high standard of living based on, at the very least, some questionable scientific conclusions.

However, for Marty, expediency and practicality, united with the glittery realities of luxury living had been overriding the quiet, insistent voice of his conscience.

"I have Mr. Arthur on the line."

"Thank you, Nancy. Norm… How are you?"

"Good… what about you, Marty?"

"Well, obviously, it's been a rather sudden turn around, and I feel like we all have just been through the wringer from the aborted trip."

"Yes… I know what you mean," responded Norm.

"Norm, I just got news that you may file an injunction"

"Yeah, Marty. The board moved ahead with it while we were on the cruise and I want you to know that I am sorry it has gone this route."

"Me as well. Before we go any further, would it be improper for me to ask if you and I could have a 'one-on-one' to see if there is another direction we could go."

"Personally, Marty, I would like that, but let me check with my attorney to see if we are clear to do that."

"Thank you, Norm, just get back to me when you can."

"Will do. Talk to you soon." The line went dead.

Marty was sure that this impulsive call had probably gotten him in legal trouble, but right now it seemed like the only possible avenue out of this muddle.

Marty spent the next few hours cleaning up administrative junk and making calls and then headed out the door just as his cell chirped.

"Hi, Myra... I am walking out of the office right now and will be home in time to be ready for dinner."

"You better be. It's 5:45 and you are catching all the traffic. We are meeting Ric and Mary Margaret at 7:30 at Tony's Steaks on the Tollway."

"No problem, My. Give our angel a kiss and a hug. See you in a few."

Marty enjoyed the company of Ric and Mary Margaret. He hoped that he would never need Ric's services as a lawyer. He generally abhorred lawyers. They seemed always to work in 'situational ethics' which meant that all boundaries were movable. He laughed to himself out loud! ...*and were you not just pondering your ethical boundaries a few hours ago. ...perhaps the 'glass houses' analogy applies.*

Having arrived home on time, Marty had finished showering, dressing, and picking up the sitter and he and Myra were 'on the road.'

"You seem subdued tonight," queried Myra

Damn it, he thought, *How can she always read me so well.* "Well, I did get into it a bit with Tom today."

"Oh... how so?"

"Same 'ol, same 'ol. He wants a quick resolution of the difficulties with COSM and it appears we are at an impasse."

Myra frowned, "I know you have been having problems with it. Are you going to be able to solve them?"

"I really don't know! To be honest, I am having my own concerns about the developing militant attitude of Tom, the company, and the industry in general. It is like they are reaching some crisis point and they need COSM to be gone."

"What do you mean... gone?"

"I don't know. There seems to be some time frame that I am not privy to and it's causing increased tension and increased focus on solving the COSM issue."

"Well, I know you'll figure it out. Now let's have some fun tonight."

Ric and Mary Margaret were already seated with their drinks when they arrived at the restaurant. After the hi's and hugs, Marty and Myra sat down and the waiter was instantly at their elbow. Marty normally wasn't a drinker nor was Myra, but the unsettling days motivated him to order a double vodka martini.

"Whoa," said Rick, "…tough day?"

Marty grimaced, "Yeah… well, it could have been better. How was your day?"

Rick shrugged, "…oh, the usual."

Mary Margaret laughed, "Oh, he always says that, but if you can pry anymore conversation from him, you find out that he's actually involved in solving the world's problems."

Ric jokingly jabbed Marry Margaret.

"Well, maybe I should give Rick my problems to solve," Marty joked.

Ric looked at him with concern, "Is it really that bad?"

"Well, let's just say at the moment I don't have any answers."

Mary Margaret tried to ease the seriousness, "And here I thought you had solved the world's health problems"

Myra snorted, "Yeah… at the expense of his own."

Marty looked at her in shock, "What do you mean?"

"Well, you haven't had a complete night's sleep for the last week."

"What?" said Marty.

"You didn't think I noticed?" scowled Myra.

Just then, the waiter arrived and they completed their order and Marty ordered another drink.

"Marty," yelped Myra.

"Oh, what the hell, Myra, I may as well get blasted. Maybe that will help the solution to magically appear."

Ric and Mary Margaret focused with concern on Marty. Ric was first to react, "This sounds serious."

Marty shook his head, "Well, I hope I am overreacting."

"Can you share anything with us" Mary Margaret queried.

"Well, as your husband well knows, there are areas that I cannot address under my nondisclosure agreement. Let's just say that I am being asked to do something that I am not comfortable with."

Myra gawked at him, "You never told me that."

Marty hung his head, "I guess I didn't want you to be concerned."

He paused, "OK… As you all know, the pharmaceutical industry has been in a battle with groups, such as COSM (Council On Safe Medicine), that constantly challenge the launch of new drugs. They are relentless and persistent in their belief that the pharmaceutical industry has conspired to coerce Congress, the AMA, and the FDA, not to mention the media, into ap-

what COSM believes are badly researched drugs. My career and spe- my specialty has been to research and try to debunk or reduce the these groups. To date, I have been fairly successful, which has heightened my profile and I might say, my remuneration."

"Chiles, Arken are about to launch a new product and senior management seems to be ramping up the intensity of attacks on any opposition. For the life of me, I can't understand what is different with this launch, yet, I have been instructed to 'go to the mattresses' on this one."

"What does that mean?" asked Mary Margaret.

"It's a Godfather reference," Ric said, "I'll explain it later." He turned back to Marty. "Surely, they're not asking you to do something illegal."

"No… And stop calling me Shirley."

Myra spewed her drink into her dinner, "I think the drinks are getting to you, Marty."

Marty watched Myra clean up her drink from her blouse and then looked back at Ric, "I would be lying if I didn't feel as though there seem to be 'no' boundaries. The exact words were, quote, 'do what you have to do' and it was strongly inferred that that's what my company was hired to do."

"Marty… that scares me," murmured Myra.

"Yeah, it didn't really give me a sense of comfort myself."

Everyone ate in silence for a few minutes.

Finally, Ric said, "So, let me get this straight. Your job has been (*and is*) to monitor and research any entities that are publicly in opposition to *Big Pharma*'s research conclusions."

"Yes," replied Marty.

"…and you answer this opposition by using the FDA approvals and other additional sources for confirmation to the public that the research is legitimate and stringent, thus supporting the efficacy of *Big Pharma*."

"That's about it," nodded Marty.

"There's something I don't understand," Ric mused, "if the FDA is the government protection agency for the public, and they have approved of the new drug, why would… what did you say the major group's name was?"

"COSM."

"Yes… Why would COSM fight the FDA approval. Aren't they both acting on behalf of the public?"

Here it is, thought Marty, *the crux of the dilemma. Do I expose my developing doubts or do I 'toe the company line' and plead ignorance'?* Either way, Ric, in typical lawyer fashion had cleared away the PR noise and asked the question that would expose what could end up as a medical, political, and financial scandal the likes of which had never been seen.

The downstream questions were only the beginning:

Did the drug companies alter, tamper with, or outright lie in their conclusions?
If the answer was 'yes,' was the FDA aware of the false conclusions?
If they were not aware... why not?
If they were aware, why did they approve the drug(s)?

Marty was not able to address the scope and the consequences of the answers and the direction his further thinking was taking him, so he had conveniently slammed the door and not addressed it further... until now.

Ric, Mary Margaret, and Myra were all staring at him, intently waiting for the answer to Ric's question.
After a long pause, Marty finally lifted his head and stared deep into Ric's eyes, "At this point, I need to ask you a very important question. If the answer is 'yes,' I can continue this conversation. If the answer is 'no,' then this conversation is over."

Mary Margaret and Myra both gasped. Ric just continued eye contact and nodded as if knowing already what the question was.

Marty reached into his pocket and extracted a $5 bill from his pocket. "Will you accept this as a retainer and represent me as my attorney?"

Ric stared at the $5 bill as he pondered the implications of his answer. Their friendship was very important to him, but he surmised that his friend was either in or approaching some 'deep water' and he felt Marty was reaching out for help. If he accepted the offer, he could always resign later.

"I will accept the retainer on three conditions. One... We end this conversation in front of the girls; Two... We can mutually terminate this relationship at any time; Three... This $5 does not represent my normal fee." They all chuckled. "...after all, I am a lawyer and I have to uphold our reputation." Again, they all laughed.

Myra chimed in, "Do we have any say in this?"

"No. Only when you are alone with Marty and he can operate under spousal privilege."

Maty nodded, "Why don't we finish dinner and then go back to our place and you and I can talk."

"Great," they chorused together.

Having arrived back at Marty and Myra's home, Marty and Ric went into the den with their drinks. Marty shook his head in puzzlement. "This is so bizarre," he offered.

"Why so?" queried Ric.

"It's just that an hour ago we were good friends having dinner and now I feel our relationship has changed."

Ric looked up. "It only has to change if we allow it," he offered, "why don't you start at the beginning and let's see where we go."

Marty took a deep breath, "First of all, most of what I am going to say is conjecture with no fact backup. My gut is telling me there is something wrong, but I can't figure out what it is. The death of the congressman has 'shaken me' more than I realized and today's events have not eased those feelings."

Ric pressed again, "Take me back to the beginning."

"Where do you mean?" questioned Marty.

"The start of your career… and describe what you do."

Ten minutes later, Marty finished the description of his software and its purpose.

"I'm impressed," said Ric, "if I understand correctly, you are working in a new genre, generically called Big Data. You have designed algorithms that are continuously scanning all facets of the internet, especially social media, mining, and categorizing that data to know how a segment is going to react to a situation. With that data, you can predict, with a high degree of accuracy, the probabilities of, for example, the voting results of a state, county, city, block, and even a house."

"Fundamentally, that is correct," replied Marty, "it is the reason Trump fooled all the pollsters and surprised everyone with his win. He was not relying on the old statistical analysis, but actual data with a high prediction probability."

Ric continued, "Your patented algorithms have taken that concept and applied it to the pharmaceutical industry."

"Yes."

With some excitement in his voice, Ric resumed, "So, with any consumer segment you chose, you could analyze their habits, likes, dislikes, moods, health, etc. and gauge the effects of advertising, purchasing, frequency of use, effects, or any other information you wished. Your system can organize this data into designated categories, alerting you instantly of any response that could cause disruption in the marketing of existing drugs as well as drugs in the approval process."

"Fundamentally... you've got it," responded Marty.

Ric nodded, "OK... now what?"

"Great question. I am in a moral dilemma. On one hand, I have just been identified in some circles as the new 'point of the spear' in promoting and defending *Big Pharma*. On the other hand, I am having serious moral difficulty, challenging every principle with which I was raised, by accepting the dubious reward of substantial material wealth with the commensurate ego inflation."

They both sat staring into space. Neither knowing how to respond.
Finally, Ric looked back at Marty, "Marty... It seems to me that before we venture down the legal road, you need to decide your personal options. You obviously understand both sides of the equation. I would guess everyone, to some degree in their lives, are confronted with decisions of this nature. Unfortunately, our society measures the results of those decisions from the material perspective."

"We don't seem to have the tools to quantify the alternative choices like contentment, serenity, peace, and self-worth to be able to counterbalance the instant gratification of the material rewards. Personally, I believe the ignorance of the value of those emotional rewards are a major contribution to the very ailments that your industry claims they alleviate. But I digress!"

Marty jumped in, "I agree that those qualities substantially contribute to our health and *Big Pharma* brings some products to that arena."

"Agreed," nodded Ric, "however, I am not suggesting a 'throwing the baby out with the bath water' proposition as the only option. Couldn't a case by case approach be an alternative?"

Marty nodded in agreement, but a rueful smile crossed his face.

"What does that look mean?" asked Ric.

Marty sighed, "My very short view into the pharmaceutical industry has taught me one thing, if nothing else. The patience required for long-term responsible testing is not a popular discussion in *Big Pharma* boardrooms. Wall Street demands returns and the shorter the delay to market, the better. They have even turned that motive into a complete marketing program."

Ric frowned, "I don't understand."

"Just look at the disclaimers embedded in their advertising. Over time they have desensitized the public to all the possible reactions from their drugs. With all the claimed research, does it not seem odd that with further testing they could've removed some of those side effects instead of the body just saying 'no' to these foreign invasions? If that isn't enough, they now are augmenting the initial cashflow by offering drugs to treat the effects of the first drug. Now that's hutzpah! As sane as your 'case by case' suggestion sounds, unfortunately, it flies directly in the face of the single greatest obstacle ... 'greed!' Ric, I am not sure that I could even begin to relay to you the money that is generated from the launch of a new drug."

"Does it cost a lot to get there? Yes! Does it take a long time? Yes! Is it monetarily worth it...? Oh yes! Is it physically worth it...? Well, statistically...who knows? Just as an example, look at the dramatic increase in cancer, autism, diabetes, high blood pressure, Alzheimer's, and on and on."

Ric interrupted, "But isn't the purpose of the FDA and the CDC to protect against that mentality?"

Once again, Marty smiled, "Even with your intellect, education, curiosity, and common sense, you haven't grasped the depth of the avarice. We talked of patience a while ago. The pharmaceutical industry has, for at least a half a century, been infiltrating and bending governments, educational institutions, and physicians' organizations with the belief that science can, will, and has usurped mother nature."

Marty continued, "A vast percentage of new drugs are found in nature, either by natural healers or the drug community. The problem is that the drug community can 'reverse engineer' the natural product and then produce a patented synthetic without the unintended consequences. Thus, the disclaimers!

"Combine that with the decades of systematic and constant denigration and criminalization of natural medicine practitioners, and we are left with doctors who are purposefully and woefully undereducated about naturopathy.

"Doctors are so bombarded daily with volumes of new scientific information that they must trust *Big Pharma*, supported by what they see as the 'protection' of the FDA, NIH, and the AMA." Suddenly, Marty stopped as he saw Ric smiling. "What?" he said.

"Your little diatribe shows me that you are much more invested in the opposing view than you realized. With all the research that your company does, you have only been focusing on countering the arguments instead of weighing the pros and cons."

A heavy silence hung in the room for a full thirty seconds and finally, Ric spoke, "Marty, I suspect that rather than looking for legal advice, you are seeking someone you can trust in airing your doubts and concerns. I am more than happy to be that someone, but it seems to me, from your comments, you have pretty much made your decision and are just trying to accept it.

"My suggestion would be to explore this further with Myra and then, perhaps, the three of us could meet to see where you go from here. However,

I think this caution is necessary. From what I can garner from your comments, you are dealing with a very powerful, determined, and ruthless adversary, and caution is obviously in order."

***

The women looked up expectantly as Richard joined them at the table in the coffee shop. After greetings and introductions and coffee orders, they settled and Richard began, "I'm sure Clay has informed you, but I need to reiterate that any information that is disclosed or exchanged here is under strictest confidence and any disclosure could bring criminal charges against you."

Both women nodded in agreement.

"OK. Fill me in."

Over the next ten minutes, Pam and Kelly retold their stories.

"Well, I have to say that you both seem to have a definite bent for detective work. Getting that license number was brilliant. Do you think you were seen by the man?"

Pam paused. It had never occurred to her before. She tried to recollect whether that was possible.

"I suppose that's possible, but I don't recall."

Richard's cell buzzed. He answered with a brusque, "Yes," and listened for a moment. "OK. Good work. Text me the mug shot right now and let me know when we track a location." Clay's eyebrows rose in question. Richard clicked off and addressing Clay, said, "They picked up a print off the glasses found in the washroom and got a hit. The mug shot is on the way."

Kelly and Pam listened politely. Just then, Richard's cell 'clinked.' He glanced down, smiled, and held the phone for the women to see.

Pam gulped audibly, "That's him… that's him. I'm sure of it."

Richard held up his hands, "OK. Now settle down. Are you saying that this is the man that was on the ship as well as the man you just saw this morning?"

Yes… Yes," squealed Pam. Just then, Pam's cell 'chirped.' She looked down and saw that it was Mr. Chiles. She looked at the two Agents. "It's Mr. Chiles. I have to take this."

"Mr. Chiles?"

"Where are you, Miss Styles. This is a work day, you know."

Pam blanched, "Mr. Chiles… I am so sorry. I got a call last night to meet Dr. Dearsome and I am with him now. I am so sorry I didn't call you."

Tom could feel the fear creeping into his bones. "What the hell does he want with you. I've got a company to run."

"Yes, sir. He is just reviewing the events I witnessed on the ship." Clay and Richard were listening intently and Pam was holding her cell so they could hear Tom's side of the conversation.

"I am almost finished. I should be there in a few minutes."

"Come and see me the minute you get here."

"Yes, sir."

They all sat in silence for a moment.

Finally, Clay spoke, "Pam, we realize this is getting dicey, but we need you to try and function in your normal way while we sort out a game plan. We definitely can't meet here again. We will communicate with you through Kelly when we need to get together. In the meantime, you go back while we talk to Kelly a little more."

Anxiously, Pam looked at Clay, "Do you think I am in any danger."

Clay quickly reassured her, "Not at all. Right now, Mr. Chiles has no idea what you have seen and although his normal paranoid nature will be active, you just have to stick with what you just told him."

Pam rose from the table, "OK."

"Don't worry, Pam. With what has developed, we will have protection around you in the next couple of hours. Hopefully, you won't see them, but they will be there. You are doing great."

Kelly got up and hugged Pam, "I will come up from time to time."

Hesitantly, Pam walked out of the coffee shop and headed across the street. She breathed deeply to calm her nerves. She couldn't help but have a feeling of exhilaration mixed with a gnawing sense that she was in danger.

***

Monk sat on the sofa with his head in his hands. What a fluke! How could she have been there? This is getting tricky and messy. Now I must take care of her. …and what about the other woman? Some serious planning was needed, which was the reason he had survived this long. The development of his disguising techniques was a large part.

On occasions, he would catch a glimpse in a mirror or window and would not recognize himself. The talent had been developed when he was a child in New York. His mother was a Broadway 'wannabe,' so he spent hours backstage watching the actors and makeup artists practice their skills.

One older gentleman actor had spent hours teaching him the subtleties of color and shading as well as artificially rearranging the face and body. He had even attempted to become an actor, but his mother quickly dampened that dream when she married a ne'er-do-well and moved to Dallas, ending his theatrical education.

He soon fell in with a rough crowd and began his criminal journey, quickly learning that there were all types and shades of underworld denizens that could commit criminal acts, but eventually, because of their lack of intellect and planning, were doomed to either die a violent death or fade away in prison.

His upbringing had left him with a total lack of empathy combined with a curiosity about death. He lacked the fear factor and labored under the egotistical fallacy that being caught was only a matter of poor planning.

Additionally, his early exposure to theatrical magic taught him that diversion from the obvious was a strong tool.

With that awareness, he started his plan. Why not begin where he was least expected – surveillance at Chiles, Arken, and Associates. He would have to take extra precautions because the woman, Pam, had already seen him twice. He also would need multiple, quick change tearaway costumes (with makeup) so he could do continuous movement.

The familiar sense of adventure and excitement started to sweep through his body. This was going to be fun.

***

Tom Chiles was between a rock and a hard place. The fear generated by Monk still chilled him. He didn't know what the secret service was doing or had done. His instincts told him that more was happening than he knew and now here he was, staring at the name on his incoming call… Albert Ashbury, CEO of the 2nd largest pharmaceutical in the world.

"Albert, how are you?"

"Great, Tom. I have Frank Morrison on the line with us."

Tom grimaced, "Hello, Frank"

"Hello, Tom," Albert continued, "Tom, we were quite shocked, as we are sure you were, to hear about the sudden death of the congressman."

"Yes… we were all shocked. My team was at the table when he suffered his attack," Frank spoke up, "well, I hope you all came through it unscathed."

Tom thought he heard an ominous tone in Frank's voice.

Albert interjected. "In that regard, I heard a rumor that the secret service has become involved."

Just what I need right now, thought Tom...*a couple of paranoid piranhas nosing around.* "Yes, and they are still involved. It's their protocol to investigate any death of a sitting congressman. They are using my offices. I would imagine they will complete their investigation by tomorrow."

"So, you are not concerned about anything that transpired?" asked Albert.

"Of course not, Albert. It was an unfortunate event but hasn't affected any of our plans other than, dare I say it, the reduction of our time and efforts satisfying his continuous requests and charges."

"Excellent," chorused them both.

There was a brief pause, then Albert spoke, "How is our new cheerleader, Marty Cooper, reacting to all this?"

"Excellent," responded Tom, "if you want, I will suggest that he call you both. He has some extremely interesting products and services you could use."

"Yes... please, do that," responded Albert.

There was some background conversation and then Albert said, "Gotta run, Tom. Thanks for the update."

"My pleasure, guys."

They all clicked off the line. Albert looked across the table at Frank, "We need to watch him. He's dangerous."

Chapter 17

Rob Schafers put down his headset with a frown. It bothered him that he was still listening to the recordings from Marty's home. Why had he not just cut off the feed?

His break with Tom Chiles had at first been both disturbing and yet somehow, satisfying. He knew he had done the right thing and yet, he still couldn't 'let go.' When he had installed all the 'bugging' equipment, he knew that he had stepped over the edge and here he was, still listening, and what he had just heard between Marty and Ric shocked him.

Rob had assumed that Marty was still somewhat 'drinking the Kool-Aid.' Far from it. He obviously had fooled Tom, Derek, and Rob about his new leanings away from the *Big Pharma* philosophies…

For some reason, this thrilled Rob. Marty was someone whose principals had not yet been totally corrupted, even in the face of the elevated life style and a rosy future.

Rob felt a desire to further this kid along his path of integrity. But he was technically out of the picture. How could he help? He noticed that no one had previously listened to any of the recordings. He promptly erased the previous stuff and then reset the system.

Now he needed to formulate a plan to warn Marty about the bugging. But how? By disclosing to Marty, he was disclosing his involvement.

Perhaps a 'mia culpa' was the best way to go. Hopefully, with Marty's changing attitude, combined with Rob's illumination, Marty would be better equipped to plot his future. …but it had to be done soon before Derek or Tom became suspicious about the late start on the bugging.

***

Marty had slept badly after his conversation with Ric. Between the fear of losing what he had, and the bright future that was blooming, together with the continuous nagging from his conscience, he was a mess.

Myra, at first, had badgered him relentlessly until, finally, he had broken down and actually cried as he imagined the bleak future. Expecting tears, admonishments, accusations, and hostility, he was shocked when Myra leaned over on the bed, grasped his chin, and boldly stared him straight in the eyes and said, "You are an idiot! Do you really think that our marriage depends on Cooper Consulting? I married you for who you are, not what you are! I couldn't be prouder of you than I am right now. If we had carried on with you going against everything you believe, then that would guarantee the end. Yes, this is scary, but together we will be fine. Now get ready for work and we can work out a solution later. I love you."

Marty was speechless and never more proud of his wife than now. He shook his head as his cell brought him back to the present.

"Hello… Marty Cooper."

"Marty, I don't know if you remember me, but we met in the Chiles hallway one time. My name is Rob Schafers and I previously did consulting work for Tom Chiles and Derek Maurrel."

"Yes, Rob, I remember. What can I do for you?"

Rob hesitated.

"Hello, Rob… are you there?"

"Yes… I am here, Marty. I have a matter that I need to discuss with you in strictest confidence, as soon as possible, and it requires that we meet outside the offices. That is all I would like to say at the moment. Do you know the I-Hop close to you?"

"Yes."

"Could we meet there in fifteen minutes?"

Now it was Marty's turn to pause. What could this possibly be about? He hardly knew this man, and yet, it sounded very important and his former relationship with Tom and Derek augured well as to his credibility.

"…um …Could you give me any more information?"

"I'm afraid not, but you will understand when we meet."

Marty looked at his watch, "Yes. I can be there in fifteen minutes."

"Thank you. That is a good decision." The line went dead.

Marty called Nancy, "I know we were scheduled to catch up on everything, but I just got a call and have to go to a short meeting before I can get there."

"No Problem, Mr. Cooper."

"Thank you, and Nancy, I don't exactly know how long I will be, but let's plan on lunch and then we can work through the afternoon. By the way, I can't tell you how much I have appreciated you 'manning the shop' while I have been away. I know I have thrown you into the deep end and I am impressed at how well you can swim."

Nancy smiled, "Of course, and thank you for your comments. Not necessary, but appreciated."

***

Pam could not get assimilated to the constant presence of someone watching her. Every time she looked up from her desk, she was aware of someone. Rather than give her a sense of security... au contraire... it just reminded her that she was in danger. She tried to assure herself that the man was not crazy enough to do anything here in the office, but then she remembered he had killed a congressman in front of an entire dining room full of people.

Tom, had not noticed the extra bodies. In fact, Pam had had no contact with Tom since she had come back from her meeting with Clay and Richard.

Just then, the door was ripped open and Tom, still looking disheveled, stormed out of the office and nodded at Pam, "I have to go out for a while. I should be back in about an hour."

"All right," responded Pam. As he walked away, she noticed he was carrying what appeared to be the same paper bag he had on the street. *How odd,* she thought.

Just then, her cell buzzed. She saw it was Clay.

"Hello"

"Pam, this is Clay. I know that Chiles just left his office, so I wanted to quickly talk with you."

"What can I do for you," responded Pam.

"We would like to have another meeting with you and Kelly tonight and would like to have Marty Cooper's assistant join us. Do you think you could arrange that?"

Pam stared at her phone for a moment, then said, "I will try. Where do you want to meet?"

"We would like to meet at the secret service offices in downtown Dallas at 7 o'clock. I will text you the address."

"Let me check with the other girls and get back to you."

"Thank you. Let me know as soon as you can."

Pam held her head. She felt she was being placed unwillingly into further danger for which she was not equipped. Even worse... she had no options because she was dealing with a secret service investigation, and they set the agenda.

She picked up her purse and headed downstairs to Kelly's desk. The door to Derek's office was open and she saw Kelly just getting up from the chair in front of Derek's desk. Derek spotted her and waved her into the office. Kelly stood awkwardly as Pam came into the office.

"Pam, how nice to see you," he exuded, "please, have a seat and please stay, Kelly."

They both sat down.

"I have been meaning to talk to you both about the recent events. I understand the secret service in occupying one of our boardrooms. Are either of you involved with them at all?"

They both looked at each other and then Pam spoke, "Only insofar as me having been on the scene when the congressman had his attack. They have interviewed me a couple of times."

Derek stared at her intently, "So, you know nothing about a suggestion of foul play"

"I only know what I just told you and after my interviews, I was told to not discuss the event to anyone. I am very uncomfortable about this conversation."

"I understand... I understand," offered Derek, "I was only curious from the standpoint of you girls being unduly distracted from your work and I wanted to tell you that if there is any problem, you can come to me."

"Thank you," they chorused as they got up to leave.

As they exited under Derek's skeptical gaze, Pam whispered, "I need to talk to you. I'll meet you in the ladies' room," and walked away. Kelly waited for a few moments and then walked down the hall to the bathroom.

"What the hell was 'that' all about?" She spouted!

Pam smiled, "I think we have a little paranoia running rampant."

"No kidding," responded Kelly.

"Anyway," said Pam, "we have been asked to come to the secret service office tonight at 7 and they would like Nancy to be able to come as well."

"Why do they want Nancy?" wondered Kelly.

"I don't know. I just know they want us there. Why don't the three of us meet at Romero's at 6 and drive down together."

"OK," replied Kelly, "I am very curious."

"Me too," said Pam, "...oh, and would you mind arranging for Nancy. I don't know her very well."

"Sure... will do. See you at 6."

***

Marty walked into I-Hop and immediately spotted Rob in the back-corner booth.

"Marty, thank you for coming. I know this is 'highly' unusual, but I assure you, it is important."

Marty smiled awkwardly, "I don't know what to say except 'I am here.'"

The waiter arrived and Marty ordered an ice tea and Rob ordered another coffee. They both were silent for a moment.

Finally, Rob spoke, "Marty, I want to preface this conversation with an apology and a warning. As I unfold the story, I would ask that you hold your anger until I have finished. You may wish to at the least hit me, and possibly, try to kill me."

"What!" blurted Marty.

Rob took a deep breath, "I would like to mitigate your response by giving you a short history of my relationship with Tom Chiles." Rob proceeded to outline their service record together and Tom's meteoric rise in the pharmaceutical industry as well as Tom financing Rob's security company.

"Thus, was born a deep bond with Tom and it has lasted for years. From time to time, he would ask me to perform certain functions that, shall we say, were questionable at best and possibly, illegal at worst. I don't offer this as an excuse, but I was able to assuage my conscience with the financial enticements and many other 'perks.'"

"I understand that," said Marty, sadly.

"I know you do, Marty, but we'll get to that in a moment."

Marty looked at him oddly.

"All in its own time," smiled Rob. He continued, "There are some characteristics of Tom that some people never see... thank God. He can be a mean, nasty, and callous person. I have seen him take fine, idealistic, honest people and mold them into materially motivated monsters and I contributed to that on occasion, even with you."

"What do you mean?" snapped Marty.

"First, let me say that the reason I am here is because I have come to admire you. You may or may not be aware of the fact that Tom and I had a philosophical 'break up' some time ago. Never mind the details, suffice to say he was proposing something that was beyond even my rationalizing capacities. The 'break' energized me to take a long look at my actions and motives, which I found wanting.

"'What has this to do with you!' you ask. Precisely this: When you came aboard, Tom instructed me to 'bug' not only all systems in your office, but your home as well."

Rob waited for the explosion.

After a lengthy silence, Marty spoke, "Are you telling me that everything that has transpired in my home has been 'bugged.'"

"Yes," replied Rob, "but let me add, as of now, no one has listened to anything, except me, and everything has been erased. And that leads me to the reason for this emergency meeting. For the moment, I have stopped any recordings either at your home or your office. However, the recording of you and Ric in your den last night precipitated this meeting. It is erased… but if I don't reactivate the system, Derek and Tom will know very quickly. It will follow that I will be blamed and as they say, 'the game is on.'"

Marty sighed, "This is so horrific I can't even grasp it. Does anyone else know about this?"

Rob shook his head, "Not that I am aware of, although, strangely enough, I suspect that your assistant knows something."

Marty held up a finger, "I remember a call from Nancy about an attack on our system…"

"Don't worry about it, that was me testing if we were secure. It's because of that I suspect she knows something. She knows computers and something she said once made me suspicious. However, that is not the issue. Me freezing the 'bugs' and your reaction to this conversation are the two main issues.

"Before you recover and decide to hit me, I want to say two more things. First, I have had an epiphany concerning my actions and I want to deeply apologize for those actions. Secondly, I want to do anything I can to help you."

"Well, thank you, but…"

"Marty, you are in over your head with Chiles. He will burn you up and discard you like an old shoe. I may have a plan that could benefit us both if you are willing to trust me."

They both sat in silence.

Finally, Marty looked at Rob, "I can't totally grasp the ramifications of all this. The fact that you have come to me certainly goes a long way toward establishing trust."

Then, he laughed, "Of course, how do I know that I am not just being 'played' again. Nevertheless, I am willing to listen. My first reaction is that I am screwed. How do I continue, with the knowledge of what you have told me about Chiles?"

Rob nodded his head, "We are in a new game and I can tell you, Marty, this is the big leagues. The greed and corruption are more than you can imagine. I am just grateful that I am 'out' when I am; however, these people do not forget. We are now loose ends and that does not sit well with *Big Pharma*."

"So, what I think you are 'not' saying is that I should be grateful that you have opened up to me before I became one of the 'owned participants.'"

Rob smiled again, "Except for the grateful part... Yes. What we really need to do is put together a plan immediately."

"First things first," said Marty, "I need to talk with Myra."

Rob's head was bobbing, "For two reasons. One, of course, your marriage... but, two, for the time being, you are going to have to live with a 'bugged' house and office until we can put together our game plan."

"My God! I never even thought of that. How do I break that to Myra?"

"I think I can hold off anyone hearing any recordings for a couple of days. In the meantime, let me work out a plan."

They both rose and as they were heading out the door, Rob turned to Marty, "Thank you for your understanding."

"You're welcome... I guess... and thank you."

Rob paused, "Could I ask you one more thing? Could you please call Nancy and tell her I would like to talk with her?"

"Of course," said Marty.

While walking to the car, Rob pulled out his cell and dialed a Washington number.

A gruff voice answered, "Yes."

Rob replied, "Remember the 306."

"Rob! How are you?"

"I'm good, Larry... And you?"

Larry chuckled, "Well, except for the usual Washington bullshit, I'm great."

"Larry, I need a favor."

"Any time, partner."

"There's a secret service guy here that I need to meet. His name is Dr. Clay..."

"...Dearsome," interrupted Larry.

"Wow! Washington really is a small town... anyway, he's the lead investigator on the Congressman Barnes case."

"Yes. I know him and I had heard he was heading it up for now. What can I do for you, Rob?"

"I need to be introduced to him immediately. I may have some information and people that could help his work. If you or someone could call him and vouch for me, then we could save a lot of time."

"I can handle that. Should I have him call on this number?"

"That would be great, Larry. I owe you big time."

"Don't worry... I'll collect. Talk to you soon."

Rob arrived downtown and entered the Chiles building through the back entrance, taking the freight elevator to the 14th floor and easing in the back door, he walked to Nancy's desk.

He watched her for a moment until she looked up.

"Hi, Nancy. I'm Rob Schafers. I think Marty may have called you."

"Yes, he did, Mr. Schafers."

"I know this is very unusual. Did Marty say anything to you regarding what this is about?"

Nancy shook her head, "No. He just said that I was to meet you and to give you a listen."

Rob nodded, "Good. I understand that you have some computer knowledge."

Nancy shrugged, "A little."

Rob smiled, "Let me explain something before we go any further. I own a security company and I pretty much know everything about you."

Nancy looked visibly rattled.

"...and I am very impressed with your resume. You are very talented, but more importantly, you have integrity. I am not here on a combative mission. On the contrary, I need your help. I would like to establish some ground rules about this meeting. First, it needs to be absolutely confidential. Are you comfortable with that?"

Nancy nodded.

"Second, I will not ask you to do anything outside of the law. OK?"

Nancy nodded again. Just then, her cell beeped. She saw it was Kelly. "Sorry. Please, excuse me." She got up and walked to the back of the room. "Hey, Kelly." She listened for a minute or so and then answered, "Ok. I'll see you guys there." As she walked back to Rob, she was frowning.

"Nothing bad, I hope?" Rob offered.

"No... just confusing. Now, where were we?"

Rob smiled, "What I am about to say will shock you, but I can assure you it is factual and I have just informed Mr. Cooper. We, and I include myself, are in a situation that none of us want to be in and I think we can work our way out of it with your help."

Rob went on for a few minutes divulging again his work with Tom Chiles, the separation, the nature of the industry, and finished with his knowledge of Nancy's previous employer.

Nancy was reeling, "How do you know my former employer?"

"Let's just say that there isn't much that I don't know about this industry, and, I must say, I thought your decision to come with Marty was a wise one. However, job security is what we are addressing right now. Cooper Consulting is about to either take a drastic turn or be out of business. It's that simple and we need your help."

"Of course. I have no idea what is going on, but if I can help Mr. Cooper and he trusts you, then I am in."

Just then, his phone beeped.

"Rob Schafers."

"Rob, this is Clay Dearsome. Larry Neal suggested I call you."

Rob was shocked, "Yes, Clay, I just spoke with him. Thank you for the prompt callback."

"My pleasure. You don't know this, but I have followed your career for many years. I am an admirer. What can I do for you?"

"Thank you. Until recently, I was a consultant for Tom Chiles. We terminated our relationship a couple of weeks ago, and I have accidentally become peripherally involved with some of his personnel and I think I may be able to contribute to your investigation."

"That's excellent, Rob. When could we meet?"

"Well… that's the purpose of the timing of this call. I have some time constraints that are developing and I would like to apprise you of my information ASAP and then from our discussions, we could outline a possible game plan."

"Well, your timing couldn't be better. I am having a meeting about that very thing at 7 tonight. Why don't you come to the secret service office and we can get together for a few minutes?"

"Great. I'll be there and thanks… Oh, by the way. I'm bringing a girl by the name of Nancy Stone and Marty Cooper with me."

There was silence Finally, Clay spoke, "She is already coming to my meeting at 7."

Rob looked across the table at Nancy who had a shocked look on her face. "I'll notify security at the front door. Look forward to seeing all of you."

Rob clicked off his cell and locked eyes with Nancy, who had no idea what to say. Rob spoke first, "Well, this is interesting." He looked away and paused, "I think you have just demonstrated your trustworthiness. You have been sworn to secrecy. Right?"

Nancy nodded.

"Good," offered Rob, "...well, it appears we are all on the same page. Just so you understand, that was Dr. Clay Dearsome of the secret service who is heading up an investigation into the death of Congressman Barnes. We are meeting him at 7 o'clock at their offices. I suspect there will be other people attending."

Nancy just stared at him.

"Nancy, as an investigator, I have a high security clearance, so you can tell me if you choose."

She blinked a couple of times and finally responded, "Yes, there will be other people there. I am meeting Pam and Kelly at 6 to travel together."

***

Tom Chiles could not point to what it was, but he could not shake the feeling that things were happening and they weren't good. Pam had been away from her desk a few times and although she never showed her feelings, he was certain she was avoiding eye contact.

Derek had been a mess since the break-in and Kelly seemed to be avoiding any opportunity to be in contact with the 16th floor. He decided it was time to call a meeting and get a reading on everyone. He picked up the phone and paged Pam. When she didn't answer, he walked out of his office as she was coming up the stairs.

"Are you looking for me?" she inquired.

"Yes," grumbled Tom, "where have you been?"

Pam flushed slightly, "I was getting some documents at Kelly's desk..."

Tom interrupted, "Come in..." and wheeled back into his office. "I want Derek, Kelly, you, Marty, and Nancy in my office tomorrow morning at 9. We will be doing a complete review of everyone's operations."

Pam stayed at the doorway. "Will that be all?" she asked.

Damn this woman. Does nothing rattle her, thought Tom. "...and I want a written report from you and Marty on the cruise. I want to know if anything positive at all came out of that fiasco."

"Yes sir" answered Pam as she turned closing the door behind her. *'Just what I need'* she thought *'more balls in the air'*

***

Monk's first problem developed when he noticed there seemed to be protection around Pam. Seeing the same man on successive days was what tipped him off. Fortunately, he had worn a different disguise each day, and wasn't noticed.

His only conclusion was that she 'had' seen him on the street with Chiles and this was probably secret service. In the past, he had gone up against strong opposition, but the secret service was quite another matter.

He pondered the situation for a long time. Her protection posed several questions. One: If they already knew who he was, should he take the risk of continuing? Why not just disappear? Two: If he was caught, what evidence could they have without her testimony? Would it be the deciding factor? Three: What about the other girl? Could she identify him?

The dilemma raged. Ultimately, his ego and the money swayed the decision. This had been his first mistake and to leave a 'loose end' like this was not acceptable. If he walked away, he would never again have a peaceful moment. The risk was worth his future peace of mind.

On another front, what about Chiles? Had he been discovered or coopted? He quickly discarded that. If Chiles had been discovered, the secret service would probably have had him try to contact Monk for some reason and set a meet. He had time to deal with Chiles later. He would wait two more days to see if the payment was made.

***

Marty had called Myra to let her know he would not be home for dinner because of his 7 o'clock meeting.

Myra immediately detected a tone in his voice.

"Are you OK," she inquired.

"Yes. I am just tired," he said, hoping it would mollify his intuitive wife.

"Who's the meeting with?"

Marty sighed, "It's with the secret service people."

Myra continued, "What do they want?"

Marty exploded, "Myra… please. I don't know. We can go into this when I get home." Immediately, he regretted losing his cool. He listened to the silence and finally, continued, "I'm sorry, I have just had a horrific day. Let's talk when I get home. OK?"

"Of course. See you in a little while. I love you."

"Me too."

***

Kelly took the back stairs from her office to the 14th floor and opened the door to Cooper Consulting just as Nancy was exiting the ladies' room. She noticed that Nancy looked a little shaken.

"Hi, Nancy. Can we talk for a minute?"

Nancy looked kind of dazedly at Kelly, "…uh …Sure."

"Are you alright?" queried Kelly.

"Yeah… I'm just a little rattled."

"Is there anything I can do?"

Nancy shook her head, "No, I'm fine. What can I do for you?"

"This is kind of strange, but I need you to come to a meeting with me tonight at 7 with…"

"…the secret service? Right?"

It was Kelly's turn to be dazed. "How could you possibly know that?" she asked, looking around to make sure nobody heard them.

"I was just in a meeting with Rob Shafers and it seems he is joining our happy little family"

"Rob Shafers!" Kelly exclaimed, "what? …I don't understand."

"Neither do I, but I just finished meeting with him and we are all going to the same place. I was about to call you, so we could ride together."

"Great. I'm meeting Pam at Mariano's at 6 and we can try and make sense out of all this."

Nancy nodded, "Sounds good. I'll see you there is a couple of hours."

***

Tom was about to send the wire for the second payment to Monk when his cell beeped.

"Yes, Derek?"

"What the hell is going on with our stock?"

"What do you mean?" replied Tom.

Derek groaned, "Look at the ticker on the financial site and you'll see."

"Let me get off the phone and I'll look," Tom clicked on the financial ticker app. He blanched, "…What the …." And then he read the banner: 'Big Pharm Ripping Off: President.'[xi] With a sinking feeling, he read the headline again and then the video came on.

The new President's comments about the pharmaceutical industry's glutinous pricing policies had, in the last twenty minutes, caused collective stock prices to plunge twenty-five billion dollars.

He had quickly reversed his destination and was back entering his office when Pam interrupted to say that a national television broadcast reporter was on the line.

"I'm not available for anyone," he shouted.

Finally, Chiles Arken's price scrolled across. He plopped down to his chair and closed his eyes; panic rushed through his body. They had lost 15% of their value. He picked up his cell again.

"Derek… Get Marty and come here right now."

As Derek raced up the stairs to Tom's office, he punched up Marty's number to no avail. It immediately went to 'answering.'

Pam stared at him as he rushed past her and threw open Tom's door. She could see Tom at his desk with his head in his hands. Derek rushed across the room without closing the door and Pam heard him say, "What the hell are we going to do?"

"I don't know yet," countered Tom, "have you reached Marty?"

"No… I left a message."

"Well, keep trying," said Tom as he stood up on wobbly legs and looked out the window. "We need to get out ahead of this 'now.'"

"Pam," he shouted, "get Dr. Kenmore on the line."

"Yes, sir," she responded.

Tom and Derek were both silent as they pondered their next move. Obviously, there would have to immediately be an emergency meeting of the pharmaceutical companies and right on cue, Pam interrupted their thoughts.

"I have Frank Morrison, CEO of Brinkly Salsman on the line."

Tom grabbed the phone, "Frank… where and when are we meeting?"

"I just spoke with some of the other guys and we are going to have a video conference meeting in the boardroom of the Petroleum Club in an hour. Come to the back entrance."

"OK. See you shortly."

Derek was just hanging up from trying Marty again.

Tom said, "If you can't reach him before tonight, we have our meeting in the morning and I may have a game plan by then. Have you got any thoughts?"

Before he could answer, Pam called through the door, "I have Dr. Kenmore on the line."

"Arthur. Have you been watching the news?"

"Well... hello to you too, Tom."

"Arthur, we don't have time for niceties. Our stock price has just lost 15% and we need to stop the bleeding. Get on the financial news channel and bring yourself up to date. Then draft a response statement and send a copy to Derek. You'll be getting calls from the media. You know what to do. Cover all the bases." *How dare the President trample on our rights... this will affect the quality of health care... Government intervention in free enterprise... children health... Blah... blah... blah."* "We need to get you out there 'now' before COSM takes this and runs with it."

"Tom... what has happened...?"

"Never mind, just watch the news and then do what I just said. This is your moment of glory, not to mention that you have just lost a couple of million dollars." He slammed the phone down.

Tom looked up at Derek, "Stay on him until we see him on TV and send me his statement when it arrives."

It was now 5:15pm and Kelly was in the middle of redoing a document when her phone buzzed.

"Kelly... It's Pam. Derek is on his way down and he is going to need you, so pack up 'now' and go out the back way and don't answer your phone. I'll explain later."

Derek was leaving Tom's office when Pam intercepted him, "Mr. Maurrel... I need a minute."

"What is it, Pam...? I am very busy."

She hesitated for a moment and then answered, "...uh ...I couldn't help overhearing Mr. Chiles asking Dr. Kenmore to send over a statement he is preparing. If it comes to me, should I call you or just bring it down."

Tom was a little confused. "I guess bring it down. Is that all?"

"One more thing..." stuttered Pam, "will you be needing me to make copies of his statement for our files."

"Pam... I don't... I guess so... whatever you need. Now I need to run."

Pam had done the best she could in delaying Derek and hoped it was enough. She quickly grabbed her purse and headed for the elevator.

Derek was looking at the stock news on his cell as he walked toward his office and didn't notice the hall door closing. "Kelly, I am going to need you..."

He stopped, looking at her desk, then glanced at his watch. Dammit! Just when he needed her. He called her cell and left a message.

***

Tom buzzed Pam on the intercom. There was no answer, so after trying her on her cell, he left a message to please be available tonight on her cell as he may need her.

Pam looked at Tom's name on her cell as she was pulling out of her parking space. *I'll listen to that later,* she thought. Her thinking was on what she had heard in the office. Something had caused a stock crisis and she wanted to have that information when she went into her meeting at 7. Once she got settled at Mariano's, she would find it on her cell.

Monk was sitting in his car when the signal activated that Pam's car was on the move. He had installed the tracker earlier in the day so that he could continue his surveillance. He had anticipated she would be working late with the news of the stock drop. She pulled out into the traffic and headed toward the tollway. He followed her under the tollway onto the access road and after half a mile, turned into a strip mall and parked in front of Mariano's.

Monk hung back while he made some notes about her driving habits and the location of Mariano's. Was this a regular haunt or just a 'one time?'

His assumption that she was protected proved correct when, after a minute or so, another car parked and a man followed her into the restaurant.

Settling in a booth, Pam pulled out her cell and started catching up on the stock news. 'Wow!' Not only was this news having a huge impact today, but it would be disastrous tomorrow, not to mention the long term. The further she read, another realization hit home! The President's words were the opening salvo of a war with *Big Pharma*.

Kelly and Nancy arrived right at 6 and the three of them huddled in the booth, sipping on their drinks and exchanging the events of the day.

Pam's news of the stock drop was very unsettling for Kelly, as she was in a stock option program, while Nancy wondered how this was going to impact Cooper Consulting.

After a couple of minutes, none of them noticed the stooped over bearded man with the Fedora that quietly slipped into an adjoining booth. He opened his newspaper and ordered a coffee.

Kelly was speaking, "So, what do you think this meeting is about?"

"I'm guessing they are verifying all the bits of information they have collected and forming some sort of a picture," ventured Pam.

"Well, it makes me very nervous. I have never been involved with the secret service before."

Monk's head popped up when he heard 'secret service.' What meeting were they talking about and why would they be invited?

This confirmed for him that he did not have much time before he would have to go back to deep cover for an extended period. *I better check on the payment when I am done here, after which I can't afford any further involvement with Chiles.*

However, the immediate problem was this Pam woman. She could identify him.

The girls engaged in some more innocuous discussion and then got up to leave. As they passed by the adjoining booth, Pam happened to glance toward the man holding the newspaper and panic engulfed her. She stumbled and Kelly grabbed her.

"Are you OK?" enquired Kelly.

Pam nodded and hurried forward. She was ashen.

"Pam… what is it?" asked Nancy.

"Just get us out of here fast," squeaked Pam.

Kelly threw $20 on the counter and they ran out the door. When they arrived at the car, Pam jerked open the door and scrambled in, followed by the other two. She started the car and even before the girls had closed the doors, she rammed the car into gear and squealed the tires out of the parking space. As she made the turn to enter the tollway, she glanced up at the mirror and thought she saw a man staring at the car.

Kelly turned to Pam, "What was that all about?"

Pam was trying to catch her breath. She took a few deep heaves, "Nancy, I haven't told you about being beside the congressman when he had his supposed 'heart attack.' Prior to his attack, a man at an adjoining table had stumbled and fallen against Chet…er… Congressman Barnes. As he was getting up, I noticed he had a very unusual ring." She paused.

"…and…?" asked Kelly.

"The man in the booth behind us just now had the same ring!"

Kelly gasped. "It was him!" she shrieked.

"Who?" shouted Nancy.

"The man in the street," said Kelly, looking at Pam, "right?"

"I think so," offered Pam, "I want to talk to Dr. Dearsome."

Meantime, Monk was cursing himself as he climbed into his car. Whatever had spooked the girls. Their sudden departure had left him 'in the dust.' He couldn't imagine what had happened. He hadn't even pulled the paper down, so she couldn't have seen him. *…Hmmm.*

With the device on her car, he could follow, but it was pointless. Besides, with the secret service following, it was a waste of time. He needed to get a plan, carry it out, and 'go to ground' as quick as possible.

***

Rob and Marty pulled up to the security gate at the secret service entrance and showed their ID. A check on the list, a quick phone call, and the attendant opened the gate just as the girls arrived behind them. Rob and Marty waited for the girls to park and they all started toward the elevator.

Kelly started to snicker, "I feel like we are going to a funeral or something."

"Maybe we are," quipped Rob. They all looked at him.

Marty said, "Whose?"

Rob smiled, "That's the reason for the meeting."

The welcoming committee of Dr. Clay Dearsome and Agent Richard Guy were waiting in front of the elevator as the group exited.

"Good evening, folks," greeted Clay, "I think we all know each other."

They walked down a long hall and entered a room labelled Room C. It was a sparsely furnished mini board room with a table that seated twelve, dry erase board, video screens, credenza with glasses, cups, water, soft drinks, and coffee.

"Richard and I are sitting here by the dry board, the rest of you can sit wherever.

"You need to understand that bringing you all together like this is highly unusual. Normally, we would interview you separately, and we will, later, but because of some of the unusual and wide sweeping paths this investigation is taking, we decided this is the best way to quickly get the beginning of a total picture.

"First, the rules: We are the secret service and have powers that are different than other enforcement agencies. As of now, you are sworn to secrecy and nothing that is spoken in this room tonight can be discussed with anyone.

"Marty, in your case, because your wife was on the cruise and you, no doubt, have talked about the events, you have a pass with her, but she is under the same restriction."

"Good," responded Marty.

"After this meeting, if anything occurs to you that we have not discussed tonight, or you notice anything unusual or odd, you will notify us immediately."

Clay looked around the table. "Everyone on board?" he asked.

All heads nodded.

"Good... then let's get started with Miss Styles. First of all, ...Why were you on the cruise?"

"Mr. Chiles suggested that I would be a good addition to the pro *Big Pharma* team as a… schmoozer, I guess."

"Please, run through your experience right from the boarding incident to the death of the congressman."

For the next fifteen minutes, Pam relayed her experiences interspersed with questions from Clay and Richard. Everyone else stared in rapt silence.

"Thanks, Pam. Now, Marty. We haven't talked and I don't know if you have any observations from the cruise."

Marty squirmed a little, "Not really. I was so totally focused on delivering our message."

"Did you notice anything about the man who stumbled into the congressman?" asked Richard.

"No. I was on the other side of the table, talking with Dr. Kenmore."

Clay looked around the table, "OK… those are the only eye witnesses, so to speak, from the cruise. Now, let's move to some circumstantial situations. Kelly, please, tell us about your events back in Dallas."

Kelly revealed her overhearing Mr. Chiles' response to a cellphone call saying 'I just heard. It will be wired shortly.'

"Was that call on his normal cell?" asked Richard.

"No," responded Kelly, "I saw him reach into his desk drawer and answer it and then, when he was done, he dropped the phone into the trash. After he was gone, I put on some plastic gloves and opened the back of the phone and copied all the numbers from both inside and outside, then I noticed a fingerprint on the phone so I took some scotch tape and copied the fingerprint. I don't know if that is even useful, but I have the numbers and the tape with me."

"Good," responded Clay as he accepted the envelope.

"Nancy… you're next."

Nancy hesitated, looking around the room and finally settling on Marty, "Before I start, I want to apologize to Mr. Cooper. I didn't tell you what I am about to say because I… didn't know 'what' to do. I am sorry, Mr. Cooper."

"Go on, Nancy," nudged Clay.

"Mr. Cooper, one of the things that did not show up on my resume was that I am an amateur electronics and computer geek… as a hobby. As I was setting up the electronic equipment for the new office, I became aware that there were either physical or electronic bugs on everything."

Rob's eyebrows shot up. *I'll be damned,* he thought, *she knew all along.*

"Did you do anything?" asked Richard.

"No. As I said, I didn't know what to do. I confided in Kelly because I thought she would know what to do."

Richard turned to Kelly, "Kelly, did you do anything?"

Kelly shook her head.

"Just to clarify, no one else, that we know of, is aware that the 'bugs' have been discovered, other than the man who installed them… Rob Schafers."

After the buzz from this revelation, Richard turned to Rob, "Rob recently severed his relationship with Tom Chiles as a security consultant and has agreed to cooperate with us fully. His rapport and past services with Chiles are invaluable. Rob, why don't you start at the very beginning of your relationship with Tom Chiles."

Haltingly, Rob traced his history with Tom Chiles from their military comradeship to the rancorous split a few days ago. "This is difficult for me on many fronts. Although some of my services have bordered, at the very least, on illegality, it became apparent to me that his intentions had reached a level of revulsion that I could not suppress.

"Which leads me to the case in point. Yes, I installed all of the surveillance systems in both the Cooper Consulting offices and Mr. Cooper's home."

He turned to Marty, "It's small solace and I am not offering this as an excuse, but it was all installed at the request of Tom Chiles. I tell you this to expand your awareness.

"In my opinion, Tom Chiles will go to any extent to further his own avarice and expand the unconscionable greed of *Big Pharma*."

Until now, they all had kept their thoughts to themselves. …But …time seemed to freeze as Rob's scathing indictment left no doubt as to the next logical conclusion.

Before anyone could put the words to this presumption, Clay raised his hands. "Hold it," he commanded, "now it is Richard and my turn to talk." Everyone exhaled as if on cue.

Richard began, "I'm sure all of you remember the long running TV show, 'Law and Order.' Well, let's not move to the 'Order' part of the show before we complete the 'Law' portion.

"Through Clay's efforts on the cruise ship itself, we lifted a fingerprint from some evidence that certainly ties in with some other witness IDs we will hear about later. Additionally, the preliminary autopsy report indicates that the congressman may have been injected with a little-known drug called Aconite which causes heart failure. The drug degenerates rapidly in the blood, but we were fortunate to be able to capture some blood before any deterioration occurred. The blood analysis confirmed we have a murder on our hands."

This was the first time that the word had been used and it put a further damper on the mood.

"Additionally," continued Richard, "we have received confirmation from the fingerprint and identified the presumed assassin. That is the good news. The bad news is, he is in Dallas and has made contact with Mr. Chiles, as witnessed by Miss Styles and Freeman."

Noticing the shocked looks on Marty, Rob, and Nancy, Clay jumped in, "Yes, the two girls, by accident, happened to see a brief encounter between Mr. Chiles and the suspect and Miss Styles recognized him. Unfortunately, he recognized her as well."

Clay couldn't help but notice Pam, Kelly, and Nancy looking at each other. "What is it, ladies?"

They looked back and forth until, finally, Pam spoke, "We were finishing our drinks just before coming here and as we walked by a table, I noticed the ring on the man reading the newspaper at the table directly behind us. It was the same ring that was on the hand of the man on the ship."

Clay became very agitated, "How could he possibly have known you were there?"

"I don't know," offered Pam, "perhaps he followed us and we didn't notice."

Clay looked over to Richard. They both shook their heads in disgust. Richard picked up his cell and punched a number as he walked out of the room.

Kelly and Nancy looked at each other and finally, Kelly spoke. "That means he knows all of us. Are we in danger?" she asked, looking at Clay.

Clay hesitated for a moment, "I don't see why. You and Nancy don't pose him any threat."

The girls both signed in relief.

Richard opened the door and asked to talk to Clay. As Clay walked into the hall, Richard clicked off his cell. "He saw an old man walk into the restaurant about a minute after Pam and sat reading a newspaper in the booth behind them. He showed no interest in them. When they left, he was still there when our agent followed the girls."

"How did he not see the man 'tailing' them?" asked Clay.

Richard responded, "The guy wasn't there when our agent got out of his car."

"Then how did the guy know where the girls were?"

There was silence.

Then Richard said, "Maybe he put a 'bug' on her car. I'll go down and check."

"OK," agreed Clay and went back into the room. "Sorry for the interruption. Basically, we have covered the things we know. Is there anything else that anyone has to offer?"

Rob spoke up, "Before the cruise, there was an incident with Pam in Tom's office." Rob went on to describe the attack and his subsequent conversations with Tom Chiles.

Once again, Marty and Nancy were shocked.

"Are you saying that Derek Morell attacked Pam?" asked Marty.

"Yes," said Rob, "but it has nothing to do with this situation. It related to Derek's insecurity and trying to read a file in Tom's safe."

Clay spoke up, "Rob, do you think Derek should be a suspect in this investigation?"

"No, and here's why. Chiles always compartmentalizes everything. In the overview, he has been training Derek for years to be his second-in-command. That grooming has been in the nature of eroding his basic moral fiber to handle the much larger illegal and amoral functions required in a *Big Pharma* executive. In Tom's mind, Derek has not degenerated to that stage."

Rob turned to Marty, "Marty, I guess this is as good a time as any to tell you that you are the 'next one in the barrel.' You are being groomed to be squeezed for everything, including your algorithm patents, and then tossed to the wolves." He turned back to the group just as Richard reentered the room and nodded at Clay, confirming the 'bug' on the car.

Rob continued, "The ends to which these people will go is boundless. We are sitting here, investigating the assassination of a United States congressman solely because he had the temerity to question the research findings of a new drug. Here's a few questions that I finally had to ask myself:

'Why is *Big Pharma* the largest lobbying entity in Washington?'

'Why has no one ever questioned the veracity of FDA edicts when a substantial portion of their budget comes from *Big Pharma*? No chance of a conflict of interest there!'

'Why has *Big Pharma,* with the help of the FDA, doctors, and medical educational institutions consistently, over the past seventy-five years, denigrated the historical proof of natural solutions?'

'Why have natural solutions (verified by reputable medical experts) to major medical issues like cancer, Alzheimer's, autism, diabetes, vaccines (to name a few*)* been systematically vilified, along with their proponents, to the point of extinction?'"

Rob continued, "I am ashamed that I have participated in these unspeakable enterprises for all these years. The only saving grace is that I never crossed any legal boundaries. The moral boundaries are a different issue, to be dealt with by my conscience."

He looked around the table, "I think I am safe in saying that those of us in this room working in the industry have been, to some degree, coopted by the money.

"Why do you think that thousands of good people, with even a glimmer of intelligence, continue to silently propel this hypocrisy forward?"

……Silence.

"Fear and 'contempt prior to investigation' are both major components. But let's never forget the famous line from the Tom Cruise movie… 'Show me the money.'"

Everyone stared silently as Rob shook his head, "I will climb off my soapbox now. But let me just close with a view from my experience in the industry.

"Nothing… and I mean 'nothing,' is off limits if anything or anyone threatens this trillion-dollar industry. Mysterious accidents, frivolous lawsuits, anything and everything is on the menu.

"Marty… the breakthroughs you have made with your algorithms, proven by the last presidential elections, are monumental for *Big Pharma*. They will be able to target the marketing of a specific drug for a specific patient's specific problem to any of the patient's communication devices. The manipulation potential is enormous. It's George Orwell's 1984 on steroids.

"Whether we like it or not, we all are in this monumentally evil game and we are not equipped."

A hush fell over the room as the ominous ideas settled in their collective consciousness.

"Thanks, Rob," responded Clay, "your insight to *Big Pharma* is valuable as well as frightening. As large as this case is, it's obvious this investigation has ramifications beyond this room. Further, to your comments of the dangers involved, Richard has some further enlightenment."

Richard nodded, "I just investigated Miss Styles' car and discovered there has been a 'bug' attached to the vehicle, which is how the man was able to follow her.

"Our security man had already entered Mariano's when he pulled into the parking lot, so we were unaware of his arrival. He appeared to be just another customer.

"I have left the device on the vehicle so the perpetrator will not know we have discovered the 'bug'. I also have added our own 'bug' for further security."

Clay interrupted, "This demonstrates the necessity of constant vigilance. Although it appears Pam is the only target, who knows what could happen if *Big Pharma* gets 'wind' of our speculations, so please be careful.

"We will be continuing tonight to follow other leads, but please contact me if you have any other thoughts. I want to evaluate this meeting and then come up with a plan, so for the moment, just operate in your normal manner."

Clay rose as a signal that the meeting was over and they all started filing out. Clay grasped Rob's arm, "Could you and Marty stay for a moment?"

"Of course," responded Rob and waved to Marty.

When the others had left, Clay began, "As of now, I believe that Chiles is unaware that we have expanded this investigation to include him, and if that is the case, then our presence in the building could raise suspicions. I would like you to be our 'eyes and ears' in the building in case we need some immediate reaction. Marty, I am not expecting you to put yourself in danger and, hopefully, Rob can be nearby most of the time."

"I was hoping you would keep me involved in some way," responded Rob, "we just need to keep in mind that I am no longer involved with Chiles, Arken, so I must be fairly covert."

Marty was looking a little awkward. "This is certainly out of my expertise, but I will do what I can," he said.

"Good. Thank you both. Rob, I will be in touch with you tomorrow. Thanks, gentlemen."

***

As Rob and Marty started back toward the office, Marty realized that in all the excitement, he had not turned his cell back on. He had three calls from Derek and two calls from Tom. Obviously, something was up.

He dialed Tom.

"Where the hell have you been?" growled Tom. Fortunately, Tom did not wait for an answer. "Have you seen what's going on with our stock?" he yelled.

While frantically trying to pull up a headline on his cell, he tried to fake it. "Is it as bad as it looks?" he fumbled.

"What do 'you' think!" barked Tom, "the Hong Kong board looks like we will lose at least 15% of our value when we open in the morning. If I could get my hands on Trump's neck…"

Marty saw an opening, "What 'exactly' did he say?"

"Never mind what he said, I need you here so we can 'game plan' a response before the market opens."

Marty didn't want to talk anymore until he could learn something, so he just said, "I'm on my way," and clicked off.

Rob looked questionably at Marty, "Trouble?"

"Apparently, Trump made some statement about *Big Pharma*," replied Marty as he looked at his cell, "…and the entire industry is tanking on the Asian market."

Rob couldn't help but chuckle, "Well, at least now they have a heavyweight in the ring with them."

Marty sighed, "With the situation the way it is right now, I don't know how to respond. He will be wanting me to put out a bunch of 'flack' and my heart is not in it."

"Why did this have to happen tonight," he muttered as he punched up Myra's cell. "Hi, My, I just finished my meeting, but Tom called and I have to go in and handle some sort of crisis." He paused, "…No, I don't know how long. I'll fill you in when I get home."

Chapter 18

Monk had made another mistake! He just didn't know it… yet! In his zeal to bully Tom into the second half of the payment, he had called an old acquaintance, Billy, from his childhood criminal days, and hired him to drive the car when Monk had picked up Tom. Monk had paid Billy a handsome fee and dismissed the event.

Had he taken the time, he would have learned that Billy worked for the same organization for which Monk, in his past, had done services.

When Billy reported to his bosses whom he had seen and what had transpired, they expressed a serious interest in speaking with Monk.

Billy and two very large men sat in a car down the street from the motel where Billy had originally picked up Monk.

Billy was telling his fellow passengers that he hoped Monk had not checked out when the room door opened and out stepped Monk. Or was it? Monk had donned another disguise and had Billy not been watching the room, he would have missed the target.

They cruised the car up to the parking lot and the two men jumped out and confronted Monk. His confidence in his disguise was such that he was genuinely confused by the interruption until he saw Billy. He slumped in the men's arms as they dragged him into the back seat and the car roared off.

Monk had no time to struggle as the chloroform-soaked rag was jammed over his mouth.

***

"Good Morning, sunshine," growled a voice. Monk tried to open his eyes, but to no avail. They seemed to be glued shut. He heard voices, but couldn't comprehend the words.

The voice spoke again, "I think he's coming around Boss," and then Monk felt a sharp slap across his face.

"Mr. Monkman, I presume," said a different voice. Monk's eyes finally popped open. The room swam for a few seconds and then slowly came into focus as he stared into a face that was vaguely familiar.

"Ah," said 'the face,' "I see a small glimmer of recognition. Well, it has been over twenty years. I can understand the confusion," laughed 'the face,' "well… we are going to recollect some old times and when we are done, I am sure you will reach full recognition."

As if rising from a murky swamp, some memories started to emerge and with them, came a deep dread. Then he knew! Tony Scaliarie!

Tony laughed again, "…aha… so, you remember now. I must admit, Monk, I had forgotten about you and that's not like me. I always 'make it right' when someone screws me and now it looks like I will keep my record intact."

Monk squirmed, "Tony, I…"

"No… No… Monk, I'm doing the talking and you are doing the listening. Those are the opening ground rules. As I recall, before you disappeared, you had an outstanding debt with me of $100,000. Is that correct? Just nod yes or no."

Monk nodded.

"Good," said Tony, "we're on the right track. Now I believe we contracted a certain job that, although completed, resulted in a house burning down for which we knocked off $50,000. Is that correct?"

"Tony… Please."

"Just yes or no."

"Yes… but."

"Good. We're getting along splendidly," Tony pulled up a chair and sat down in front of Monk. "Now my calculations say that there was a remainder of $50,000 that has not been remitted for these past twenty years. I haven't calculated the interest on the figure, but with my normal returns, we both know it is substantial."

Monk hung his head.

"Having been associated with our enterprises in the past, I am sure you are aware that this situation, to say the least, is embarrassing. Sooo… How are we going to rectify it? I suppose, if you had the wherewithal, you would suggest that you just pay it and we all go on our merry way.

"That, however, leaves me with a difficult dilemma. I can't have everyone just disappearing and hoping that they can reappear like magic, pay back the amount and go their merry way, with no retribution."

The fear started spreading outward from Monk's stomach.

"Ah…" said Tony again, "I see I have your total attention now. Excellent." And then he stood up and punched Monk square in his face, breaking his nose. Wiping the blood from his hand, he sat back down, "I normally find no delight in physical violence, Monk, but in your case, it gave me a lot of pleasure."

Tony signaled one of his men, "Get the man something to wipe his face."

Monk grabbed the towel and tenderly daubed at his smashed face.

"Now I am finished with our one-way conversation. It's time that we talked together. Your friend, Billy, who, by the way, you should thank for you still being alive, told me about your adventure with a man in the car."

Monk's head snapped up!

"Yes," said Tony, "and I was very intrigued. Something about some bigshot owing you $500,000. I would like you to tell me about that."

Monk tried to talk but blood gushed out and the words were unintelligible.

"Take your time, Monk, we've got all night." Tony stood up and walked toward a counter. "Would you like some water?" he asked as he poured himself a glass from the pitcher.

Shaking his head, Monk looked around the room. It seemed to be some old warehouse office with a bathroom off to the side. He pointed to the bathroom. "Yes, of course" said Tony as he pointed at one of the men, "Lucky, help Monk get cleaned up and then we'll have a nice conversation."

***

Marty received a cell call just as the women arrived back at the office.

"Mr. Cooper, Mr. Maurrel has asked us to attend an emergency meeting upstairs in Mr. Chiles' office and he wants Nancy and Pam there also," said Kelly.

"Thank you, Kelly. I was in contact with Mr. Chiles, so let's all go now."

Rob stood by the door. "I'll leave you folks and we'll talk later. Good luck."

***

One by one Nancy, Kelly, and Marty filed into Tom's office, followed by Pam with her note pad.

"I am assuming that you have all brought yourselves up to date on the idiotic pronouncements from our esteemed President," suggested Tom.

There was a collective head nodding.

"Good. I have been in contact with one of our spokespersons, Dr. Arthur Kenmore, and he is currently preparing a statement to be issued shortly. I want you all to make yourselves familiar with it and we will meet here tomorrow morning at 8 and integrate his statements with whatever points that emerge tonight."

He continued, "I'm sure I don't need to emphasize the scope of what has happened, but I want you all to understand that tomorrow morning at the opening of the bell, the pharmaceutical industry is going to lose over $25 billion dollars in valuation. Our company will lose at least 15%. That, of course, is a huge issue, but more importantly, it is going to dramatically impact our image which we have been protecting for decades."

Tom started pacing. "I want our response to reflect our revulsion at the irresponsibility of our President for deliberately jeopardizing the health of our nation, the indirect besmirching of the thousands of men and women who toil in our industry, the denigration of the oversight agencies controlling our medical, financial, and educational institutions, …etcetera."

Tom paused to take a breath, "By tomorrow afternoon, I want us to have blanketed the airwaves and print with our outrage at these accusations. TV, radio, social media, blog interviews, anywhere and everywhere."

He pointed to Derek, "Coordinate your stuff with Derek and Kelly. I realize that this is a short meeting to have come in for, but I wanted you all to understand the seriousness of the situation and perhaps, some of you may decide to work at your desk. That's it. Thank you for coming in on such short notice."

As they all started to file out, Tom called Pam, "Pam. Could you stay for a few minutes?"

She looked at him oddly and then nodded. As she turned to go back, she made an anxious face at Kelly and Nancy.

Derek started down the stairs and Marty, Kelly, and Nancy headed to the elevator as Nancy said, "I did not like that look from Pam. Do you think she is in trouble?"

"Who knows," said Kelly, "why don't we go to your office and call Rob?"

***

Just as the meeting was being convened at Chiles, Arken, Monk was emerging from the bathroom with a clean towel over his nose.

"You look much better now, Monk," observed Tony. "Come over here and sit again and we'll have a talk."

Monk shuffled to his chair, where Lucky roughly pushed him down.

"Now," started Tony, "take me from the beginning about this man in the car."

With obviously much pain, Monk began his history with Tom Chiles. How he had, from time to time, done jobs, ranging from terminations, to psychological and physical intimidation of investigative reporters, to dirty tricks against *Big Pharma's* antagonists.

"How did this $500,000 item emerge?" questioned Tony.

Monk went on to explain the hit that had been completed.

"Whoa..." Tony uttered, "are you telling me that you were the one that put the hit on Congressman Barnes?"

Monk nodded.

"My... My... you have come a long way, Mr. Monkman. I'm impressed. ...and your fee was $500,000?"

Again, Monk nodded, at which point, Billy interjected, "Boss, I don't think that is quite right."

"Why do you say that, Billy?"

Billy puffed up with pride and said, "When Monk talked to the man in the car, he said I want the 'balance,' which means there was a previous payment."

"Excellent deduction, Billy. Do you agree, Monk?"

There was silence.

Tony started pacing, "Monk, I am disappointed that your previous story was not complete. As I stated earlier, I personally don't enjoy violence, but our friends here seem to get pleasure from inflicting it. My observation is that you have reached another fork in the road. Either talk or pain. I am anxious to hear your decision."

Monk started shaking, "Tony, I am not holding out on you. The balance of the million is in an account in Grand Cayman and I was going to tell you."

Tony paced some more, then leaned over the chair and stared into Monk's eyes, "Monk, you have used up whatever credibility you may have had, so I have one more question and I would suggest you consider your answer carefully. Do you have any other money on deposit in Grand Cayman?"

Staring into Tony's black, dead eyes, Monk knew any resistance was futile. "Yes, I have a balance of around $700,000."

"Excellent," burst Tony, "I always enjoy entering a new partnership with sufficient capital."

Monk groaned.

"Oh, don't worry, Monk, you will be treated fairly," chuckled Tony. "Now," he said, "I would like to start on a method to acquire these funds. Do you have any thoughts?"

Silence again.

Then finally, Monk spoke, "There is one other matter that we would need to handle."

"Do tell!" said Tony, menacingly.

Monk outlined the situation regarding his identity being breached to Pam.

"...and who is this woman?" asked Tony.

"She is the executive assistant to Tom Chiles."

"Interesting," mused Tony as he paced back and forth in deep thought. When he finally spoke, he had a sly smile on his face. "OK," started Tony, "my first assessment is that our man... what is his name?"

"Tom Chiles," responded Monk.

"Right... Mr. Tom Chiles is in a rather compromised position, being responsible for the killing of a United States Congressman. A daunting problem. It seems to me that he would be amenable to a nondisclosure agreement."

Monk shook his head, "Tony, he is the CEO of a major pharmaceutical company and has resources that are beyond even you."

"That may very well be, Mr. Monkman, but let us not forget that he can only maintain that position as long as his secret stays secret, and there is a price for that."

Tony paced some more, finally stopping in front of Monk, "I want you to call and tell him that he needs to meet you right now. You have a situation that requires he have the money tonight and you are willing to negotiate. Tell him if he is not at this address within the hour, you are prepared to anonymously report his involvement in the assassination to the secret service tonight. Tell him to also bring his assistant, Pam, with him. If he asks 'why her,' just tell him it is for all our protection."

Monk was shaking his head, "He will never go for that."

"And why not?" asked Tony, "it's a win-win for him. He gets you off his back and he thinks he's going to get a better deal."

***

Tom and Pam had just sat down to work when a cellphone buzzed in his desk drawer. He looked guiltily at Pam as he held it to his ear.

"Yes," answered Tom.

"Where are you right now?" said Monk.

"In my office," responded Tom.

"Are you with your assistant?"

Tom glanced again at Pam, "Yes."

"Have you made arrangements for the balance?"

"Not yet, I was…"

"Never mind. Listen to me carefully. I am prepared to offer you a better deal, but we need to do it tonight. This is not a suggestion. If we don't meet tonight, our deal is off and I will anonymously notify the secret service of your involvement in the death of the congressman. I have recorded all our calls from the past, so don't think you can negotiate an alternative.

"I want you and your assistant at this address within the hour. 1774 Harry Hines Blvd. around the back and I will be waiting. Bring this phone with you in case of emergency. Have you got all that?"

Tom stood up, "Wait… it's 9:30…"

"Just do it, or else."

…click

"Considering your nasal condition, Monk, you did splendidly. Now… while we are waiting, I want to hear the details as to the where's and how's of our money. We won't have any problems with this discussion, will we?"

Monk, still holding the towel to his face, muttered a begrudging, "No."

***

Tom stared at the cell for a long time, trying to conjure up a believable reason for asking Pam to accompany him. He couldn't understand why Monk would want her there, but that was not the issue.

Finally, he spoke, "Pam, I need to ask you a favor. That was one of our major shareholders and he wants to have a meeting right now regarding the President's announcement. He asked if I could please bring you."

"Why would be want me there," she exclaimed.

Tom smiled, "Well, there are a couple of reasons. One, he has often told me how he respects you. Two, I would like you there with me for support."

A rush ran through her body, sending danger signals. How could she say no without raising suspicions? She hesitated. She just couldn't come up with a good excuse. If they went in Tom's car, she could only hope that the SS had put a tracker on him. That would be some small sense of safety.

"I realize what an imposition this is, but he sounded very insistent."
Finally, she nodded accent.

Chapter 19

When Kelly and Nancy unlocked the door to Cooper Consulting, they both jumped when the light flicked on and there sat Rob. He smiled and said "…and just where have you girls been all night?"

It broke the tension they were feeling as they all laughed.

They relayed to Rob the content of the meeting and the ending. He did not look pleased. There were some odd things happening and he did not like coincidences.

The SS tail had reported that Monk's car had not moved for a couple of hours and there were no lights in his room and now Pam being alone with Tom did not sit well.

He rubbed his chin while pondering what to do. He could not remember if Clay had told him they had a tracker on Tom's car.

He addressed the girls, "You guys stay here. I am going to check something downstairs. Leave your cells on."

He rushed to the elevator, which took forever to arrive. Exiting the parking floor, he started looking for Tom's car in the executive area just as the elevator pinged its arrival. Ducking behind a car, he watched Tom and Pam walking toward him.

As they climbed into Tom's car, he heard her say, "I don't understand why he would want me there."

As the car backed out, Rob pulled out his cell and entered Clay Dearsome's number.

"Rob?"

"Clay! Tom Chiles has just entered his car with Pam Styles. They are pulling out of his parking space at the building. I don't know if you have a tracker on his car. I am going to try and follow them. Notify the tail on Pam and see if he can follow them. Call me back."

Rob ducked down as Tom's car slid past. When they turned the corner, he jumped up and ran to his car. It would be a miracle if he caught them.

Just making the turn from his parking space, Rob's cell buzzed.

"Yes, Clay."

"We have no tracker on Tom's car and the agent for Pam is not responding."

"Shit," burst Rob, "stay on with me while I see how I make out in catching them. Better still, why don't you alert your team to be on standby and then call me back."

***

Considering her fear, Pam was remarkably calm. She knew the worst thing she could do was show any concern, but she was certain the motive for this trip was not the feeble excuse he had offered. His nervousness was palpable, which further heightened her anxiety.

Questions raged! *Had the secret service agent seen them leave? Would the girls try to find me? Where were we going?* Finally, she was able to reign in her imagination and confront her situation. ...and the thought struck her like a thunderbolt.

As they exited the parking garage and entered the tollway toward LBJ Freeway, she feigned a yawn and semi-closed her eyes. She saw Tom glance over to her and then back to the road.

Ever so slowly, she slid her hand into her purse, feeling for her cell. She felt along the face of the dial pad until she hoped she was over the 7.

She opened her eyes, looked over at Tom and calmly asked, "Where are we going?" She asked as they swung off the tollway onto LBJ Freeway.

"Our investor said he was at a funky little restaurant on Harry Hines Blvd.," responded Tom.

That was all the confirmation Pam needed to justify her fears. No one went to Harry Hines Blvd alone at night. Pam leaned over with her free hand and turned on the radio as she hit the cell button with her other hand.

"Maybe we can get some stock news," she offered.

Rob had swung out of the building and just caught a glimpse of Tom's car entering the Tollway south. It was going to be tough to catch them. He dodged in front of a car and started up the ramp, ignoring the angrily blaring horn and just missing an eighteen-wheeler roaring by in his lane. With the heavy traffic, he knew his chances were slim.

Just then, his cell buzzed. He assumed it was Clay and pressed the car speaker.

"Yes, Clay," he answered. He looked down at the speaker as he heard a muffled voice say something about 'stock news.' He was sure it was Pam's voice.

"Hello," he yelled... but all he heard was what sounded like an automobile and then a radio being changed. Then he looked at the screen and saw Pam's name. A rush went through him. *Good Girl*, he thought.

He was approaching the major exchange to LBJ and didn't know which way to go, so he took the access road and pulled over. Picking up his phone, he hit the conference button, pulled up Clay's number, and called.

"Yes, Rob."

"Clay, I have lost them, but Pam has activated her cell and I have conferenced you in." He gave Clay her number. "I think she is on AT&T. Call them and put a trace on her and I can follow your directions."

Pam thought she had heard Robs voice, but she dared not check, so she kept flipping the radio until they caught the last part of a newscast saying that the *Big Pharma* news was, no doubt, going to drag the Dow Jones down at the opening.

"Shut that off," growled Tom, "We already know that."

She switched to some music and desperately tried to think of something to say. "This is going to be a great opportunity for Dr. Kenmore to shine."

Tom looked over at her like she had leprosy.

"That blowhard!" he burst, "he'll be lucky if he doesn't explode from his own wind."

"But I thought he was our frontline defense against COSM," suggested Pam, trying desperately to keep him talking.

Tom harrumphed. "A lot of good he is going to do against the President," said Tom as he turned off LBJ Freeway onto Harry Hines Blvd. which caused Pam's agitation level to rise even higher.

Rob was having trouble controlling his own emotions. As he waited, he was trying to pick up clues from Pam's muffled voice. Waiting was not his strong suit and he was about to try Clay when his phone beeped. "Yes, Clay," he said hastily.

"They were on LBJ and just made the turn on to Harry Hines, heading south."

Rob jammed the car in gear and started for the ramp to LBJ West.

"We are tracking you as well and I see you just entered the LBJ ramp," Clay continued, "we have a SS Swat crew mobilizing right now. They are about twenty minutes from being ready."

"I'm guessing they are going to somewhere on Harry Hines, or else there would be no reason to get off LBJ," speculated Rob, "is your team coming from the south?"

"Yes," responded Clay, "…hang on, Rob. …they just turned east into a driveway …wait …here's the address. It's 1774 Harry Hines. We have a chopper lifting off right now. He should be hovering in about ten minutes."

"No… No, Clay. I don't want to jeopardize Pam. Can you keep them out or earshot until I can get a feel?"

Clay frowned, "Rob, you have not been in any action for a long time. This is an SS operation now. I need you to stand down."

"Clay, you know I can't do that," he responded as he took the ramp on to Harry Hines. He could still hear the radio in the car, so Pam had not been discovered yet.

Tom located the address and made the left turn into the parking lot of what was formerly a 7-11. Pam squirmed in her seat. "This can't be the place," she muttered.

"This is the address he gave me," said Tom as he drove around behind.

Suddenly, Tom slammed on the brakes as a man jumped in front of the car. The passenger door was ripped open and Pam was dragged out of the car just as the other man waved a gun at Tom and signaled him out of the car.

Pam started to scream, but was slapped hard across her face and told, "Shut up." They both were marched through a door in an old warehouse building. Immediately, they were blindfolded and plastic cuffs secured their arms behind their back and roughly shoved into chairs.

"Ah… Our guests have arrived," Tony offered, "please, accept my apologies for the rough entrance, but we want our gathering to be rather private. We have you blindfolded only until I am certain that you will not have any untoward panic attacks. So… when you have both recovered from your rather rude welcome, we will remove the blindfolds and our evening can begin."

Tom spoke, "I don't know who the hell you are or what you want, but you are making a very bad mistake." He had just gotten the last word out when he was jerked out of the chair, punched in the stomach and then rudely pushed back in the chair.

As he sat retching and trying not to vomit, Tony was right beside his ear, "I was hoping we would not have to start our evening like this, but I tried to warn you. Are you finished with the bluster so we can begin our new friendship"?

Tom nodded his head. There was a long pause and then the blindfolds were removed. As Pam blinked and tried to orient herself, Tom immediately saw Monk.

"You son of a bitch," Tom yelled.

Monk just hung his head.

A beefy, tall, broad-shouldered man in a silk suit stood in front of the two bewildered 'guests.'

"First of all, my name is Tony, and I am your host for the evening. The gentleman you just slandered is Mr. Franklin Carol Monkman. Over there is Billy and these other two gentlemen are my assistants and you, no doubt, are wondering what this is all about.

"Mr. Monkman, …or if you prefer 'Monk'…and I did some business many years ago after which a large amount of money was to be paid to me. That money never appeared."

Tony walked over behind Monk's chair, "Monk here, seemed to have had a memory lapse and neglected to contact me and then he disappeared. As you can imagine, I was not pleased."

He then walked over to Billy and, slapping him on the back, said, "Now, Billy here had occasion to be contacted by Monk and being the good friend he is, he called me to inform me that Mr. Monkman had resurfaced, whereupon I arranged for us to meet and have a talk."

He walked back to Monk. "As you can see, he had an unfortunate accident with his face, but he should heal soon, barring any other accidents," he said, patting Monk on the cheek, which caused Monk to flinch and moan.

"So, I am sure this has all been extremely interesting so far. Now, let's get to why you are here."

Tony walked over and stood in front of Tom and Pam. "There are really three pieces of business I hope to transact with you," he said, looking at both of them.

"Number one: Mr. Chiles, you owe Monk $500,000, which you will pay me tonight. Number two: That does not pay me for my involvement, so we will be negotiating that fee and number three," he said, looking at Pam, "this young lady had the misfortune to identify Monk under some rather incriminating circumstances and therefore, she has, as we say in my world, become a liability to us all."

"You can't be serious," Tom gasped as Pam burst into tears.

"Oh, believe me, I am deadly serious."

***

Rob turned off the headlights as he drifted to a stop two doors down from the old 7-11 and drawing his gun, he slunk along the adjoining building until he saw Tom's car.

Behind the car, he saw some light through a window in the old warehouse. There didn't appear to be any guard outside, so he raced across the parking area and froze against the building just as the sound of a helicopter began.

***

Tony's head swung toward the door as he heard the helicopter. "Lucky, go outside and see what that chopper is doing."

Lucky nonchalantly sauntered to the door and stepped outside, closing the door behind him. He looked up to spot the chopper and that's when Rob exercised his old military skills and chopped him from behind, instantly rendering Lucky unconscious. Rob dragged him away from the door, then tried to see in the window. The crack gave him a slim view of Tom and Pam, with their hands tied behind and Tony standing in front.

He had to assume there were others, but how many and where? He ran to the other side of the door and tried to see through the other window. He saw the arm of another man.

The chopper was getting louder, so Rob ran back to the other side of the door and took one final look through the crack. Tony was approaching the door. Rob knew this was the moment and drew his gun. He waited until he saw the knob turning and then threw his whole body at the door.

The sudden impact knocked Tony backward off his feet as Rob crashed through on top. Rolling to his left, Rob saw Billy reaching for the gun in his belt and shot him in the middle of his chest, just before he felt the searing pain in his ribs.

One of the other men started to walk toward Rob for the kill shot when Pam bolted out of the chair straight into him, giving Rob time to roll over and get off a shot that caught the man in the leg. He stumbled and fell, but not before he wildly tried another shot.

The din of the helicopter was deafening now and Rob could only hope that the squad was almost there. He painfully rolled over and stared straight into the muzzle of a gun in Tony's hand.

Tony smiled evilly, "Whoever you are, I am sorry we will never meet."

Rob saw his finger tightening on the trigger and closed his eyes, waiting. He heard the shot, but felt nothing. He opened his eyes just in time to see Tony's disbelieving eyes staring at the hole in his chest, then toppled over dead.

Rob looked behind him, and there stood Clay.

"I thought I told you to wait for us," Clay said, smiling.

Rob tried to smile, but the pain from the rib the bullet had broken was excruciating. Just before he passed out, he heard one of the SS men say, "We have someone down over here."

Chapter 20

It was mid-morning when the surgeon finally came into the hospital waiting room. He eyed the room full of people in various states of sleeplessness, but all with hopeful looks.

Finally, he spoke, "I am sorry for the delay in getting to you. First of all, we had to stabilize the patient, which took some time and then the operation took much longer than we anticipated.

"However, I am pleased with the results and subject to no unforeseen circumstances, Miss Pam Styles should recover with no major after effects."

The room broke into cheers and nervous laughter. Kelly and Nancy were hugging and dancing, Rob, with his sling, sat with a drugged smile, Clay looked up from his cell and gave a thumb up, while Marty and Myra just sat, still in shock at the events.

The doctor continued, "The stray bullet entered her back and exited the front just under her ribs, collapsing her lung in the process. She has lost a lot of blood and will not be able to see visitors for a few hours. Thank you for your patience."

As he turned to leave, a wave of 'thank you' rained on him. He nodded and left.

Clay put his cell in his pocket. "Here is an update," he said, "Tom Chiles has been indicted on conspiracy to commit murder, kidnapping, and other charges that are pending. Derek Maurrel has agreed to assist the investigation. Tony Scaliarie and Billy Clemson died at the scene. One of the unidentified others died at the scene and the other is in custody."

***

Kelly, Nancy, and Marty sat in Marty's office the next day trying to work out the rest of their life. Obviously, their futures had had a severe adjustment that did not jibe with defending *Big Pharma*. The company, now without the financial sources that had been exposed, was no longer viable.

Nancy reached over to answer the incoming call.

"Cooper consulting."

"Nancy, this is Norm Arthur from COSM (Council on Safe Medicine). Is Marty in"

Nancy hesitated, then said, "Let me see, Mr. Arthur."

Marty's head snapped up when he heard the name. "Oh... great. The timing is perfect!" he said sarcastically. He punched the blinking line. "Norm... how are you?"

"I'm great, but more importantly, how are you?"

Marty sighed, "Well, I have had better times."

"I'm sure... I'm sure. Have you got a moment to talk?"

Marty hesitated, thinking, *What have I got to talk with him about now.* "Yes, what can I do for you?"

Norm laughed, "Marty, it's not what you can do for me... au contraire... it's what I can do for you. I hope I am not being presumptuous in assuming these developments have not only altered your views philosophically, but materially as well."

"To say the least!" stated Marty.

"Good," responded Norm, "I believe we have been presented an opportunity that will benefit both of us."

"How so?" questioned Marty.

"I don't think my detailed thinking can be covered in this phone call, but let me give you the basics of my idea. First of all, I understand more about your algorithms than you might think and I am of the opinion they will be more powerful than even you realize. Further, I don't know if you know, but we are extremely well-financed in this battle and more financing can be had. The long and short of it is that I want to partner with you in a company working on 'my side of the fence, so to speak."

Marty was stunned. He knew that his views had changed dramatically, but why would Norm have that kind of faith?

"Norm, I don't understand. You and I have been on opposite sides for years. Why would you trust me as a partner?"

"Because I am a good judge of character. In our differences, there was always courtesy and respect between us and I always knew that someday, you would see my side. ...and that day has arrived."

Marty tried to conjure up some words, but failed.

"Marty, just say we can meet and see where we go from here."

"OK," croaked Marty.

"Great," effused Norm, "how about tomorrow at 10 at my office?"

"Thank you, Norm. I'll be there."
"Oh, and by the way, your staff is included in this opportunity."

Marty hung up the phone and turned to the girls.
"We're back in business, girls."

The End

***

"…you could, like me, be unfortunate enough to stumble on a silent war. The trouble is that once you see it, you can't unsee it. And once you've seen it, keeping quiet, saying nothing, becomes as political an act as speaking out. There's no innocence. Either way, you're accountable." – Arundhati Roy

***

Research

The commentaries and references in this fictional novel are made purely as artistic expression and are not intended to represent actual real-life situations.

To demonstrate that some of these conditions may or may not be true, the author has listed below, some website links that may help the reader to further understand the storyline.

The author particularly points out item number II, which, although long, captures many of the concepts in this fictional novel.

---

[i] https://en.wikipedia.org/wiki/Cambridge_Analytica
https://www.sas.com/en_us/insights/big-data/what-is-big-data.html
[ii] https://www.youtube.com/watch?v=5rZn1xccrig&feature= youtube
[iii] https://en.wikipedia.org/wiki/Cambridge_Analytica
https://www.sas.com/en_us/insights/big-data/what-is-big-data.html
http://theinfluence.org/you-wont-believe-the-outrageous-ways-big-pharma-has-bribed-doctors-to-shill-drugs/
[v] https://childhealthsafety.wordpress.com/2010/09/14/science-free-web-saddoes/
http://www.alternet.org/news-amp-politics/fda-now-officially-belongs-big-pharma
https://therefusers.com/how-big-pharma-controls-the-fda
[vii] https://therefusers.com/how-big-pharma-controls-the-fda/
http://www.mintpressnews.com/fda-found-manipulating-the-media-in-favor-of-big-pharma/221825/
http://in-training.org/drugged-greed-pharmaceutical-industrys-role-us-medical-education-10639
[x] https://www.fool.com/investing/2017/01/15/is-donald-trump-big-pharmas-worst-nightmare.aspx